A FINAL STORM

by

PAUL STEPHENSON

Current edition published 2021

Get a free collection of short stories and a 10% discount on all my books when you sign up for my newsletter.

Published by Hollow Stone Press

CONTENTS

For Jacob, who hated the first dedication he got, so I'll just tell him I love him.

Chapter One

Let's Have An Apocalypse Now

The evening glow of London, and Max's computer screen, provided the only illumination in the building. Another hour and, no matter how fucked this code was, he'd abandon it completely and go home. Balls to what Devlin thought. Fuck him and his '*you stay all night while I go snort coke off some hooker*' approach to management.

Being a tech guy at a big banking behemoth was not the dream Max had envisioned when he'd first started coding. Hacking had seemed too exotic for a skinny black kid from a good, God-fearing family in the suburbs of London, so he'd drifted to the other extreme. While everyone he'd known from the forums back in the day had drifted towards the hard core worlds of identity fraud, Anonymous, and in some cases prison, he'd ended up on the other side, working for the Man, trying to stop his old friends from breaking in.

He'd lost all credibility, of course, but while they'd posted endless screeds about freedom and liberty, he'd spent his life protecting the freedom of your average man and woman in the street who didn't want to lose their kid's tuition fees. Christ, he'd even ended up voting Tory in the last election, not that he'd ever admit it.

Contrary to his friends' beliefs, he'd barely been rewarded for his move to the dark side. While they assumed he'd done it so he could ingratiate himself with power players and coke fiends, earn fat cat bonuses and sleep with models, he'd been passed over for promotion too many times and was yet to see a bonus big enough to cover his credit card debts. Since the banking crisis, he'd had the added perk of people looking down their noses at him when he told them who he worked for. Working for a bank was the modern equivalent of wearing a plague sign.

He rubbed his eyes. He should go and turn the lights on; he'd strain the shit out of his already damaged retinas if he had many more nights like this. He stood, stretching. Pins and needles shot through his feet. Below him, London was starting to come alive, taking the transition to night in its stride, spilling sketchy light up to him even here on the thirty-seventh floor.

'Fuck it,' he said to the empty desks around him.

He shut down his laptop and started to pack his things away. He'd take the computer home, but he'd be damned if he'd open it again tonight. Some serious Netflix bingeing was on the cards, maybe a pizza. Might have to call in at Smoky Joe's on the way back to his shitty Camden apartment, score some green. This weekend would have to be a lost one if he'd have any hope of being able to walk in here again when Monday rolled back around.

Lightning flashed outside.

Bollocks. I'd better get going.

Something about the way the flash filled the sky drew him over to the huge expanse of plate glass separating him from the sky. Whatever else he could say about this job, the views were incredible. On a clear night he could see the lights stretch for miles.

Not tonight, though. Tonight he could only see the storm. Clouds, thick with lightning, were building up, rolling in, and covering the sky.

I hope this place has lightning protection.

A flash arced across the London skyline, burning a negative of the window frame into his field of vision. He whistled, and stepped back. Below him, the world seemed to switch off, every light extinguishing as one. He peered down as much as he dared, the storm heightening his sudden vertigo.

No streetlights. No headlights. Nothing.

He looked across the skyline. The only way he could see the ground was in the reflected glow of the lightning playing across the base of the storm: great veins of electrical activity that seemed to fill the sky from end to end. They went on for miles, as far as Max could see.

What the hell is this?

He rubbed his temples. He had a hell of a headache brewing.

The darkness below him lasted a few seconds before the first of the explosions. Hundreds of sudden flares of fire sprung up below him.

A shudder rang through the building. He grabbed a desk to steady himself.

Less than a mile away, a passenger plane fell from the cloud, it's bright orange Easyjet markings whirling round in a spin.

Max stepped back.

'Holy fuck.'

It slammed into the streets below him, taking out a huge swath of the city.

A second plane appeared from the cloud, its huge nose bursting through the storm close enough to make Max gasp. He barely had time to scramble back and see the wing shatter the glass in front of him, before the pain in his head overwhelmed everything else and he blacked out.

He screamed himself awake, pulling the covers from his bed. Sweat streamed off him despite the cool night. Next to him, Ava rose, wearily.

'Storm?' she asked.

He nodded. Her head sank back to her pillow. Within seconds she was asleep, the gentle sound of her breathing slowing and moving towards half a snore. He rubbed his eyes. Light crept through the boards on the window onto the bed, the sheets bright against the rich black of Ava's skin, and the russet, reddish-brown of his own. Early morning birdsong rang out.

He got out of bed, careful not to disturb Ava. He dressed and pulled on his knackered boots. There was something comforting about them, their long service in the six months since the storm the only constant he'd enjoyed.

He went downstairs and found himself the first one awake. Mouse was usually up by now, the only one of them with night terrors to rival Max's own. Not that either of them could claim to have suffered more than the others, but they seemed to be the ones most haunted when the lights went out. It didn't seem to stop the others looking up to him. He wasn't sure how he felt about that, even now.

There were six of them in the house. Mouse had eloquently dubbed them the Shitty Six. They had found each other in the first days after the storm. There had been, what, twelve of them then? They'd lost half that number in the first week, but as soon as Mouse had come up with his less than pleasant moniker for the remainder, the deaths had stopped. So it stuck, no matter how little anyone wanted it to.

They'd lived up to the name a few times. With gangs fighting in the streets for control of the capital, they had retreated to the sewers more than once. It may have stunk down there, but they were safe from the cross fire.

Since the storm, the city had become almost unrecognisable. London had been hit by hundreds of tiny tragedies that had conspired to destroy the city completely. Deep underground a fire had burned hot enough to melt people to their chairs. A bus had ploughed into a petrol station. The fires which had swept through

London as a result made the events of 1666 seem minor. The city had burned for days, doused in the fuel of a hundred downed planes. London, once so proudly the great survivor of the Blitz, had finally succumbed.

When the rains came three days later, the survivors came out of whatever hiding places they'd found, and started to ask why. But nobody had answers. The storm had wiped out the nation's capital was all anyone knew. Word soon came that the capital was just the start of it. Outside of the M25 the scenes of devastation were as widespread, and nothing Max had heard in the months since had given him reason to leave the city. When Ava, their final member, had joined their number, she'd told them that even as the fires raged, gangs had taken control of the motorways, killing those trying to flee. Things were bad here, but leaving sounded worse.

He checked the cupboards, but found them as empty as he knew they would be.

'Morning,' Mouse said behind him. 'You're up early.'

'Couldn't sleep.'

'I heard.'

'You did?'

The boy nodded. Mouse was sixteen and weighed less than the average household pet, to look at him. A timid, nervous boy, but sweet. Most people would write him off as soon as they met him.

Their loss.

Mouse was the first person Max had met after the storm. Max had woken on the floor of his office, looking up at the sky where once there had been ceiling. Covered in his own blood, his skin raw to the touch. A crow sat on his foot, staring at him inquisitively, no doubt sizing up his suitability as a tasty treat.

He shooed the creature away and edged his way towards the mess of twisted metal that had been the frame of his nearest window, past which smoke from the fires billowed up into the clear blue sky above him.

Hobbling down over thirty flights of stairs, his panic had grown. He'd gotten as far as the third floor when the fires stopped him. He had to get out before the flames worked their way up, or worse, brought the building down around him, but he had no way through. So he'd stayed there, hoping the fires wouldn't come higher, staring at the buckled and warped window frames, trying to work out how to get out.

Mouse had appeared at the window opposite, waving at him. Max was so startled by the appearance of a skinny white kid he waved back gormlessly. Then the boy was gone. He returned an hour later, as Max struggled with the smoky air, having found a long rope. Mouse threw it over, and Max tried to summon the courage to use it. He finally made the five metre crossing, clinging to the rope as smoke billowed around him, his burned skin chaffing painfully with every inch.

When he'd finally made it across, he'd hugged the boy. Mouse had been so appalled at the physical contact he'd run away. By the time Max found him huddled behind recycling bins a block away, the sun had set on the first day and the fires were intensifying, not dying out. He'd not touched the boy uninvited since.

'What's for breakfast?' Mouse asked.

'Nothing,' Max replied, with a sigh. 'I'll need to go out.'

'I'll go,' Mouse said.

'No, you stay here, look after the others.' He grabbed his coat and started to remove the barricades from the door. 'Lock up behind me.'

Max stepped out into the street and looked around. Down at the far end a fresh body hung from makeshift gallows. He looked around, pulled his coat tight and headed towards it.

Chapter Two

Yes, I Am a Long Way From Home

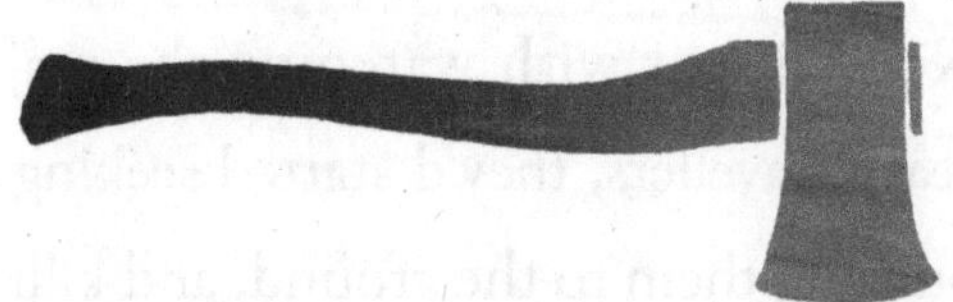

'What do you think?' Mira asked.

'I think you should take the shot,' Tana replied, chuckling.

She cricked her neck and raised the bow. She pulled the arrow tight and lined up the arrowhead with the deer across the field. Her heart thumped, and she took in a long breath.

'I can't,' she said, lowering the bow.

Tana laughed again. 'Don't worry about it,' he said. 'But at some point, you are going to have to learn how to do this.'

She nodded. In the months since the storm, her vegetarianism had gradually fallen away, but as their group struggled to adapt, she had balked at getting her hands dirty like the rest of them. None of the others had put pressure on her, but she knew she needed to pitch in. Once the deer had been in her sights, however, her intentions fled. It wasn't just the helpless nature of the beautiful animal — she'd struggled with any violence for months, since she'd had to cradle Jen's body in her arms while she passed out of existence.

'I'd have missed it, anyway,' she said.

The deer finally twigged to their presence and fled.

'They're getting bolder,' Tana said.

'Nobody around but us,' Mira said.

'Wish that were true,' Tana said, packing up the bow.

In the last few months the bandits out on the roads had grown bolder too. Not content with watching the major roads and picking off weary travellers, they'd started seeking out fledgling settlements, burning them to the ground, and killing the people inside. On their own travels they'd found two such scenes, enough to convince them they should stay on the move.

As for the government forces they'd fled three months back, they weren't so sure. Some bandits wore army uniforms, but whether they were part of the Birmingham government and its roving capture squads or rogue militants was unclear. They had no desire to get close enough to them to ask them personally.

'Let's get back,' Tana said.

Their current camp was by a lake, their caravans pulled far enough off the road to stay invisible. Scarcely a handful of Tom's group remained, the rest scattering after they left Dalby Forest. Father Leonard had wanted to stay there, but Mira and Tom couldn't bear to be so close to where Jen had died. Only Mira, Susan, Tana, Chen, and Tom remained of their group, although Mira wasn't sure how much of Tom was truly still there with them.

Next to the lake, Susan had the fishing lines out, while Chen washed clothes in the water. When he saw Mira and Tana returning, he stood, looking to them expectantly.

'Nothing,' Mira said, grumpily.

'Never mind,' Susan said, but Mira caught the look of disappointment flash between her and Tana.

'Sorry,' Mira said, and walked to the caravan she shared with Susan.

She sat on the hard bed and stared at the door, wanting someone to knock. And not. What she really wanted was for Jen to come and sit with her, tell her everything was going to be okay.

But that's not going to happen.

Tears welled in her eyes. She wiped them away.

She stood, washed her face in cold water, and headed back outside. Tana and Susan were deep in conversation. No doubt discussing her lacklustre performance. Maybe they'd get bored and want to get rid of her completely. Her gaze fell on the last of the caravans, and she walked over to it. She knocked on the door. There was no answer, but she opened the door anyway.

'Tom?' she called, entering the dingy rust bucket their former leader had chosen as his new home.

The smell of booze hit straight away. Empty bottles and cans covered the counters. Mira didn't know how he managed to find new ways to get so steaming drunk every night; they hadn't passed anywhere for him to stock up in days.

'What do you want?' he barked from his bed.

'Nice to see you too.'

He sat up. He'd slept in his clothes again. He winced as he moved and grasped his knee.

'Sorry,' he said, bashfully. He rubbed his eyes.

'Time to get up,' she said.

'Wouldn't want to miss another exciting day in the apocalypse,' he said sarcastically. He flashed a smile, and she got the briefest glimpse of the Tom she used to know.

She felt the familiar mix of pity and anger. He was the only one who understood what Mira had gone through, the lines she'd crossed.

The people he'd lost. Compared to him she'd got off easy, in a way. Nobody had ever strapped her to a chair and tortured her.

But he was also the reason, accident or not, that she'd lost Jen. She wasn't sure she could ever truly forgive him for that.

She smiled back and left him to it. Outside, Tana and Susan were still talking, Tana staring off into the distance, shaking his head.

'What's going on?' Mira asked them.

'We're trying to decide our next move,' Susan replied. The nurse had become their de facto leader as it became clear Tom had abandoned the post.

'This place is pretty exposed,' Tana said.

'Yes, but we've not seen or heard anything since we got here.'

'What are we going to do, stay?' Tana asked. 'If we're going to dig in it needs to be somewhere we can live off a bit better than an empty lake. We need a farm, a place to store food, somewhere to keep warm. Somewhere isolated.'

'Everyone in the country is looking for that place,' Susan said. 'We've not found it once. Besides, spring is coming.'

'Even more reason to find somewhere we can plant crops, prepare for next winter.'

Mira started to tune out. This argument had been had many times. She could see both sides. Susan wanted to stay mobile, flexible, and adaptable. Tana wanted to find somewhere to stay. Eventually they'd pull up sticks and be on the road again. Mira didn't much care, one way or the other. Move, stay, it all blended into different flavours of the same meal.

Chen stood up, looking beyond the others. 'What was that?'

'What?' Tana replied.

Tom stumbled out of his caravan, clutching his knee and wincing as he came down the step.

Chen studied the tree line. He raised a hand to hush them.

On the edge of the wind, Mira heard it. Engines. Deep, full-throated engines.

'Shit,' Susan said.

'Guns,' Tana said.

They scattered to their caravans. Susan and Mira had their guns stashed under their bunks. Both were armed and back out of the door in seconds.

There was no mistaking the approaching thunder of motorbike engines, sending the birds out of their treetop homes in panicked flight.

'What do we do?' Mira asked.

Tana looked around, weighing up their options. 'We're too exposed here,' he said.

The lake was a tranquil and peaceful place to pitch themselves, and far enough from the road not to be noticed, but should those bikes cross over the ridge, they'd have nowhere to hide.

They ran for the trees. Once they reached cover they lined up their guns and trained them back at the caravans.

Waiting was the worst part. The sound of engines drew closer and louder. Mira marvelled that anyone would choose such a conspicuous method of transport in these perpetually dangerous times. Unless, of course, they were the kind of people who didn't have to worry about other people.

A lion doesn't have to hide its roar, does it?

For the briefest of moments it seemed like the engines might roll on by, but they slowed, and stopped. Whatever Tana and Susan had thought about the seclusion of their convoy, it evidently wasn't secluded enough.

The first heads appeared over the ridge. Bandits, decked in denim and leather. Men, four in total. Mira's finger tightened on the trigger of her rifle.

'Hold your fire,' Tana said in a hushed tone. 'We don't know how many there are.'

The bikers looked around. They could see the place was inhabited, or had been moments earlier. Their eyes scanned the trees on the edge of the clearing, looking for signs of movement. The biggest man called one of the others over and said something to him. The other man disappeared back over the ridge.

'Shit,' Tana said.

'What?' Susan asked.

'I'd wage good money he's been sent to scan the tree line.'

'What do we do?'

He furrowed his brow. 'Stay here. Line one of them up in your sights. Be ready to fire.'

He started to back away.

'Where the fuck are you going?' Susan hissed.

Tana hushed her with his finger and disappeared into the woods.

Mira focused back on the men in front of her. One of the men kicked open the door to Susan and Mira's caravan, somewhat unnecessarily. It wasn't even locked. He disappeared in. Mira's stomach turned at the thought of some gross biker going through her things.

Another man picked through the small trailer they used to store their food. He started to unhitch it from its coupling to Tana and Chen's caravan.

'Motherfucker,' Chen hissed.

The man came back out from Mira and Susan's caravan, laughing and brandishing a pair of Mira's knickers. He held them up and the other two men roared heartily.

I'm definitely taking you out, you fucker.

She lined him up in her sights. Chen took the man scavenging their food, while Susan trained her gun on the big man in the middle. Tom moved his barrel on each in turn.

Something cracked behind them. Mira's heart froze.

'Now then,' the fourth man said behind them, his voice thick with Mancunian brogue. 'You three hold it right...'

Another crack rang out, louder this time. Mira squeezed her trigger, pulling the rifle up as she did, missing her target. It didn't matter. Tom, Susan and Chen found their marks, and the three men fell in an instant.

Mira spun round and saw Tana standing over the body of the fourth man, rifle pointed at it, willing it to make another move.

'Well,' Tom said. 'That was easy.'

The bushes around them rustled. Four more men burst through them.

'Don't fucking move,' one of the men snarled.

'Drop the guns,' another barked.

Rather than quibble at the conflicting instructions, they lowered their guns to the ground slowly and raised their hands. Tana's face betrayed his disgust at not having seen the play before it was made. Susan and Chen's showed their understandable fear, while Tom had the same look of blank resignation which seemed to perpetually haunt it.

'Well,' a man snarled at Mira, leaning in close enough for her to smell the fetid stench of his breath. 'Aren't you a pretty one?'

She picked a point on the grass ahead of her and fixed it with a stare.

The man on the floor coughed, and started to move, making Mira and the others jump.

'Fucking hell,' the body said, coughing again. He stood, and removed his leather jacket, revealing a black vest beneath. The back of the vest had a bullet lodged in it. He removed the vest and the other four chuckled.

'Told you it fucking stings,' one of them said.

'Which one of you cunts did this?' the shot man asked. He held up the bulletproof vest as an accusation.

None of them answered.

'I think it was this big cunt,' he said, moving to Tana. 'Was it you?'

'Jesus, Gra, he's a big fucker,' one of the other men said, laughing. 'You might want to watch yourself.'

Gra raised the pistol in his hand, and whipped the butt across Tana's face.

Tana fell to the ground, sparked out by the blow.

'Not such a big cunt now, are you?' Gra said, before spitting at Tana's unconscious body.

Tom let out a roar, but before he was even halfway out of his kneeling position he was taken out with the butt of a rifle. Mira looked up at the man with the rank breath in time to see his rifle butt smash into her face.

Chapter Three

The Storm Before The Calm

Trying not to stare at her own feet dangling high above the ground, Lydia took a deep breath and tried to calm herself.

'What do you reckon?' Greg asked, above her.

'Of what?' she replied.

She craned her neck to see what Greg held in his grease-smeared hands. It looked like a generic machine part.

'What is it?' she asked.

'The answer to our problem,' he said, smiling broadly.

'If you say so.'

She looked down again, unable to stop herself. They were high up a radio mast, hitched in by a series of ropes Greg had put together. Lydia hoped they were secure enough to prevent her falling to an untimely death. One thing was for sure, surviving a plane crash hadn't diminished her fear of heights.

She had no idea why she was even up there. So far, her only contribution, as the burly red-headed engineer tinkered away above, her was to hang uselessly below him. She could as easily have stayed on the ground and shouted up encouragement for all the use she was.

'Two minutes,' he said.

'I hope there's a bottle of wine waiting for us when we get back,' she said, idly.

'I get the impression Burnett is trying to ration the booze a bit more.'

'I don't know why. There must be a thousand supermarkets and off licenses in Birmingham. You'd think booze would be the one thing we wouldn't run out of.'

'Scouts have been everywhere up to the boundary. Don't think they found as much food and drink as they were hoping for.'

'Either that or our scouts have a nice little stash of their own.'

'Could be,' Greg said, chuckling. 'Right.'

There was a clunk.

'Is that it?' she asked.

'Let's find out.'

They descended, Lydia taking it inch by terrifying inch. The sun was setting, the shadows in the streets around them starting to elongate. They reached the bottom and Greg unhitched them both from their safety harnesses while Lydia tried to coax her legs out of jelly mode.

Greg walked over to the wheeled generator hitched to the back of their jeep and started it up. The putter of the engine filled the streets around them, and smoke billowed out the rear. Satisfied with its performance, he busied himself with the large box next to it.

Lydia pulled her coat tighter around herself. Winter might be starting to shake loose its grip, but it was still far from warm once the sun went down. Still, they'd made it through the coldest months, and there was something to be said for that. In the three months since the fall of Grayling's regime, she and Greg had struck up a firm friendship. He was a good man, albeit carrying a more bruised nature than the man she'd first met wheeling a shopping trolley around York.

Once Burnett had taken down Grayling, Greg had stuck around while Lydia had recovered from the bullet hole through her abdomen. Together they had searched the prison and the surrounding streets, looking for their friend Samira. They had asked others from the yard, but there was no sign of her. Lydia refused to give up hope. It was the only hope she dared still keep.

Once Lydia had healed, Greg had wanted her to go with him back north. But Burnett had begged them both to stay. He sold them both on the dream of a new government, one built around compassion. A new dawn. Lydia had bought it, but not for the reason Burnett had assumed. She wasn't ready to give up on Samira just yet. Every chance she got, she went out looking for her. Either way, she'd agreed to stay. Greg had been less sure, but had followed her lead.

A few weeks later Greg had tried to hit on Lydia, when they were both more than a little tipsy. He'd taken her knock back well and had been the same jolly Greg the next morning. The subject had never come up again. She did wonder, however, if that was Burnett's plan all along – to ensure Greg had a reason to stay. Certainly without him Burnett's good intentions wouldn't have gotten off the ground. A gifted engineer, Burnett had relied more and more on Greg to get them back up and running.

It wasn't that she didn't find Greg attractive – although his balding ginger hair and thick, bristly beard were not particularly high on her list of desirable qualities in a man – it was more a question of timing. Lydia still thought of herself as married, and wasn't ready to give up the husband who'd died in the storm. She suspected she never would be, like she would never get over the deaths of the children who'd died with him. Since the storm, there hadn't been many nights when she hadn't woken in a cold sweat, wondering where her babies were, or the man who gave them to her. The pain of their loss was still too much to bear, and no amount of jovial red-headed kindness could help her to let them go.

Greg flicked a switch and the panel on the front of the box lit up. A strange, high-pitched wail filled the air. It didn't sound too encouraging to Lydia, but Greg fiddled with the knobs and dials on the front until the sound eased into static, and silence.

'Aha,' Greg said. 'Got you.'

'It works?'

'Let's try the handsets and find out.' He pulled off one of the small walkie-talkies from the top of the box and tossed it to Lydia. 'Go into the next street and wait for a minute.'

Lydia walked four streets over, to be sure, and waited, marvelling at the alien glow of the digital screen on the front of the handset. She hadn't seen anything like it since the storm.

She looked around. She had no idea where she was. This wasn't her city, and more than once she'd wondered why she didn't leave. This new civilisation was nothing but a thin veneer of respectability on a permanently treacherous situation. The city was constantly poked and prodded by bandits, lawless thugs, and the former soldiers of Grayling's army. Even here, in this street, she wasn't safe.

The handset chirruped. She nearly dropped it in shock. She pressed the button.

'Yes?'

'Mic one, mic one, isn't this a lot of fun?'

She laughed. 'Roger that,' she said.

She started back. Burnett would be pleased. If the handsets worked, and if Greg was right about the reach of them, the job of keeping the city secure would be a lot easier. They would be able to maintain contact with the various security outposts around the edge of the city, giving them more visibility than the current system of flares and torches.

The last of the daylight disappeared over the horizon as she rejoined Greg, thick clouds above them separating them from the night sky.

'It works,' she said.

He didn't look up. He stared at the box, frowning.

'What's up?' she asked.

'I've got a signal from somewhere,' he said. 'I just can't tell where.'

'How far can this thing reach?'

'Well, I've boosted the range, so the technical answer would be that radio waves can reach round the globe. But I'd be amazed if this could reach London.'

He adjusted a knob and pushed a few buttons, causing another squeal of static, followed by a sudden burst of angry sounding foreign words.

'Luegs der no einisch a. Ren ueber d numeros. Ha da oepis fautsch, das wird dir z gnick braeche.'

They looked at each other, blankly, each hoping the other might recognise the language.

A second voice joined, away from the microphone. '*I ha das fautsch lueg doch schnaeu use!*'

Greg gave her a wide smile, picked up one of the handsets, checked the frequency, and hit the button. 'Hello?'

The voices at the other end of the line stopped. A low crackle and the buzz of the generator were the only sounds for a second, until finally a tentative and guttural 'Hello?' came back.

'Hi,' Greg said. 'Do you speak English?'

'Naturally,' the voice replied, a little haughtily.

'This is England. Birmingham, to be precise. I'm Greg. Who am I speaking to?' He spoke in a slow, measured way, then gave Lydia a look to ask if he'd been too patronising.

'This is Geneva.'

'Hello, Geneva.'

'Can you see the storm?' the second voice added.

'What storm?' Greg asked.

Lydia surveyed the sky. The dense clouds which had formed above them looked ordinary enough.

'Do you know about the first storm?' the first man asked, his voice calm and even.

'Well I barely managed to survive it,' Greg said.

'No,' the man replied, struggling to keep his own patronising tone under control. 'Do you know what caused it?'

'Solar storms,' Lydia and Greg said in unison.

'Correct,' the man replied.

Lydia felt like a child getting the right answer in science class.

'Specifically,' the man continued, 'the storm acted as a sustained EM pulse, which both destroyed active electrical equipment and overloaded the neural cortex of a huge majority of humans.'

'Except smokers,' Lydia said, leaning over to speak into the handset.

'Correct. Not only smokers, though. We survived because we were deep underground, where the pulse couldn't reach. Almost every researcher at CERN survived, initially.'

'Is that where you are?' Greg asked.

'Close to it. A fire...' The man's voice trailed off.

Lydia had heard that tone before, too many times since the storm. The tone of someone who couldn't bear to relive their experiences.

'There's a second storm,' the second voice said, taking over from the first. He sounded a lot less calm than his friend. 'It doesn't look as severe as the first storm, but still. You should know.'

Another burst of indecipherable language passed between the two.

'We're going to head underground,' the second voice said. 'We suggest you do the same. Try this frequency again. We'll be listening.'

'Good luck,' the first voice said.

'You too,' Greg said.

There was nothing but static.

'Shit,' Lydia said.

Above them, the first arcs of lightning played across the base of the clouds.

Chapter Four

The Hawkman Is Coming

Blinking his way back to consciousness, Tom's first thought was that he'd again had too much to drink. Every morning started the same way: regret, recrimination, self-loathing, and a drink to make it go away. A pitiful cycle to be stuck in to be sure, but it was his cycle, and goddamn if he didn't own it.

But he'd already done the waking part of the day, he remembered, as he tried to pry open his eyes. And the first drink. Not only that, but the pain in his head wasn't the usual tight knot he woke to. He remembered the buzz of motorbike engines, and everything flooded back to him. He forced his eyes open, and became aware of sticky blood congealing on his face.

He sat up. Beside him Tana and Chen both lay unconscious.

Mira and Susan were gone.

He leapt to his feet, but the dizziness in his head and the weakness in his knee conspired to bring him straight back to the ground.

'Tana! Chen!'

He crawled over to where they lay and tried to shake them out of their slumbers. Tana's face carried a huge welt over his left eye, while Chen's sported a run of sticky redness similar to his own.

Tana bolted upright. 'What the fuck?'

'Mira, Susan,' Tom replied. 'They're gone.'

Tom managed to get to his feet. Their camp had been looted and trashed, the tyres on their cars slashed, the caravans burnt out.

'Oh, Christ,' Chen said, waking up. He got to his feet with considerably more ease than Tom.

'What do we do?' Tom said, shaking the life back into his useless legs.

'We have to find them,' Tana said, firmly.

'How the fuck are we going to do that?' Chen asked, not unreasonably, kicking the flat tyres on the lead car.

They stared at each other for a moment, each wanting one of the others to come up with an excellent plan.

'Fuck,' Tana said, when it became clear no such plan was forthcoming.

Tom climbed the ridge and looked at the long road the bikers had come down. Tyre tracks headed off into the distance. Or maybe that's how they'd arrived? He climbed down and investigated. Next to one of the tracks lay a small pool of blood. It turned his stomach.

'We need a car,' Tana said, joining him at the road, staring it down like he wanted to fight the expanse of tarmac. 'Those fuckers made a lot of noise. If we can get close, we should be able to track them easy enough.'

'I take it our guns are gone, too?'

'Yep.'

Chen joined them and, without bothering to club together supplies, the three of them headed down the road, following the rubber tracks, which ran for a few metres. It was the only lead they had.

They walked in silence, Chen and Tana stopping every mile or so to let Tom catch up. He was suffering. Sweat dripped down his back and beaded constantly on his forehead. His legs screamed pain, and his stomach cramped.

How stupid had he been? He'd given up, safe in the knowledge there was nobody left for him to lose. He'd lost his best friend to a murderous bastard and Jen because of his own stupidity and carelessness. He'd decided it was better to remove himself, not let anyone else get hurt on his account. Now, he'd lost two more people. The two people Leon and Jen had cared most about, to boot. He'd let them down.

Again.

He hadn't been this long without a drink in weeks, the booze keeping the demons at bay. As his feet pounded the tarmac and sweat poured off him, he let them back in, gladly.

This was his fault.

If this was his *roads to Damascus* moment, bring it on. He deserved nothing less than to die out here. But first, he was going to find his friends.

'We should stop,' Leon said, next to him. Tom's heart soared at the sound of his friend's voice, but when he turned, it was Chen.

No more Leon for you.

'No,' Tom said. 'We need to keep going.'

The road ahead cut through endless countryside, and they'd seen nothing to suggest where their friends had gone. There were no cars for them to try, and no turns to puzzle over. Three straight hours of walking, and it was as though they hadn't taken a step.

'Let's take five,' Tana said.

Chen stopped, slumping to the ground. 'I need a drink.' He looked up at Tom. 'Water, I mean.'

'Me too,' Tom said. He turned away to hide his blush.

'How the fuck are we going to find them on foot?' Tana called out, loudly.

'We need a car,' Tom said.

Chen stretched out on the tarmac. 'We need a fucking miracle.'

Tom wished they hadn't stopped. His muscles ached, his knee spasmed randomly. There was too little left of him, both physically and mentally.

They sat for a moment longer, until Chen stood back up and dusted himself down. Tom and Tana took that to mean they were ready to set off again. They walked on, falling back into the regular pattern of Tana and Chen letting him catch up every mile or so.

'So,' Tom said, approaching the two of them, their hands on their hips, patience visibly wearing thin. 'Say we do find these fuckers. What then? We don't have weapons, we're tired, and we're dehydrated.'

'We'll figure it out,' Tana said.

Tom snorted and the big man turned on him.

'You know what, Tom,' he said, 'I've had enough of your shit. You've had a tough time of it. Boo hoo. We all have. None of us blame you for what happened to Jen, not even Mira. But it used to be people could rely on you. Not anymore. If the only things you're good for are slowing people down, cynicism, and breath like a distillery, you can fuck off right now.'

Tom hung his head. 'I'm sorry.'

'Don't be sorry,' Tana said, turning back to the road. 'Be Tom.'

The two men set off again. For a moment Tom considered turning round and heading in the other direction.

Fuck me, I need a drink.

He didn't mean water.

When they finally came across a village, night was falling. They'd tried to revive the first few abandoned cars they came across, but to no avail. These days it was pretty rare to coax a car back to life if it hadn't been used since the storm. Anything that required a computer was knackered from the off, and anything old enough to predate that was unlikely to restart after six months inaction, even if the battery did still work. Then there was the petrol, most of which was expiring. Still, they had to try.

There were no signs of life in the village. If the bikers had stopped here, they'd already moved on. They didn't strike Tom as the kind of people to sit quietly of an evening, their feet up in a pretty village cottage, reading a book. As for what Mira and Susan might be going through, it didn't bear thinking about.

Tana kicked in the front door of a house, and they trudged in. The corpses inside were more preserved than the skeletons outside, having not been exposed to the elements, but they were still leathery, their stench long since dissipated into a deep, musty awfulness that was somehow as bad.

It was the knowledge that they were breathing in people.

Without a word, they each took a room. Tom fell into a child's bed, checking it was empty first. Wherever that body was, it wasn't his problem tonight. His own body protested at being made to stretch out, but his muscles soon thanked him for it. His mind started to drift, until the nagging part of it won its battle, whispering one word in his ear... *Drink.*

He got up.

The house was in total silence, so he crept out of his room as quietly as he could and back down the stairs. If this house had been sealed up since the storm, there had to be something to drink in here. At the bottom he let his eyes adjust to the darkness, or at least fathom out which direction the kitchen was, but as he took a step out, the floorboard beneath him creaked.

'Thirsty?' Tana asked.

'Yes, Tana,' Tom replied. 'I am. There was a time when you would have joined me in a drink, too.'

'There was a time you could get through the day without one. Go back to bed, we have to leave early in the morning. Susan and Mira need us.'

'What about some water, at least?' Tom asked.

A bottle landed at his feet, the plastic thudding dully against the carpet.

'Thanks,' Tom said, and picked up the bottle.

He headed back up the stairs, cursing his friend. He downed the bottle of water, pretending it was something else, and climbed back into bed. Slowly, he drifted off, to dreams filled with Jen, blood spreading across her white top.

Chapter Five
The Warden

Burnett looked at the stack of papers on his desk and sighed. If the storm had brought about the end of human civilisation, why the fuck was he still doing paperwork? Before him lay reams of briefings from the various department heads of his fledgling new government, most of them scribbled on scraps of paper. All he could do was stare at them, trying to work out how the hell he'd come to be in this position in the first place. Sure, he'd either killed or imprisoned everyone from the last government, but that shouldn't have meant he'd take their place. This wasn't a kingdom of old, this was supposed to be an attempt to revive democracy. So how had he ended up in charge?

Because you were an idiot and said yes.

It was the only rationale he could come up with. Everyone looked at him because he'd acted decisively. That was, apparently, all it took. He'd been rewarded for that decisiveness with paperwork.

He picked up a report by Greg, their nominal Chief Engineer, who again had come to that title by being the sole survivor they had found so far who could fix things. He was bloody good at it, but he didn't half like to write a report. This one was telling him, in language far too complex for his understanding, that they could restore some element of the power grid, but at a cost. They could turn all the lights on for a day or two, or ration it out to the areas most in need for a longer period. At least, that's what he thought it was telling him. He'd read the bloody thing four times and still couldn't be sure.

He grabbed a pen and scrawled 'approved' on top of the report in handwriting so illegible it had once nearly cost him his career in the force. He added it to the out tray on his desk. Soon a man whose name Burnett could never remember would come in and clear the tray, and that would be that. He'd give Burnett one of the differential bows he liked to give, and that would be the last Burnett would hear of it until there was a problem. For all Burnett knew, the officious little man went straight out and burned the reports.

Sighing, Burnett leaned back in his chair. He didn't have a clue what he was doing here. He basically said yes to every request passing his desk, trusting his department heads knew what they were talking about. He'd sense check them to make sure nobody was going off and ordering gas chambers or anything stupid, but that was it. It staggered him that this laissez faire approach marked a dramatic improvement over the previous administration.

Of course, the lack of a slave army meant things weren't moving forward with much urgency, but that couldn't be helped. Hell, some days he was even slightly glad Grayling had at least managed to clear the streets of the dead, even if he had used slave labour to do it.

There was a knock at his door.

'Come in,' he said.

Rather than the nameless differential man, it was Tyler, the woman he'd entrusted to run security. Tyler had the hardest job of Burnett's section chiefs, in that she had responsibility for the one area Burnett knew anything about, and as such the one area he was constantly interfering in.

'Evening, boss,' Tyler said. She was young, a former officer of the law herself. Before the storm, she'd been a sergeant in the Birmingham force, one of the unlucky sods who spent their evenings and weekends trying to corral the pissheads and wastrels of the Midlands into not killing each other, or themselves. To Burnett's mind that made her the perfect person for the job. If you could stand firm and calm in the face of an England World Cup match, there wasn't much you couldn't handle.

'What have you got for me?' Burnett replied. It came out curter than he'd intended, but he was too tired to care.

If she took offence, she hid it well. 'Raiders. Think it was more of Grayling's old lot. Had the uniforms and the guns. Tried to strong arm one of the gate posts.'

'What were they trying to do?'

'Dunno. Tried to capture a few of them to ask 'em, politely of course, but they ran off. Could be they came back to try and liberate their friends, or could be after food. Who knows?'

When former Minister Grayling had started up his tin pot regime, he'd turned to the surviving local thugs and gangs to be his muscle, with predictable results. Most of them had died, some had scattered, but a few of them now served as company for the Minister at the local prison. If their gang friends managed to free them, they might actually have a shot at taking on Burnett's own men. He made a mental note to boost security at the prison, before remembering it was Tyler's job, not his.

'Beef up security at the prison?' he said.

'Already done,' she confirmed. 'Still, that's the second attack this week by men in army gear. Either they're getting organised, or more desperate.'

'I'm not sure which is worse,' Burnett said. 'What do you need?'

'More volunteers to man the barricades?'

'Fine, we'll put out a call tonight. Careful though, I'm not convinced we've gotten rid of the bad apples.'

She nodded, flashed him a quick smile, and left. No small talk; he liked that. But now he had to go to the Bullring.

I hate that fucking place.

Once home to his little counter insurgency, Birmingham's huge shopping centre and the buildings surrounding it were now home to nearly every person living in Birmingham, three hundred or so of them. The shops and offices around had been transformed, with clothes shops serving as dormitories, pharmacies serving as hospitals, and formally chic chain gastro pubs serving as dispensaries for some of the worst food Burnett had ever tasted.

Not everything has changed.

He chuckled at his own joke, and readied himself to leave. The vast majority of residents would be together right now, eating their evening meal, and he wanted to address as many of them as he could, mainly so he wouldn't have to repeat himself ad infinitum, but also so he could cut down the chances of being cornered by small groups bitching and moaning at him about how their apocalypse wasn't meeting expectations.

Night had fallen, but warmer than in recent evenings. As he approached the curved outside of the shopping complex, he was as surprised as ever to see people climbing poles to light the night lanterns. Six months since the storm and he still couldn't quite wrap his head around how far back they'd been knocked. Greg had rigged up generators, but fuel was limited, and an oil lamp would burn longer and stronger than a bulb, which would drain the limited power offered by the gennies. They'd already spent many a long day arguing back and forth about what constituted an essential service, and had settled on the canteens and infirmaries being the only thing that needed the power. Greg said they had enough fuel to keep them going until the end of spring if that was all they used, so until he got the grid up and running again, that was all he was going to have.

'Evening,' he said to the security guards who manned a cordon around the shopping centre. They nodded back, and continued their vigilance. Burnett had recently named the security force as being a 'tier one' service, along with the cooks and the doctors. Now they got an extra half ration of food, and an extra booze ration on the weekend, so it should be easy enough to persuade a few extra to join the ranks. Mind you, maybe incentivising based on the food currently on offer wasn't much of a motivational tool.

One day, if we're lucky, a proper chef will turn up.

People *had* been turning up, especially in the last few weeks, as word got around Grayling was gone. From what intelligence he could glean, the world outside his domain was spiralling into chaos. The people who turned up looking for sanctuary seemed more desperate with every passing day.

On the one hand, he needed people. He needed to grow this into something that could one day pull the whole country back onto its feet. On the other, every new arrival was a new mouth to feed, a new drain on their resources. Most of them were in no shape to be of use, for the first few weeks at least.

As he walked into the former Slug and Lettuce pub, he realised he was too early for the main evening crowd. Pretty much anyone who'd taken a work detail was still out working it, so the people left in here were the ones who hadn't. He was appalled to see just how many weren't pulling their weight.

He'd been averse to setting mandatory work details – that was one step too close to Grayling's methods – but seeing well over a hundred people tucking into their gruel, laughing and enjoying each other's company while others out there toiled and worked, his blood boiled. If he hadn't been so tired he might not have overlooked how emaciated they were, or the tremors in their hands, or the crutches so many of them had propped against their chairs. But he *was* tired, and by the time he stood on one of the benches, he *was* angry.

'Right,' he barked, and the room fell into a hush. 'How many of you have been to work today?'

Some hands shot up, but not many.

'There are people out there, watching the perimeters for you, risking their lives, every minute they're there. There are doctors missing out on tonight's meal because they're too busy. There are people, beyond the city limits, venturing into territories outside of our control, trying to get the lights back on, find stuff for you to eat. All so you lot can sit in here, eating food made for you by yet more people. So, how many of you, tomorrow morning, are going to be turning up for work? For security detail? For farm duty? To help in the kitchens?'

Silence settled on the room, and Burnett realised he'd had his fists balled the whole time.

'How dare you?' a voice called from the other side of the room.

Slowly, a woman stood. She looked old and frail, and for a second it looked like the equally elderly man beside her would have to help her to her feet, but she managed it on her own.

'What work is it you'd like me to do, sir?' she said. 'You'd have me out there, tilling the fields? You could assign me a soldier, make sure I'm doing my bit. He could check my knuckles at the end of the day, make sure they're good and raw? Might not get as much done as some others, but you won't have to worry about keeping me alive for long.'

Her words hung heavy in the hall. The crowd turned to Burnett, whose anger had transformed into a burning heat in his neck.

'I...'

'What about Al here?' she continued, cutting him off. 'He lost his legs in the storm. Left for dead. What should he do tomorrow? Go on a security patrol?'

'Look,' Burnett said, trying to regain his composure. 'I appreciate not all of you can work...'

A low booing sound rang out around the room. Burnett saw the things he'd ignored before. The crutches, the frailty. He wanted to climb down from the bench and find a nice dark hole to crawl into.

He was spared further embarrassment by Greg and Lydia, who burst into the room. The burly engineer panted, his cheeks a deeper red than his heavy beard.

'Mr Burnett,' he called. He stopped trying to take in the scene of angry faces before him. 'Can I... uh, can I talk to you?'

'You can talk to all of us,' the old lady shouted.

Greg looked to Burnett, who nodded.

Anything to get me out of this.

'The storm,' he said. 'It's back.'

Burnett turned and looked to the window behind him. Sure enough, a heavy cloud hung in the sky, green arcs of electricity playing across its surface. He turned back to the crowd, his mouth open.

Maybe not anything...

The old woman started to scream, and everyone else followed suit.

Chapter Six

Not For You

As he approached the gallows, Max chanced a look up. Whoever the poor sod hanging at the end of the rope was, it wasn't anyone he knew. He looked at the boots at the end of the dangling legs, and wondered. Not like the Kurgan and his boys to leave nice boots like that hanging off a corpse.

He stopped.

He didn't like this. The body swinging above him still had a pistol tucked into its waistband to go with the nice boots on its feet. Too tempting.

A trap.

Max stepped back, slowly. He needed to get past the body, but somewhere there'd be a tripwire, or a net, or something to ensnare the poor idiot who decided they wanted to take those boots or that pistol. That's if he was lucky. If he was unlucky, the Kurgan and his boys already had him surrounded, and would spring out at any second.

No. If that was the case, I'd already be dead.

Fucking Kurgan.

Some people had taken to the apocalypse better than others. Max considered himself in that bracket. Years of computer games and a taste for disaster movies had prepared him for the harsh realities of a burnt-out world. The Kurgan, on the other hand – he'd not just survived. He'd *thrived.* Max had no idea who Kurgan had been before the storm, but one apocalypse later he'd reinvented himself as the villain from an eighties fantasy film, given himself a Mohawk, and started collecting heads.

Where maybe a few thousand had survived the storm and the fires, there had to be less than a hundred people left, dotted around the boroughs. Hundreds had died of sickness and fire, others had fled. Of the rest, half must belong to the Kurgan's crew of merry torturers, rapists, and scumbags. Max reckoned the Kurgan and his men had killed at least two hundred people since the storm in his quest to have total dominion over the ruins of the old capital.

Max had seen them up close too many times. The Kurgan had taken a singular dislike to Max and his family, which probably had something to do with Max stealing his precious collection of water filters from right under his nose. He'd traded it for close to a month's worth of food.

That was a fun day.

He assessed his options. Kurgan wouldn't know where they lived; they'd been too careful. This must be a random trap, like dozens of others around the city. Chances were even if he did get caught, it'd be hours before someone came to see what they'd captured.

The buildings on either side were burned out, so he chose the left and stepped through a broken window, deciding to risk the structural instability within. Once inside, he let his eyes adjust for a moment and checked the long knife he kept hanging from his belt.

Before the storm this must have been a travel agents'. One wall, still standing, had a huge mural of the nose of a passenger jet painted across it. His stomach turned.

Had quite enough of that view.

He climbed the stairs.

The first floor stretched into a second building, the partition between the two lying in rubble. The melted plastic chairs and scorched computer terminals betrayed the second building as a call centre. Bones lay scattered, remnants of the unlucky sods who'd spent the last few moments of their lives on the phone to disgruntled people across the country, moaning about whatever. Unless, of course, this was a cold-calling room, in which case fuck 'em.

At the far end, the floor had collapsed. The building below was completely gone. Max eased himself down into the rubble and back into the street. He was past the hanging body, so he pulled his coat tight and walked on.

Finding food became more of a problem with every passing day. On the day before the storm there'd have been enough to keep its millions of inhabitants fed for weeks, even months. The fires had depleted that stock considerably, time even more so. The meat, vegetables, and dairy had gone off. Even the wheat was useless. Now they were down to whatever tinned goods and dried food they could scavenge.

With so few people still alive to fight over what remained, it shouldn't have been hard, but the Kurgan used most of his considerable strength in numbers to find and hoard every morsel of food he could. He wanted to starve the city into having to bow to him.

Max had no intention of going down that road. What he needed was to find one stash, somewhere, enough to feed him and his family for a few months, and they needn't go out again. They could hide away until the Kurgan forgot about them, or until someone finally killed him. Hell, it might even be one of his own people.

A floorboard creaked in one of the shops behind him. He froze, his hand going to the hilt of the knife.

'No need for that,' Mouse said, stepping out from a shadow.

'What the hell are you doing here?' Max hissed.

'What?' Mouse said, looking affronted. 'If you find a decent stash of food, you'll need help carrying it back, right?' He had a large black holdall slung over his shoulder.

Max shook his head. 'Fine. Keep an eye out though. You see the body?'

'I did. Trap?'

'Have to think so.'

Mouse nodded. 'So where we going today?'

'I thought I'd go beyond the scorch. See if we can't find something out there.'

'Beyond the scorch. Even the Kurgan doesn't go out that far.'

'Which is why we're going there.'

Mouse didn't argue with Max's logic, because they both knew it was bullshit. Nobody went beyond the scorch. Beyond it were people who made the Kurgan look civilised. Most of the people who'd survived the fires in the first place had ended up on pikes or in gallows, which was why Max never ventured that far. He had, once, in the first days after the storm, and he'd lost good people.

'Or we could try south of the river?' Max said.

Mouse shrugged. Neither option held much promise. Max didn't even know if they could still get across the Thames. But things were desperate. Today wasn't the first time he'd been out, looking for food. Every day he came back empty handed. There would come a point when that was no longer an option, and looking in the cupboards this morning, he'd known that time had come. Pretty soon his family would be forced to go out searching on their own, and none of them were strong enough to stand up to the Kurgan, if it came to it. Not Max, not Mouse, not even Eva. Even together, it wasn't likely. The Kurgan might be the pissant king of North London, but Max doubted he had the same grip over the South. Besides, Max hadn't scavenged there, and when he'd looked south from the few towers which still remained, the scorch looked a hell of a lot less severe south of the river.

Yeah, but that means people.

They headed south, walking for miles through the borough of Camden, of which Max felt sure he'd scoured every inch, and past Regent's park, once an endless expanse of green, now either burned black or gone to seed. Max had tried to search the park once before, but it was home to too many of the city's feral dogs. He'd beaten a hasty retreat that day.

How long until dog meat is on the menu?

'How about we jump on a boat and sail away?' Mouse asked, as the river appeared on the horizon.

'Nice idea,' Max said. 'You want to be caught on a tiny boat if you come under attack?'

Mouse shook his head.

Max was uneasy this close to Buckingham Palace. While he wasn't completely sure the Kurgan used it as his central base, it made too much sense not to be true. It was big, ostentatious, and although the fires had reached it, it had fared much better than the rest of the government buildings in Westminster. A few hundred metres away from them, the Houses of Parliament lay in ruins, the huge clock tower of Big Ben the only part of the structure even half recognisable. Whitehall, too, was completely destroyed. In fact, it took Max a moment to realise they now stood in the ruined entrance to that once grand building.

He frowned, something tugging away at his consciousness, as he stared at an exposed interior doorway. He looked through it, until it dawned on him what he was staring at. A sign, small, on the door.

'To Bomb Shelter Area.'

The penny dropped.

'Mouse,' he said, not able to take his eye off the sign. 'You ever hear about the secret nuclear bunker under Whitehall?'

Mouse shrugged. 'Dunno. Makes sense though. Hey, that'd be worth trying to find, eh? I bet it'd be full of food, and medicine, and water. Shit, probably loads of guns, too.'

'Look at that sign,' Max said.

Mouse picked a way through the rubble. Most of the building was dust and broken bricks, but underneath it the bulk of the ground floor was intact, with the door stood tall amongst it, its small sign scorched but still legible.

'Well,' Mouse said. 'Shit.'

They made their way over to it as carefully and methodically as they could. Both had been through enough broken buildings to know how perilous they could be, how easy it was to turn your ankle and be left hobbling with no doctors to fix you.

They reached the door, both hesitating for a second. Max stretched out a hand and tried the handle. It didn't budge an inch.

'That was predictable,' Mouse said.

Together, they worked their way around the ruin, trying to find another logical way into the bunker or any hint that getting in might be possible. For hours they poked and prodded, wanting as much to convince themselves of the bunker's existence as they did to get into it.

Evening came, and with it came the realisation they'd completely wasted the day. A day in which they had an immediate need to get food. Max would have to return home empty handed and try again tomorrow. How desperate would they be, then? What if he didn't have the strength tomorrow?

He kicked a stone in anger, regretting it instantly. On top of the pain, a lump of rubber fell off the sole. Maybe he'd try getting the nice new ones off that corpse on the way back.

Mouse had given up, too. He sat on a piece of fallen masonry, looking up at the sky. 'What does that look like to you?' he asked.

Max followed the boy's gaze, and saw the storm clouds above. They were lit with electrical arcs that played within, casting a green hue over everything. The hairs on the back of his neck bristled. 'We need to get back to the house,' he said, in a quiet voice. There was no reason to think the house would be safer than anywhere else, but he had to go and make sure everyone else was okay.

'I dunno, lads, should we let them?'

Max's stomach lurched again.

The Kurgan stepped out from behind a broken wall, joined by three of his ludicrously attired men, each armed with a hefty looking club to go with their Day-Glo spandex and leather ensembles.

Mouse grabbed hold of Max's arm, and stepped behind him.

'It's okay,' Max said, not thinking for one second that it was.

'I was hoping you'd get into the bunker for me,' the Kurgan said.

It had been a few months since Max had seen him, and the intervening period had done nothing to wash the crazy from him. His muscled and tanned torso was bare, emblazoned with crude tattoos and body art which looked to be going septic. His ears were pierced and stretched, and around his neck hung a chain, decorated with several small bones.

'We've been trying all day. If there's a bunker down there, there's no way in.'

'We'll be the judges of that,' the Kurgan said. He spat on the ground by Max's feet.

'You're more than welcome to try for yourself.'

The Kurgan nodded to two of his men, who went over to the door, and started to hammer at the heavy wood with their clubs.

'What about that?' Max asked, motioning to the sky.

'What about it?'

'You remember the last time the sky looked like that, I take it?'

'Didn't kill me last time. Don't see why it would this time.'

Max nodded. The man may be a lunatic, but he had a point. 'So,' he said. 'What now?'

'What, you think I'm gonna let you two little pissants go?'

Max sized it up. Both he and Mouse were tired, hungry, and weak. Kurgan and his men looked fit and healthy, and all they'd been doing was watch them toil. Max and Mouse could run, but he didn't like their chances. At least Kurgan's men weren't carrying guns.

'I was kind of hoping, yeah,' Max said.

The Kurgan leaned in towering over Max. 'I'd think again.'

He raised his own club. Max braced for its impact, the sinking feeling in his stomach telling him this was the end of the road. He held his breath for some reason, as though holding on to it would save him.

Mouse stepped forward out of Max's shadow, and waved something. A line of crimson red sprouted across the Kurgan's side, and Mouse's small hand slid into Max's.

'Go,' he whispered.

They ran, sprinting as fast as they could away from the howl of anger behind them.

Chapter Seven

Nobody's Fault But My Own

Waking without a hangover was a novel experience for Tom, but the crashing guilt that normally accompanied it was still there. So were the usual aches and pains which came from rousing his broken body. All told, it wasn't much of an improvement.

It took a few moments to remember where he was. The sun hadn't yet risen and the room was filled with a murky light. He sat, rubbing his legs to coax them into action. He woke Chen and Tana on the sofa, both of whom got up and dressed without a word, and went down to the kitchen to try and rustle up some breakfast. They were in luck; the kitchen was well stocked, with both coffee whitener and bottled water.

They went through the house quickly, stuffing a rucksack full of tins, water, and spare socks. Chen had managed to find clothes that fit him, while Tom and Tana had to stick with the ones on their backs. It was a shame — Tom's reeked .

Tom found one cupboard full of booze. Whisky, vodka, wine. He stared at the bottles for a second, and even started to reach in, but pulled his hand back at the thought of Mira and Susan. He closed the door. Tana had been watching him.

'I didn't...'

'I know. Come on, let's hit the road.'

The village was tiny, barely more than a few houses along a stretch of tarmac, which forked in two almost as soon as the buildings ended. No way of knowing which way the bikers had gone.

'What do you think?' Tom asked.

Tana assessed both directions and the sign between them. Neither name meant anything to Tom.

'No idea,' Tana said.

'I don't think they stopped here overnight, right?' Chen asked. 'They must have a base. If they were going somewhere when they found us, it's less likely they were taking turnings. The way to the right looks more like a straight line, so... fuck, I dunno.'

Tom shrugged. 'It's better than anything I've got.'

'Me too,' Tana said. 'Let's do it.'

They set off, Tom's legs aching and weary from the previous day's walk. Still, he felt happier than he had in some time. Having something to focus on, as unpleasant as it was, was better than sitting around with nothing to do.

The sun had risen to its peak by the time they came to another sign, declaring them to be approaching the village of Willingham by Stow. They stopped and passed around the water bottle. Tom was sweating profusely; the others let him take as much as he needed.

'Can you hear that?' Tana asked.

Tom focused. Below the sound of birdsong and the wind in the trees, he could make it out – the low, sputtering rumble of an engine. Several engines, perhaps.

Motorbikes.

They quickened their steps. The village was quiet, and as they reached the centre they stopped again; straining to hear the engines once more.

The sound was gone.

They'd passed the doctors, a school, and a bakery before. Like most English villages, the centre consisted of a church, a pub, and a post office.

Laid out in the car park of the pub were four bodies. Each had taken a bullet to the head.

'Fuck,' Tom said.

'No women,' Chen said.

Tom's stomach lurched. If these bikers were rounding up women, it would be for the obvious reason.

'We can't have missed them by much,' Tom said. 'We need to find a car.'

That proved difficult, despite the number dotted about. This had evidently been a wealthy place before the storm, so most of the cars had fancy-pants computer systems in them that had been fried. Of the others, most of them had been idle too long, their batteries drained, the petrol in their tanks useless.

The sky darkened before they admitted to themselves they were on a hopeless mission. They would have been better off chasing their prey on foot. Finally, having failed to coax a Ford Focus into life despite a full tank of petrol, Tana snapped. He got out and slammed the door repeatedly, until the window shattered.

'Might as well stay here for the night,' Chen said, ignoring Tana's outburst.

'They could be fucking miles away,' Tana shouted, venting his frustrations once more with a firmly planted boot to the car's side mirror, which flew off onto a nearby patch of grass.

Tana sighed. 'Fine.'

They found a house with no corpses and three clean beds. Chen headed straight for the kitchen to find food, while Tana stormed off to one of the bedrooms. Tom headed for the lounge and sank into the sofa, glad to be sitting down. He massaged his knee and took off his shoes to rub his feet, recoiling at the smell. Thankfully, food smells wafted through almost immediately. Not for the first time, Tom counted himself glad to have survived the apocalypse with a chef by his side.

'Guys,' Tana shouted from upstairs. 'You'd better come see this.'

Tom eased himself out of the sofa and followed Chen up the steps. The door to the master bedroom was open, Tana's broad shoulders filling the window. Lightning arced across the sky, a kaleidoscope of colours playing out across a dark cloud canvas.

'It's back?' Chen asked.

'What do we do?' Tana asked.

'Nothing,' Tom replied. 'There's nothing we can do.'

'I wish I had a fucking fag,' Chen said.

Tom nodded. It had been months since any of them had had a cigarette. The idea of trying to sustain that addiction while keeping yourself clothed, fed, and watered had seemed like too much effort for most of them. In Tom's case, he'd swapped one harmful addiction for an even worse one. Chen might want a cigarette, but Tom wanted a drink.

Shit, I'd take both.

He thought back to that first night, when he and Leon watched the storm on their back patio. Tears sprung unbidden, and he wiped them away as quickly as he could. His breath caught in his throat.

He missed his friend.

It occurred to him that he had two pretty good friends here, and two more out there somewhere, God knew where. He wondered if Mira and Susan were watching the same storm. He hoped they were okay.

He hoped *he* would be okay, too. Not such a shock, perhaps, but it was both surprising and gratifying to find he did care, after all.

They watched in silence. On the night of the first storm the intensity had ratcheted up within a few minutes. The headaches had started and they'd blacked out. Tonight, as the storm started to ease, there were no headaches, no blackouts. Instead they watched a crescendo of light, before it stopped, plunging the world below into darkness. A few minutes later the rain came, heavy droplets hitting the window. Still they stood, watching.

'Well,' Chen said, finally. 'I'm guessing dinner will be ruined.'

Sure enough, Chen's lovingly crafted risotto had been reduced to a decidedly sub-par one. Chen tried to convince them to let him start again, but neither Tom nor Tana were willing to wait, so they crowded around a single candle and ate. Tom didn't care how burnt it tasted. None of them could muster conversation, so they sat in sullen silence.

'What does it mean, do you think?' Tom asked finally, breaking the silence.

'I should have taken it off the heat,' Chen replied, sullenly.

'Not that.'

'Does it have to mean something?' Tana asked.

'Ewen said the first storm was due to solar flares,' Tom said. 'If there's going to be more of them, we could be in serious fucking danger.'

'We're in serious fucking danger every day, in case you hadn't noticed,' Tana said. 'I don't see how one more risk, one we have no control over, makes a difference.'

'Well,' Chen said, leaning back in his chair. 'You're a cheery one tonight.'

Tana didn't laugh. 'What's the plan tomorrow?' he asked, wiping his mouth.

'I still say we need some wheels,' Tom said. 'I say we set out on foot, see what we can find.'

'And if we don't?'

'Well, fuck, Tana,' Tom said, standing up. 'You tell me. I want to find them as much as you do, you know.'

Tana stood up, picked his plate up and tossed it into the sink. He stormed out of the room without another word, his heavy footsteps the only sound in the silence.

Chen smiled uncomfortably, shrugged his shoulders, and stood up.

'Good night, Tom,' he said.

'Good night.'

Chen went to his room, and Tom was left alone in the dark, staring at the candle's flame. In the flickering light, he composed himself, and remembered how much better he'd been today than yesterday. Or the the day before, or, well, pretty much any day in the last few months. Not that he'd achieved anything. Mira and Susan were still out there; they'd made exactly no progress.

But you didn't have a drink today.

Why would he even want one? Why punish himself? Life was hard enough, and twisted enough, without adding that particular demon into the mix. The way Tana and Chen had looked at him, the disgust in their eyes. He didn't want that. He couldn't bear it.

Walking through to the kitchen again he piled the plates quietly onto the side. He opened the cupboards one at a time, until he found the one he wanted. He took a glass, a half bottle of gin, and returned to the candle.

He placed them onto the table, his hands shaking. He stared at them.

I don't need you.

He stared at the bottle.

Poured a glass.

Stared at it.

His head swam, like he'd already taken his first sip. He could taste it on his lips. Could smell it. Jen's face, the look of surprise as she saw the blood spreading over her shirt, rose unbidden in his mind. Shaking, he lifted the glass to his mouth, and drank.

Chapter Eight

Beautiful is this Burden

As panic swept the hall, Burnett stood useless for a moment, trying to work out what to do. In the end he opted to climb back onto a table and bellow at the top of his lungs.

'Stop!'

The pandemonium halted immediately.

'Panicking will achieve nothing, except get a few of you killed. If this is the same kind of storm as before, there's nothing we can do to avoid it. We survived last time.'

Faces stared up at him. He climbed down from the table, and suppressed the urge to sprint for the doors. Calmly, he walked out into the street. Outside, the air was warm. There was no rain, despite the heavy clouds above. People followed, so he kept moving. Others joined them from the Bullring until the square filled with people, everyone staring at the sky with a mix of horror and fear playing across their faces.

'Is this what it looked like last time?' he asked Greg and Lydia, who had followed him from the restaurant and stood gawping upwards.

'You didn't see the storm?' Greg asked.

'I was in an interrogation room,' Burnett replied.

'Don't ask me,' Lydia said. 'Last time, I was at ten thousand feet. To begin with, anyway.'

'Okay,' Burnett replied. 'You win.'

'This looks pretty much the same,' Greg said. 'There's more, too. I'll tell you after. If we survive.'

The light show continued its dance, but the longer it went on, the less people seemed to fear it. The mood in the crowd moved from total horror to something more akin to a November Fifth fireworks gathering until, finally, the lights ceased to play, and the clouds turned a heavy grey. The first smatterings of rain hit Burnett's face.

People crossed themselves, or whispered prayers to the clouds, or simply watched distrustfully, as though they might change their mind and unleash fury. Finally, people dispersed, going back to whatever they were doing earlier.

'There's more?' Burnett asked, turning to Greg.

'Come with us,' Greg replied.

They jumped into a car, Lydia driving. Burnett sat alongside her, with Greg in the back. As soon as their seatbelts were on, Greg leant forward.

'So,' he said, failing, if he was trying, to conceal his excitement. 'You remember I said I might have worked out a way of getting communications back up, at least operationally?'

'Vaguely,' Burnett replied. Truth was, Greg had more ideas every day than Burnett could feasibly complete in a whole month, so Burnett had developed a selective attention span for his friend's myriad plans.

'Basically, I found a crate of old satellite phones, circuitry intact. I knew there wasn't much chance the satellites themselves would have survived the storm, the first one, I mean. But I thought maybe I could repurpose them, hack into the radio waves.'

'Didn't the radio waves go down in the first storm?' Burnett asked

'No. Radio waves are a constant. Not man made. Anyway, we came out here, to find a big radio mast. That *had* blown, so I had to fix that. But once I did, I was able to repurpose the radios and, hey presto, we have a super-charged CB radio system, and five handsets to pass out to the perimeter.'

'Sounds excellent, Greg, but why do I get the impression that's not the whole story?'

'Because it isn't,' Lydia said. 'Greg, why don't you cut to the chase; this isn't that long a journey.'

'We found a signal,' Greg said. 'From Switzerland. Two scientists at CERN. They'd seen the solar flares, and knew another storm was coming. But get this, they didn't survive the first storm because they're smokers. They survived because they were underground. The effects of the EMP generated by the first storm caused huge devastation on the surface, but had no effect deeper underground.'

'So?'

'So, if there are going to be more storms, not like tonight, but a real storm, we can protect against it.'

'How?'

'Well, we'd need to go underground.'

'We're here,' Lydia said, pulling up to the mast.

'You left everything here?' Burnett asked.

'We didn't exactly have time to pack up,' Lydia said.

Greg got out and immediately started fiddling with dials.

'You think he's right?' Burnett asked Lydia.

She shrugged. 'I guess so. I think the Swiss guys were genuine, but what the hell do I know? Could have been two Scousers shining us on. Who knows? But it felt right.'

Greg picked up a radio. 'Hello?'

Silence greeted his query. He waited a moment and tried again.

'Hello, Switzerland?'

'Hello, England,' a voice came back, weak sounding. 'You made it?'

'We're fine. You?'

'Not so good. David is dead. He got a... nosebleed. I have a headache.'

Greg looked over at Lydia and Burnett, frowning. 'I'm sorry to hear that.'

Silence.

'Are you still there?' Greg asked.

'Yes,' the man replied. 'My nose is bleeding.'

Lydia turned away.

'I'm sorry. I need to ask you something. Is that okay?'

'Yes.'

'What depth? To be sure? How far underground would you need to go?'

'I am not sure. But you need to work it out soon. We were a hundred metres down, but you might not need to go down that far. Maybe you need to go deeper.'

The last word turned into a wet, sickly cough, and the line went silent for a moment. When he came back to the microphone, he sounded weaker still.

'You have to hurry. Tonight's storm was only the beginning. The levels of activity we are seeing on the surface of the sun, they're unprecedented. There will be more ejections. In the next days, maybe weeks. Much worse than the first storm. You need to get to safety. You need to warn people.'

Silence hung over the airwaves again. Greg stared at the radio, ashen faced.

'Are you still there?' Greg asked.

'Goodbye,' the man said. 'And good luck.'

The line went dead.

'Jesus,' Lydia said.

'What do we do?' Burnett asked.

Greg finally broke off eye contact with the radio. 'We need a bunker. Damn big one.'

'Where the hell are we going to find one of them?' Lydia asked.

'We don't have time to build one,' Greg replied.

'Have either of you ever heard of Pindar?' Burnett asked.

Both of them looked at him blankly.

'Government bunker. In London. Right under Westminster, I think. I heard about it in our anti-terrorism briefings.'

'Burnett, London's gone,' Lydia said.

'You're right. We've heard nothing good come out of London. By all accounts it's a wasteland. Not to mention the trouble between here and there. I'm open to other suggestions.'

'I can't think of anywhere else,' Greg said. 'I mean, a hundred metres down? That's deeper than you'd think. Maybe the deepest parts of the Underground, but that's not exactly better. There's cold war bunkers all over the place, but without the internet I don't know how we'd find one, let alone know how deep they were.'

'We'd need to see if it's viable, before we start trying to kart everyone down there. Where the hell would we even start?' Lydia said.

She was right. It would be a hard enough sell to everyone here to go to London. Going down there in blind hope wouldn't be enough.

'You're right,' he said. 'You two head to London, scout out the bunker. See if it's a viable option.'

'What?' Lydia said, holding up her hands. 'Hold on. I said *we* should scout it out. I didn't mean the royal fucking *we*. What the fuck good am I going to be in London? Neither of us are fighters, or good with guns.'

'We don't need fighters,' Burnett replied. 'We need people I can trust, and that's a pretty short list. People who understand the gravity of the situation. I need Greg to go down there, because he'll have the best shot at being able to get into the bunker, if you find it.'

'Fine, send Greg down there with some armed guards. I don't see why the hell you'd need me to go down there.'

'Hang on,' Greg interjected. 'I'm not sure I'm happy with either option.'

'You heard the man on the radio,' Burnett continued. 'We might have hours, or days, to get down there. Do you think we've got time to get a team together, brief them on what we have to do? You're more than capable, both of you.'

He grasped Lydia's shoulders.

'If it weren't for you, none of us would have made it this far. It would still be Grayling and his men running the show.'

That much was true. She had saved his life in the prison, when everyone else was using him as a carpet. She put her own life in danger, took a bullet even, to warn them about Slater's planned ambush.

'Oh come on,' she scoffed. 'All I did was get shot.'

'You did a hell of a lot more than that, and you know it.'

She shook her head and threw up her hands. 'It's just... Samira. If I leave that means I've given up on her.' She shook her head and stared at the ground. 'Fine.'

'Good. Greg?'

He nodded.

Burnett fished out his pistol from his waistband, and the spare magazine he carried for it. 'Take this,' he said, and handed the gun to Lydia. 'Hopefully you won't need it. Take the car, take a radio. Greg, you need to rig up two radios for me.'

'Two?' Greg asked.

'He needs one to talk to us, and one to broadcast to as many people as possible,' Lydia said.

'Exactly.'

'You sure?' Lydia said. 'Could be dangerous.'

'You see another option? Besides, I can't ignore a man's dying command.'

'Fair enough.'

Lydia took the gun and went to prepare the car. Greg busied himself with preparing the radios. Burnett stood, watching, thinking. How the hell was he going to convince a few hundred people to abandon the world they were starting to rebuild? Especially given the destination. There were some people who had barely made it out of London with their lives; he couldn't begin to imagine how he could convince them to go back there. It wouldn't take long for their concerns to spread through the rest of them, either. That was even before he got to the logistics of it. It made his head swim.

'Here,' Greg said, as Lydia rejoined them. He handed Burnett two handsets. 'This one is to talk to us. This one is set to broadcast on all frequencies. Don't get them confused. Take the generator back to base and keep the handsets charging. We'll turn ours off until we're ready, one way or the other. Try not to run the battery down.'

'How are you going to get back?' Lydia asked.

'Don't worry about me. You two get on the road. Be safe, and watch out for bandits.'

'We will.'

'I don't have to tell you how much is riding on you both, do I?'

'I'd rather you didn't,' Greg said, with a chuckle.

'Okay. Good luck, both of you.'

'You too.' Lydia said.

They climbed in, Lydia behind the wheel, and drove off. They kept their lights off, navigating by the little moonlight breaking through the clouds.

The rain had stopped, and the night turned cold once more, the heat of the storm slowly ebbing away. He looked at the trailer housing the generator and the transmitter. There was no way he could drag it back, but he didn't want to leave it here, either. The chances of bandits straying this far in were remote, but he still didn't want to risk it.

Burnett rubbed his head and turned the generator off. He wheeled the trailer behind a hedge, and pulled some branches off a tree to make it harder to see from the road. Satisfied, he tried to get his bearings, and headed back to the city centre.

Chapter Nine
Backlit

Resting her head against the window, Lydia tried to get some sleep, a pointless endeavour given the adrenaline and fear coursing through her body. Beside her, Greg drove, their car crawling slowly along the roads. He had no lights on, despite the almost total darkness, so it was slow going. If the morning mist starting to cling low to the surrounding fields developed into fog, he'd find it almost impossible to navigate, and they'd have to stop.

Lydia had driven for the first part of their journey, getting them out of Birmingham and onto the country roads. They had decided to avoid the main routes into the capital, figuring they'd be less likely to run into bandits on the back roads. Problem was, they were a mess. Thankfully their car was a quiet runner, so in the darkness they were near invisible. They'd have to be unlucky enough to run straight into a band of bandits to be seen. Not that it would be out of keeping with their luck to do exactly that. Once the sun came up, it'd be another story.

At some point they'd need to stop for food, water, and sleep. Getting to London could take days at this rate, and there'd be no point making it that far only to be tripping their tits off on sleep deprivation and dehydration.

Six months ago they could have done Birmingham to London and back again already, with time to stop for a McDonalds along the way. That was before the world got flip-turned upside down.

Great. Now I have the theme tune to The Fresh Prince of Bel Air *in my head.*

She squirmed in her seat, struggling to get comfortable. She gave up.

'How are you doing?' she asked Greg, as much to make sure he hadn't fallen asleep with his eyes open as out of concern.

'Fine,' he said. 'This fucking kills your eyes though.'

She knew what he meant. Her own eyes were still sore from having to stare, unblinking, at near perfect darkness, trying to make out the road ahead of her.

'You need to stop?' she asked.

'No, I can keep going until the sun comes up. Then we can work out where the hell we are. Maybe stop.'

She closed her eyes again, but it didn't feel like a minute had passed before the sunrise prised them open. As it rose, angry, red, and beautiful, she wondered whether the burning orb might hold some kind of malevolence towards humanity. Wiping out the bulk of it with solar storms once looked like carelessness. But by the third attempt it looked more like mischief on the part of their star.

'I wonder why those scientists died,' she said. 'I mean, I didn't even get a headache.'

'Maybe surviving the first storm the first time hardened our brains, somehow. They wouldn't have been exposed to it.'

'Or,' Lydia said, 'maybe we're the chosen people of the great sun god, Ra.'

He smiled. 'Who knows? I can't say I feel particularly chosen.'

'Me either.'

They rode on in silence for a few minutes, as the light grew around them.

'Studely,' Lydia said, as they passed a sign.

'Why, thank you,' Greg said.

'That's not...'

'I know. Just fucking with you. We've not made it far.'

'I don't know this part of the world.'

'We're thirty miles or so south of Birmingham, and we're kind of heading in the wrong direction,' Greg said. 'We should stop somewhere. Let's find something to eat, get some sleep, and work out which way we're going.'

To their right was a built up residential area. Lydia was about to suggest they investigate, when Greg took an impromptu left off the road, and headed down a small lane.

'Where are we going?' she asked.

'There's a big pub down here. Quite nice, I've been there before.'

'You realise it's probably closed, right?'

'The thought had crossed my mind.'

They pulled into the car park of the Hollybush Inn, which stood untouched by the events of the last six months, a beautiful old-fashioned public house, covered in ivy. The gravel crackled under the wheels of the car. Greg pulled up by the entrance.

'You reckon the beer will have gone off yet?'

'I imagine so.'

'Shame, I'd love a pint.'

The doors were open, and they entered the musty main bar. Bodies all around, at every table. She held her breath, aware her lungs were already full of the people who had died there.

'Fuck me, that's a fair old stench,' Greg said, pulling his jumper over his mouth.

They worked methodically, searching the place to find anything edible. Lydia found bottled water and soft drinks. Greg found crisps and pork scratchings, something Lydia had never tried before.

'You've never tried pork scratchings?' Greg asked, incredulous.

'I'm Greek, Greg. We don't tend to deep fry pork skin.'

'Well pardon me, your majesty.' He ripped open a packet. 'You should try these. Lots of protein. Good for you.'

'I doubt it,' she said, watching in horror as he took out a curled piece of fried fat and popped it in his mouth.

He offered her the bag. They looked like deep fried baby fingers. She took one, and gingerly placed it inside her mouth. She bit it in half, her mouth filling with salty crispness. She balked at it, but began to chew.

'Well?'

'It's horrible, but...'

'But you want another one, don't you?'

She nodded, shamefully. 'I really do.'

Once the packet was gone, she washed the taste out with a bottle of Coke, but the residue of fattiness lingered.

They continued to look around.

'There's nothing here,' she said.

'We could break in upstairs. Might be somewhere to crash for a while.'

'We should hit the road.'

'That's the scratchings talking. I'm beat. Besides, we shouldn't be driving in the day.'

They found the doorway leading to the living quarters, where they found one bed which was corpse free.

'I don't mind, if you don't,' Greg said.

'It's fine,' she said.

Greg took his trousers off and climbed under the covers. She did the same, fiddling around under her top to remove her bra too. Now she really wished he hadn't hit on her, and she could sense the same in him. To his credit, he turned his back straight away.

Lydia climbed in next to him and lay her head down on the pillow. She had started to wonder about the bed's previous inhabitant, and where their body was, when sleep took her.

Lydia woke, and saw day was turning back to night. Beside her, Greg still slept, his back to her, his breathing on the verge of a snore. She pulled herself up in the bed, making him stir. He turned to her and gave a sleepy smile. He turned back.

The warm musk of having a man next to her, a concept so totally alien in recent months, stirred something. The grief and pain and everything else was compressed, for a moment, into nothing, and something... *else* swept through her.

She leaned in further.

He turned slightly, and gave her a quizzical look, but she could already sense his anticipation of what was to come.

Fuck it.

She leaned over and gave him a soft kiss, which he pulled back from for a second in confusion, before reciprocating. Her hand worked its way under the cover, under his top. She caressed his back, and pulled his body closer, so his soft belly pressed against her. He stiffened against her thigh.

Reaching down, she slid her hand into his boxers and took hold of him.

'You know this doesn't mean anything, right?' she said, softly.

'Do you hear me complaining?'

It must have been at least six months since either of them had found themselves in this position, but they took their time. Greg seemed to sense this might be his one and only chance at this, and applied himself with dedication, as though auditioning for a part he never expected to be available to him. When they rolled away from each other some time later, panting, sweating, and sated, she looked back at him and laughed.

'Thanks,' she said. 'I think I needed that.'

'No,' he replied, still smiling a broad smile. 'The pleasure was mine.'

They got up, each wanting to cover the nakedness they'd been enjoying in each other a few minutes earlier.

'I'll go check the bathroom,' she said, wrapping a sheet around herself. She went through and stared at herself in the mirror.

What the hell was that about?

She washed as best she could with the dribble of water from the tap and returned to the bedroom, where Greg was going through the wardrobes of the Inn's previous inhabitants. He was wearing his boxers, his stomach hanging slightly over the front of them, the thatch of red hair on his chest matching a small patch at the base of his spine.

'Hi,' he said. 'Looks like there's some stuff here you might want to look at. Nothing my size, unfortunately.' He patted his belly, embarrassed.

'Cheers,' she replied, aware of the blush flushing her cheeks.

'Listen,' he said. 'I want...'

'Let's get dressed first, eh? Then we can talk.'

He nodded, and the two of them dressed in silence, whatever passion had been in the air before slowly seeping away.

Greg was right, though. The woman who had lived here was her size, and had good taste in functional clothes. Lydia found herself a whole new outfit in minutes. She contemplated packing a bag with more, until she remembered the task in front of them.

As soon as she remembered what they were supposed to be doing, the guilt flooded back. They should be in London, not sleeping the day away, or having romps in bed. They had to get back on the road as soon as they could.

'Okay,' Greg said. 'Are we allowed to talk now?'

'If you like. Before you say anything though...'

'Jesus, woman, are you going to let me talk?' he said, laughing.

'Sorry,' she replied, her cheeks flushing again. 'Go on.'

'I like you. And that was fantastic. But the situation we're in is not exactly conducive to a long-term, healthy relationship, even if we both wanted one. I know you don't want one, and I don't think I do, either. If you ever want to do... *that* again, sure, it'd be a grand old time. But I'm not expecting anything from you, okay? Now, we've got a job to do.'

She stood, stunned. 'Well,' she stammered. 'If you're going to go and take the words right out of my mouth...'

He leaned forward, planted a kiss on her cheek, and turned away. 'Let's get on the road, shall we?'

Lydia offered to take the first shift, and as they got back into the car the last light of the sun slipped away to nothing beyond the horizon. Neither spoke, but it wasn't an uncomfortable silence. Next to her, Greg pored over the map as best he could in the low light of the moon.

'If we're going to avoid the motorways, we're going to come into London at a funny angle. I don't know the city well.'

'We'll manage,' Lydia said.

They rode on in silence for a moment.

'Greg,' she said. 'I do have one question.'

'Yes?'

'Well, you don't know the area well, but you knew that pub?'

'Ah,' he said. 'Funny story, actually. That was where I met my wife.'

Chapter Ten
From Where Its Roots Run

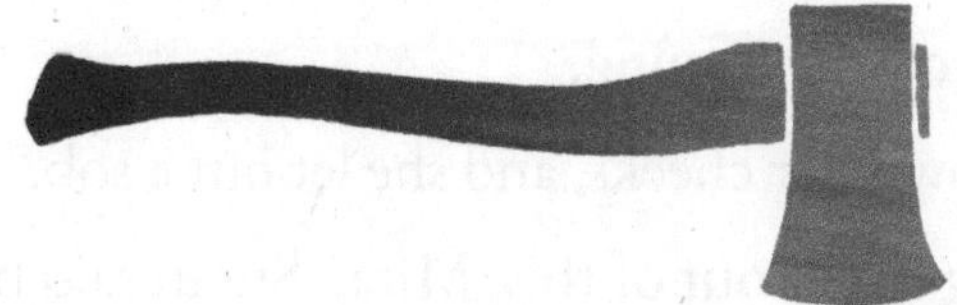

Mira tried to free her hands from the heavy rope that bound them. It was no use. She, like Susan and the other women beside her, had been strung up in an old horse box, which bore them down a dark road to who knew where. Along with Susan and Mira, there were three other women, all unconscious. Mira didn't know where they'd come from. All had been there when she woke.

'Shit,' Susan said next to her. 'I need a piss.'

'Me too,' Mira replied.

Arms aching, she craned to get a better view of the world outside, but the air slits in the horse box were too high, and she didn't have the strength to pull herself up to get a better view.

In the absence of anything else to do but hang there and think, she ran through a mental list of the terrible things that were likely to happen to her when the box came to a halt.

The face of Ewen, the monster who had killed the only boy she'd ever loved, floated to the front of her mind. He'd been psychotic, certainly, but these people, whoever they were, seemed worse somehow. Institutionalised sociopathy. The fact she and Susan had woken in this cart, and Tom, Tana, and Chen hadn't told her enough of a story. It was too much to hope they were still alive, that they might be out there, hot on the heels of the motorcycle gang.

There was no help coming.

Tears ran down her cheeks, and she let out a sob.

'We're going to get out of this, Mira,' Susan said beside her.

'How?'

'Same way we've made it this far. By being badasses.'

'I don't feel much like a badass.'

'Sure,' Susan said. 'But it's pretty hard to feel like a badass when you're hanging from the ceiling of a moving vehicle that's hurtling towards your almost certain doom.'

Mira laughed, and a bubble of snot escaped her nose, joining the tears streaming down her cheeks. She wished she could wipe it away, but it just hung there.

'I'm scared,' Mira said.

'Me too, sweetie.' Susan's voice was lower, softer. 'I know what you're thinking. Wherever we're going, I don't think it's anywhere good. Together, we'll try to get out of it, I promise. But if things get beyond us.... There's no shame in looking for an easy way out, rather than... the alternative.'

Mira nodded.

The truck pulled up. Shadows played inside the box from people moving around them. The sound of the bike engines fell to nothing.

'Stop right there,' a voice called.

A shotgun cocked somewhere outside. Mira's heart soared, wondering if this could be the rescue she hadn't allowed herself to dream of.

'Alright, wankers, no need to get yer fucking knickers in a twist,' a voice replied.

Mira's heart sank again. This was no rescue.

The door to the horse box opened, filling the inside with bright sunlight that forced Mira to squint, until a burly-looking biker climbed in and blocked out the light again. He had a knife in his hand, which glinted as he brought it up to Mira's face.

She moaned, a noise she had no control over. The man lifted the knife up to the rope binding her hands. In a flash, he severed it from the hook in the roof of the truck, leaving her hands still bound.

Mira fell to the floor, her legs unable to take her weight. Her elbow smashed to the floor, hard, sending a jolt of pain up her arm. She cried out. If the man had any concern for her, he didn't show it, and moved straight onto Susan, who eyed his approach with a wild stare.

'Hey,' the second of the voices called from outside the box. 'What's going on in there? Don't you be bruising my goods.'

'Fuck your goods,' the first voice replied. 'What about our payment?'

Mira tried to get up, wanting to edge to the door and assess her chances of escaping, but couldn't summon the strength. The big biker returned, having cut down the other three women. He lifted Mira up with one arm, dragging her and Susan out onto the street.

They were on a deserted road, albeit one scattered with occasional car wrecks and long-decomposed bodies. There were no buildings, just miles of rolling farmland, going slowly to seed.

On the road, the bikers stood facing a new group. Not bikers, but mean-looking bastards nonetheless. Their leader, a tall skinny white man with an angry scar down his face, held his hands out in front of him.

'Come on, lads,' he said. 'You show me yours, I'll show you mine.'

Another man ushered Susan and Mira forward at the barrel of a shotgun. Behind them, the other three women from the truck had been revived and shoved forward to join them, groggily becoming aware of the trouble they had collectively found themselves in.

'Nice,' the thin man leered. 'Hello, ladies. I'm Bill, and I'll be your new boss. Well, I say boss. I'm much more than that, ladies, as I'm sure you'll come to know.'

He moved towards Mira.

'Not so fucking fast,' the big biker said. 'Where is it?'

'Easy, Gra,' Bill replied.

He motioned to one of his men, who lowered his weapon and went back to their Land Rovers. When he came back, he struggled with a large crate. He walked to the middle ground between the two groups, and opened the top. He pulled it back with a flourish, revealing the goods within.

Mira and Susan shared a quick look of incredulity.

'What the fuck?' Susan said. 'You're selling us for *food*?'

'Food's scarce,' one of the bikers said. 'Women less so.'

A chuckle rippled through both groups.

'So,' Bill said, clapping his hands together. 'We got a deal?'

'Let's take a look,' one of the bikers said. Mira recognised him as the one with the rancid breath from the lake.

He moved forward to the crate, and Mira could feel the tension ratchet up a notch. Fingers tightened on triggers both sides of the aisle, and nervous glances went from man to man. Mira thought she could see more of the tension in Bill's men. The hairs on the back of her neck stood to attention.

This isn't going to go well.

The biker got to the box and started pulling out tins. He checked they went all the way to the bottom and picked one at random to open. He pulled back the lid and put his nose to it. He recoiled away.

He dropped the can and stood, pulling out his pistol. 'What the fuck?'

'Hey,' Bill said, smiling. 'You asked for tins. I got tins. Didn't much care what was in them.'

'You miserable b–'

As one, Bill's men opened fire, cutting down the rank-breathed biker, and half of his compatriots in one fell swoop.

Mira dived to the ground as the remaining bikers opened fire. One of the women from the horse box, barely out of unconsciousness, was caught in the middle. A spray of blood splattered over Mira.

'You bastards,' the main biker said, through a mouthful of blood. He fell down beside Mira, spilling the pistol from his hands and right into hers.

She worked her hands up from underneath, wrists still bound by rope. The bindings covered most of her hands, limiting her grip, but she managed to claw at the pistol until she had it.

She couldn't get her finger loose enough to grip the trigger so she sat up, dropped the pistol into her lap and started to work at the ropes with her teeth, trying to free her index finger.

Shots continued to ring out, but the battle became increasingly one-sided. Two bikers remained, both cowering behind the horse cart, firing rounds indiscriminately behind it. One of Bill's men lay dead.

Her finger free of the binds, she picked up the gun. She rose to her feet. Susan jumped up beside her, and Mira pulled her friend behind her. She held the gun out, pointed at Bill, who had just noticed this new development.

'Alright, darling,' he said, the smug smile leaving his face for the first time since they'd met. 'No need for that.'

'Fuck off,' Mira said. 'We're leaving.'

'You sure about that, love?'

The two remaining bikers were flanked and killed, and the roar of gunfire stopped immediately. The guns turned to Mira. The two other women stood, and closed in behind her.

'Stay back,' she said, her finger tightening on the trigger.

'Shoot him,' Susan urged.

'Why don't you give me that, little girl?' Bill said, moving forward.

Mira's hand started to shake, and sweet beaded on her forehead. She saw Ewen's brains splatter on a wall. Jen's shirt blossoming with red.

Stars danced on the edge of her vision. She resolved to shoot. She was going to kill this fucker. She aimed for his head, and pulled the trigger.

Except she didn't — her finger not obeying the impulses in her head.

She felt faint. She tried again to pull the trigger, but couldn't. Tears welled in her eyes. She felt the strength go out of her arm, her legs.

'Shoot him,' Susan hissed.

'Give me the gun,' Bill urged once more, his voice lower.

He moved forward, growing bolder at the visible shaking of Mira's hand. He reached forward in a flash, and took the gun from her. She didn't have the strength to fight back, and it slipped from her grasp.

He leaned in. 'I'm going to make you fucking pay for that, sweetheart,' he whispered. He planted a kiss on her cheek, his dry lips pressing on her wet skin.

She cringed away from it, a shudder of revulsion sweeping over her.

Bill turned and motioned to his men. 'Pick up the crate, get the women on board. Let's get back home.'

Somewhere inside, some part of Mira broke. She collapsed to the ground, her legs unable to take the weight of what felt like a metric tonne of shame, regret, hatred, and fear crashing down on her shoulders at once.

'Come on,' Susan said, pulling her up. 'You'll be okay. We'll be okay. I promise. We'll get through this.'

Three of Bill's men moved toward the four women, their guns pointed at the faces of their new prizes. They ushered the women over to a white van.

They climbed into the back. There were no seats, only the crate of spoiled food. Without a word, the door closed on them, throwing the four of them into total darkness.

One of the women screamed and started hammering on the side of the van.

'Hey,' Susan said. 'Don't do that.'

'Why not?' the woman shot back.

'Because it's annoying, and it's not going to achieve anything,' Mira said, flatly. She groped around the edge of the van, trying to find anything she could sit on.

'As opposed to you giving him that gun?' the woman shot back.

'Hey,' Susan shouted.

There was a scuffle. The truck teetered for a second as someone was shoved against against the wall of the truck.

'Stop,' Mira said, weakly. 'I'm sorry. I just...' She fought back the tears.

The truck moved, and all four of them fell to the ground. Mira felt two bound hands press against her, pulling her into as close an embrace as possible.

'We'll get through this,' Susan said. 'I promise.'

Mira nodded in the darkness, knowing full well how much of a lie it was.

Chapter Eleven
Your Hand In Mine

'Sorry, say that again?' Lydia asked.

'I met my wife in that pub. Well, my ex-wife. It was, shit, it must have been fifteen years ago. I was at university; so was she. I was in York; she was in Leeds. Both of us did engineering courses. You know, going to factories, research labs, stuff like that. There was a night out after some trip to a plastics factory, the kind of thing where everyone is drowning their sorrows at the realisation they are going to end up working somewhere tedious like a fucking plastics factory. That was the closest pub to the hotel we were being put up in. That's where we met.'

'Huh. So...' Lydia said, unable to find the words she needed.

'Yeah.'

'You said ex-wife?'

'We lasted five years. No kids. Not even kept in contact since then. We were much too young to get married. Funny I ended up back there, though.'

'Well, you did drive us there.'

'Yeah. Sorry, it feels a bit weird given...'

'Don't worry about it,' Lydia said. 'You think she survived the storm?'

'I dunno. She smoked, so I guess there's a chance. Although that was ten years ago, so who knows? The only way I could think to find out is checking Facebook, so I guess that's off the table.'

She laughed. 'Well, I'm going to try not to be offended by the fact you seduced me in the same place you met your ex-wife.'

'Hey, you seduced me, remember?'

'True.'

'So, what about you?' he asked.

She had known it was coming, but still wasn't prepared. She opened her mouth to answer, but nothing came out.

She was saved from having to find the words by something catching the corner of her vision. She turned to the movement.

'Holy shit,' she said.

The truck barrelled at them from a side street and smashed into the passenger side. Lydia grabbed the wheel, spinning it hard, trying anything to get away, before slamming on the brakes.

Glass exploded everywhere. Wet splattered across her face. The car turned over, something slammed into her head, and darkness closed in.

The darkness swirled into pain, and light. She opened her eyes. Her cheek and nose hurt, and she couldn't feel anything below her waist.

That's probably not good.

In the passenger seat, Greg sat motionless. She tried to focus her vision. Two hands reached in through the shattered window and pulled Greg out, roughly.

'Greg,' she called out, weakly.

Two hands reached in on her side. Before she could protest they grabbed her shoulders and roughly pulled her clear of the car. The arms dragged her a few metres, over which she lost her bearings before being dumped onto the ground. The jolt seemed to reconnect her with her lower half, which responded by letting her know how much pain she was in. She howled.

'Dump that one here,' someone said, a man's voice, thick with a cockney accent.

'Fuck's sake, he's a right fat cunt,' another man replied, struggling.

Lydia could barely see out of one eye. She strained to move her head to see anything other than the dark clouds above them. A man dragged Greg's unconscious body over to where she lay.

'Don't,' she said, or tried to. It was hard with a mouth full of blood.

'Search 'em, see what they got,' the first voice said. 'You, search the car. They got to have some supplies with 'em'

The radio.

No matter what happened, she couldn't let them take the radio. It was the only way to contact Burnett.

What do you care? You're not making it off this road, let alone to London.

Greg was finally dumped, unceremoniously, next to her. She watched him for signs of life. The way his body fell to the ground, however, all but extinguished her hope.

'Don't think that fat fuck will be telling us anything,' the second voice said, panting at the exertion.

'Car ain't got fuck all in it,' a voice called out.

'Look again,' the first voice said. 'They got to be carrying something.'

She strained to lift her head to look at the men who'd run them off the road. Four of them, sporting filthy beards and filthier clothes. Their hair ranged from wild to non-existent.

'Well, fuck,' the first man said. 'What kind of fucking luck is that? First fucking car we've seen in a pissing week, and it's two dozy pricks ain't carrying so much as a fucking bottle of Evian between 'em.'

'What do we do?' the second one asked.

'Fuck 'em, leave 'em here.'

Lydia lay her head back down.

The men got back into their van, struggled to turn the engine over, and finally drove away. The whole thing was over in a matter of minutes.

She blinked. It seemed to be the only thing she could do, save from turning her head. It was a start. Next, she tried to move her fingers. They let her know how unhappy they were with the command, but complied nonetheless. She continued for a while, testing out various parts of her body, trying to work out what was damaged, and what wasn't. Somehow, she hadn't broken any bones. She felt tenderised, bruised beyond anything she'd experienced before, but more or less intact.

She couldn't bring herself to try sitting up. Her spine felt completely hammered, and moving her head further than she'd already done might cause irreparable damage.

Out of the silence, Greg's breath rasped, suddenly. He was alive, but barely. Lydia let out a sigh of relief, her eyes welling with tears.

As the night rolled on, the ground grew colder. The breathing next to her grew shallower. She tried to sit up, but couldn't move. Even the small movements she'd managed before were gone. The realisation gripped her, and she started to hyperventilate.

This is it. This is how you die.

In the end, it wasn't the cold that shocked her into action, or the deteriorating condition of the man next to her. It was the dogs.

She heard the growl before she saw them. She managed to move her head and saw one pair of eyes staring at her. Another set joined; a third; a fourth. Four dogs circled her, on the periphery of her vision in the barest light of the moon. They snarled at her, daring her to move.

She did, careful not to alarm them. It wasn't until she sat up that she realised what she'd done. There was no time for self-congratulation though. With every muscle screaming at her to lie back down, she stood.

'Back off,' she called out.

They ignored her and continued to circle, snarling. None of them came closer. She locked eyes with one of the dogs, more wolf than pet, and held it in her gaze. She fished around in her pockets, desperately trying to find something, anything, that might drive them away. If she could get back to the twisted mess of metal that was their car, she might be able to find the gun the inept thieves had missed. If she made that move, though, she'd be dead before she got there. Either that or Greg would be.

Her fingers closed around a lighter, long since abandoned, its top stuffed with lint.

She pulled it out, turned it up to full flame, and lit it, hoping to God it worked. A flame spouted from the top, and she waved it in front of her. The dogs didn't retreat, but they lost some of their confidence, snarling but staying back.

The fire started to burn her. She held it as long as she could, but had to let go, wincing at the pain in her thumb, seemingly the one part of her not already hurting.

The circle paced closer again, emboldened by the disappearance of fire.

She took off her coat, and then the jumper underneath, her body aching with the movement. She made sure not to break eye contact with the dog she'd designated as the lead predator, a large mongrel of some kind, dark as the night and with a fierce stare. She took the lighter and lit the sleeve of the jumper, hoping the woman she'd stolen it from wasn't the type to go for flame-retardant clothing. For a second, nothing happened, and her other thumb started to feel the burn of the lighter's top. Finally, fire licked up the long sleeve.

The dogs hesitantly took in this new development and stopped circling. Looking around, Lydia decided to go on the attack. She let out a blood curdling roar and waved the burning rags about.

The dogs hesitated and started to break off, scattering to the safety of the adjacent roads.

Lydia collapsed, exhausted. No sooner was she down, than she realised she couldn't afford to rest. She placed the still burning jumper next to Greg and headed for the wreck of the car. It didn't take long to locate either the gun or the radio, both of which had nestled safely in the pocket of the driver's side door. She loaded the weapon, and looked over the radio. She had no idea how to use it; Greg hadn't shown her how.

She went back to Greg and checked his pulse. It was still there, but very weak.

'You flirting with me?' he rasped.

She jumped back in fright. 'Jesus, Greg.'

He laughed, weakly. 'You thought I was a goner, huh?'

'Never for a second.'

'Don't rule it out yet,' he said. 'I don't feel very well.'

'Don't be silly,' she said, leaning down to stroke his hair. 'You'll be fine.'

'No,' he said. 'I don't think so. My arms are definitely broken. My neck feels weird. I can't feel my legs.'

She looked over the damage by the light of the fire. It was every bit as bad as his assessment. His legs lay at funny angles, cut to ribbons, blood still oozing from the wounds and collecting in pools beneath him. One of his arms was snapped in two, the forearm bone jutting through his blood-soaked top. His complexion was pale, and his eyes had a misty glaze.

'You have to keep going,' he said.

'Don't be stupid,' she said. 'I'm not going anywhere.'

'Yes, you are. And it's considered bad form in some circles to berate a dying man and call him stupid,' he said. He tried to laugh at his own joke, but ended up wincing instead. 'Lydia, everyone is counting on you.'

She wiped her eyes. 'I don't even know how to work the bloody radio.'

'There's a switch on the side, should already be coded to the right channel. If not, it's seventeen. There's nothing stopping you. You know where the bunker is. Get there. See what it's like. Tell Burnett. Don't let me down.' The words came in short bursts, each seemingly more difficult to deliver. 'Don't you stop for me.'

She nodded, and wiped her eyes again. 'It's bloody typical; I was starting to like you.'

'I know,' he replied, smiling. 'Sod's law. Now go.'

'I'm not leaving you, Greg. There's dogs around.'

'I like dogs.'

'You wouldn't like these ones.'

She waited for a response, but none came. She leaned over him, but the shallow breathing was gone. She felt for a pulse, but it too had gone.

'I can't believe your last words were, 'I like dogs',' she said, half laughing, half sobbing. She leaned down, and gave him a firm kiss on the lips.

She stood, somewhat shakily, and looked around, wiping the tears from her eyes. In the light of the moon there wasn't much to see. No houses, no cars. Nothing but the road and the wreckage. Tucking the pistol into her waistband, she grabbed the radio and set off.

Chapter Twelve

Steel That Sleeps The Eye

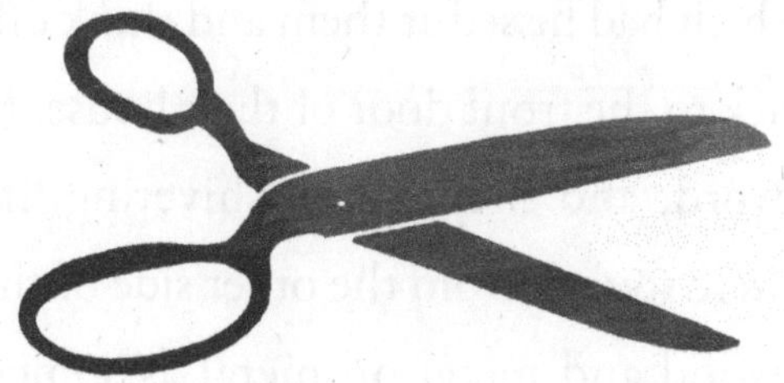

The body still hung from its noose as Max and Mouse picked their way through the rubble to get past it. Neither had said a word since fleeing the Kurgan and his men. Max had taken them on several detours on the way, trying to shake any pursuers they might have had on their tail. Hopefully it had done the trick.

They were back on the same Camden street as their home, the dangling corpse and the trap it was attached to the only thing between them and their sanctuary.

'You think we lost them?' Mouse asked, panting.

'I can't hear anything,' Max replied, although he knew full well that didn't mean shit. Kurgan's men might not be the subtlest of adversaries, but there was a reason they'd survived when everyone else hadn't. They could be sneaky, devious bastards when they wanted to be, as evidenced by the fact neither Max nor Mouse had heard them creeping up on them back at the Bunker.

He climbed back down into the street, and looked around. 'We should go round again, to be sure.'

'Okay,' Mouse said, with a weary resignation.

They wandered around again, in and out of alleyways and side streets, until the soles of Max's feet couldn't take it anymore, and Mouse's gait had turned to an exhausted shuffle. At one point a sound made Max freeze, but it turned out to be a bedraggled looking cat, which had hissed at them and slunk off.

They got back to the front door of their house. Mouse tapped out the password, and they stood, shivering, in the cold of night. There were sounds from the other side of the door: wood scraping on wood and metal on metal as someone removed barricades and opened latches. The door creaked open, and an elderly woman peered through the crack, her expression one of mean intensity.

'You know,' she said, not opening the door further. 'If you're going to abandon us for an entire day, you might want to think about letting somebody know, so the rest of us don't spend hours going out of our minds with worry.'

'I did,' Max protested. 'I told him. He decided to follow me.' He motioned to Mouse, who hung his head.

'Sorry, Nana.' Mouse said.

Nana was the oldest of the Shitty Six, and could lay a reasonable claim at being the oldest person left alive in the country, at the ripe old age of eighty-four. She was a spry old dear, though. She moaned less than some of the others and had lived through the Blitz, which she'd said was a lot like now, except there were currently disappointingly few handsome American men running about.

'Come in then,' she said, finally, opening the door scarcely wide enough for them to squeeze through. 'I don't suppose you found food on your travels?'

'No food, sorry,' Max said.

'We ran into the Kurgan, though,' Mouse said, beaming with excitement. 'I cut him up!'

That earned him a hefty clip round the ear.

'Mouse!' Nana boomed. 'What have I told you about getting yourself into trouble?'

'Sorry, Nana.'

The house inside was warm, thanks to the various candles covering every surface. Back in his university days, he'd doubted whether you could ever heat a house with candles, now he knew you could. You just needed enough to cross the threshold into them being a fire hazard to do so. There was a chimney, but they hadn't dared utilise it, for fear of giving their position away.

Max walked through to the kitchen, which doubled as the single communal area. The other three sat around the table, notable for its total absence of food. As soon as Max entered, all three demeanours changed.

Darren was the first out of his chair, a jovial and massive man with what would charitably be called a simple disposition. He came over to Max and gave him a bear hug, squeezing the air out of Max's lungs. Jess and Ava didn't stand up. Ava gave him a hard stare, her dark eyes and set jaw letting him know exactly how much trouble he was in. Jess, on the other hand, looked up and gave him an absent smile that seemed to signify she'd not even noticed he'd been gone.

'Hi,' Max said.

Ava looked away.

'Hello,' Jess said. 'Don't suppose you have any food, do you? I'm famished.'

'No, sorry,' Max replied. His stomach growled at the mention of food.

'I stabbed the Kurgan,' Mouse declared proudly, on his own entrance into the room.

'You did what?' Ava said, looking even angrier with him than she had with Max. 'You did *what*?'

'I stabbed Kurgan,' Mouse repeated, less confidently.

'It's true,' Max said, in response to the querying eyes of the rest of the family. 'Well, more of a surface cut, but... he did.'

'Wow,' Darren said, slowly. 'Good work, Mouse. You showed him.'

'Cheers,' Mouse said, and sat at the table.

'Would you like to tell us what actually happened?' Ava asked Max.

'Sure,' he said. He sat down at the table, and the others did the same, except Nana, who fussed around behind them, pretending not to listen. 'We headed out, looking for food. Well, I did, and Mouse followed me. We thought about going south of the river, when we came across something.'

'A bunker,' Mouse interjected.

'Right. Down by the river, right by Whitehall. I mean, it makes sense, right? They'd have somewhere to evacuate the Prime Minister, key government types, if there was a nuclear attack, right? Well, we think we found it.'

'Only we couldn't get in,' Mouse said.

'Right.'

'And the Kurgan turned up, with his goons.'

'Yes.'

'And I stabbed him.'

'Kind of.'

'So,' Ava said, holding up her hand to shut the pair of them up. 'Let me get this right. Instead of looking for food, you tried to break into a top secret military bunker, failed, and got attacked by the most homicidal lunatic in London. You attacked him, and ran back here, presumably with him right on your heels?'

'No,' Max replied. 'Well, yes and no. There's no food. It's gone. I've been out on those streets, and so have you, Ava. There's nothing left. I was going to try and get south of the river, try my hand there, but the prospect of a bunker? That was too good to pass up. Think about it. There must be all kinds of supplies down there. Food, water, blankets, beds. Nobody even knows it's there.'

'Except the Kurgan.'

'Well, yeah.'

'And maybe whoever is already in the bunker.'

'There's not going to be anyone in the bunker,' Max said, scoffing.

'Why not?'

'There was no nuclear war, for one thing. If anyone had gone into the bunker during the storms, they would have come back out as soon as the fires cleared. They'd have to. They're the government.'

'If you say so.'

'In the meantime,' Nana interjected. 'There's no food at all?'

'No,' Max said. 'Sorry.'

Five faces stared back with disappointment. Nana's lips tightened, and she leaned against a cupboard and looked away from Max. Darren wore his usual empty expression. Max wished the big man could be of more help to them, but at the first sign of trouble he'd retreat into himself and refuse to move, which made him too much of a liability to count on. Mouse, full of bluster and bravado. Jess and Ava, two women of such diametrically opposed personalities Max was continually amazed they hadn't killed each other yet. Jess was a flouncy artiste, a formerly middle-class woman whose idea of pitching in was to offer derisory critique from the side-lines, or perhaps a sketch of your toils, while Ava was the kind of person for whom the hardest part of the apocalypse was the inability to go for a morning run or be able to schedule your day to the nth degree. They had been together for months, and he had no idea how she felt about him.

They look so tired.

'Which is why,' Max said, 'I think we should leave.'

The room erupted in raucous consternation.

'I can't be going out there at my age...'

'What about Darren...'

'Where will we go...'

'Are we leaving London...'

'Can we go to the zoo...'

Max held his hands up, and all five fell silent. 'I'm not saying we have to go. I'm saying it's what I think we should do. I'll leave it up to everyone to decide for themselves.'

'What, leave people behind?' Mouse asked.

'I don't want to stay on my own,' Jess said.

'Darren doesn't, either,' Darren said.

'No,' Max said. 'We'll take a vote. Either we all stay, or we all go.'

'We can't leave,' Ava said. 'It's too dangerous out there.'

'We can't stay, either,' Max said, losing control of his tone. 'We. Have. No. Food.'

They stared back at him, shocked. Max never lost his temper. Usually he didn't see the point. Things were what they were, what was the point of getting het up about it?

'Talk it over,' he said, quieter. 'I'm going to bed.'

'Wait,' Ava said, before he reached the door. 'Have some food first.'

'We don't...'

Ava stood, and opened a panel behind the broken sink Max had never seen before. He'd seen it, obviously, every day for the last six months, but his eyes had skirted over it every time. Once Ava opened it, of course, it seemed absurd he hadn't spotted it.

Of course it's a secret compartment, look at it.

Ava reached in and pulled out three tins and a pack of crackers. One more reach in yielded four small bottles of water.

'Jesus, Ava,' Mouse said. 'You been holding out on us?'

'No,' she said, affronted. 'I kept it for a dire emergency, and I'd say having not eaten for two days counts. Besides, if this is going to be our last night here...'

She fixed Max with a look, and he knew he'd won her over, at least. If he had, he'd won everyone. He didn't think he was out of the doghouse, though, not by a long shot.

'Good thinking,' he said, seeing if he could thaw the ice quicker.

Trouble is there's always too much bloody ice.

'Don't suppose you've got any cigs squirrelled away in there?' Mouse asked.

'Oh, cigarettes; yes, please,' Darren added.

'Sorry,' Ava said, putting the panel back in place.

'I'll get the hob on,' Nana said. She started to potter about. They knew better than to offer assistance.

'So,' Ava said. 'Where would we go?'

'Well, call me crazy, but I still think the bunker's worth a shot.'

'I had a horrible feeling you'd say that.'

Nana brought out the food, a strange concoction of spaghetti hoops, baked beans, hot dogs and tinned spinach, the latter ruining the meal completely. Max didn't care, he wolfed it down eagerly, taking care to sip his water to make it last.

They went to their rooms rejuvenated by the food and without further discussion about leaving. Max could tell, though – they were going. He'd hoped he could mend whatever bridges he'd burned with Ava, but she retreated into her room and closed the door without a word. He went into his own, and started to pack.

They were well practised in the art of having a bag ready, and Max had his packed in a few minutes, stuffed with the few items of clothing he'd found which actually fit him. He headed back down.

Nana hadn't gone to her room. She sat at the table, walking cane between her knees, staring at boards that had long ago replaced windows.

'Nana?' Max said, setting his bag down. 'You okay?'

She looked up at him, her eyes brimming. 'I can't go, Max.'

'What? Why not?'

'I'll only slow you down. Maybe get you all killed.'

'Don't be silly,' he said, sitting down next to her. He took he

frail hand in his own. 'We'll be fine. And we're not leaving yo

behind.'

'I... I don't know if I can. My ankles hurt, and my back hurts

I'm on my feet for too long.'

'We'll make it work, Nana. If we have to stop and rest, we st

and rest.'

She gave him a weak smile. She clearly wasn't sold, but M

couldn't leave her behind. Neither could he stay and wait fo

to no longer be an issue, as blunt as that sounded. Besides,

knew Nana. She was made of stronger stuff than even she kn

How else could you explain her continued survival in the fac

so much destruction?

He looked around the house, at its crumbling, wrecked w

its complete lack of a light source that didn't have a wick in it;

dirt, the grime.

I'm going to miss this place.

'Come on, Nana,' he said, helping the old lady out of her c

'Let's go get you packed.'

CHAPTER THIRTEEN
PATHS OF GLORY

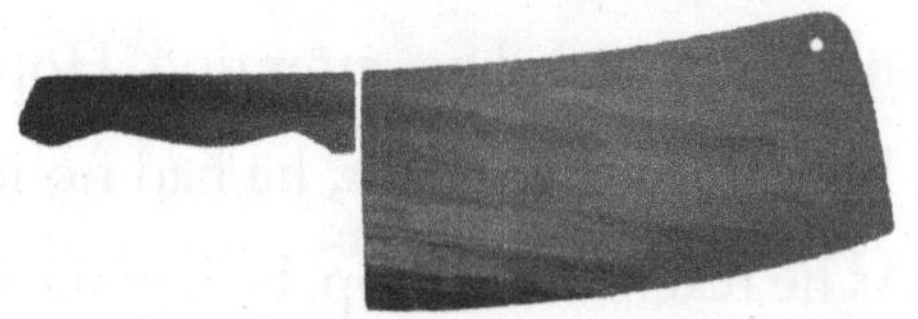

By the time he got back to the Bullring, Burnett was cold and exhausted. One of the armed guards almost fell over at his sudden appearance and nearly took his head off in startled excitement, before realising who he was.

'Get a truck, meet me here in a few minutes,' he growled at the man, who scurried off before Burnett could follow up by asking where Tyler was.

He trudged onwards to the shopping centre. People still milled about, watching the skies with distrust.

If they knew what I know, they wouldn't take their eyes off it again.

At some point, he'd have to talk to them, but he'd be damned if he was going to try converting people one at a time. Thankfully, they were too absorbed by the sky to notice him skulking past.

Inside, everything was quiet. Most people had turned in for the night, fed and scared. In fact, most people tended to sleep the whole night away these days, before waking at the crack of dawn, as though the darkness was something to be avoided at all costs.

Burnett was of the opinion that if night was when the monsters came out, you needed to be awake to face them.

Tyler had set up her security office in an outdoor clothing shop deep inside the shopping centre, and tended to sleep there most nights. She said she didn't want people coming and raiding the sleeping bags, and it was useful to be there in case there was some urgent situation which needed her attention. Hopefully she'd be there tonight, because if she wasn't, he had no idea where else she might be. As he reached the shop, he saw she was thankfully getting ready to go to bed in for the night.

'Come with me,' he said.

She rolled her eyes, and pulled her jeans back up.

'Do I need a gun?' she asked.

He nodded. 'Grab one for me, too.'

She tossed him a pistol from the stash she kept under the tills, which she used as a desk.

'Where are we going?'

'London. Not yet though.'

She shot him a quizzical look and followed him out the door. She knew better than to press him further in public. When they reached the front, a van waited. They both got in, Burnett taking the driver's seat.

'Oh,' Tyler said, buckling herself in. 'Before I forget. You wanted our scouts to check on a holiday camp. In Scarborough.'

Burnett's heart stopped. He'd sent that mission out so long ago he'd not dared to mention it since, sure he'd gotten some of his own men and women killed on a wild goose chase.

'Yes?'

'No,' Max said. 'We'll take a vote. Either we all stay, or we all go.'

'We can't leave,' Ava said. 'It's too dangerous out there.'

'We can't stay, either,' Max said, losing control of his tone. 'We. Have. No. Food.'

They stared back at him, shocked. Max never lost his temper. Usually he didn't see the point. Things were what they were, what was the point of getting het up about it?

'Talk it over,' he said, quieter. 'I'm going to bed.'

'Wait,' Ava said, before he reached the door. 'Have some food first.'

'We don't...'

Ava stood, and opened a panel behind the broken sink Max had never seen before. He'd seen it, obviously, every day for the last six months, but his eyes had skirted over it every time. Once Ava opened it, of course, it seemed absurd he hadn't spotted it.

Of course it's a secret compartment, look at it.

Ava reached in and pulled out three tins and a pack of crackers. One more reach in yielded four small bottles of water.

'Jesus, Ava,' Mouse said. 'You been holding out on us?'

'No,' she said, affronted. 'I kept it for a dire emergency, and I'd say having not eaten for two days counts. Besides, if this is going to be our last night here...'

She fixed Max with a look, and he knew he'd won her over, at least. If he had, he'd won everyone. He didn't think he was out of the doghouse, though, not by a long shot.

'Good thinking,' he said, seeing if he could thaw the ice quicker.

Trouble is there's always too much bloody ice.

'Don't suppose you've got any cigs squirrelled away in there?' Mouse asked.

'Oh, cigarettes; yes, please,' Darren added.

'Sorry,' Ava said, putting the panel back in place.

'I'll get the hob on,' Nana said. She started to potter about. They knew better than to offer assistance.

'So,' Ava said. 'Where would we go?'

'Well, call me crazy, but I still think the bunker's worth a shot.'

'I had a horrible feeling you'd say that.'

Nana brought out the food, a strange concoction of spaghetti hoops, baked beans, hot dogs and tinned spinach, the latter ruining the meal completely. Max didn't care, he wolfed it down eagerly, taking care to sip his water to make it last.

They went to their rooms rejuvenated by the food and without further discussion about leaving. Max could tell, though – they were going. He'd hoped he could mend whatever bridges he'd burned with Ava, but she retreated into her room and closed the door without a word. He went into his own, and started to pack.

They were well practised in the art of having a bag ready, and Max had his packed in a few minutes, stuffed with the few items of clothing he'd found which actually fit him. He headed back down.

Nana hadn't gone to her room. She sat at the table, walking cane between her knees, staring at boards that had long ago replaced windows.

'Nana?' Max said, setting his bag down. 'You okay?'

She looked up at him, her eyes brimming. 'I can't go, Max.'

'What? Why not?'

'I'll only slow you down. Maybe get you all killed.'

'Don't be silly,' he said, sitting down next to her. He took her frail hand in his own. 'We'll be fine. And we're not leaving you behind.'

'I... I don't know if I can. My ankles hurt, and my back hurts if I'm on my feet for too long.'

'We'll make it work, Nana. If we have to stop and rest, we stop and rest.'

She gave him a weak smile. She clearly wasn't sold, but Max couldn't leave her behind. Neither could he stay and wait for it to no longer be an issue, as blunt as that sounded. Besides, he knew Nana. She was made of stronger stuff than even she knew. How else could you explain her continued survival in the face of so much destruction?

He looked around the house, at its crumbling, wrecked walls; its complete lack of a light source that didn't have a wick in it; the dirt, the grime.

I'm going to miss this place.

'Come on, Nana,' he said, helping the old lady out of her chair. 'Let's go get you packed.'

"Don't be silly," he said, staring down at her. He took her [illegible] hand in his own. "We'll be fine. And we're not leaving you behind."

"I don't know if I can. My ankles hurt and my back hurts if I [illegible] for too long."

"We'll make it work, Nana. If we have to stop and rest, we stop and rest."

The grandmother took a smile. She clearly wasn't sold, but Max couldn't leave her behind. Neither could he stay and wait for [illegible] to no longer be an issue, as blunt as that sounded. Besides, he knew Nana. She was made of stronger stuff than even she knew. How else could you explain her continued survival in the face of so much destruction?

He looked around the house, at its crumbling, wrecked walls, its complete lack of lighting—one that didn't have a window left in the [illegible] he came.

[illegible]

"Come on, Nana," he said, helping the old lady out of her chair. "Let's get you packed."

'Empty. No bodies though. Not recent ones, anyway. Seems like your friends moved on.'

He nodded, pleased to have the guilt off his chest. He wondered if Tana, Tom, and Jen were still out there, somewhere. He hoped so. Maybe, if this came off, he'd see them again.

These thoughts occupied his mind during the short drive to where he'd left the radios and generator, until Tyler finally got bored of waiting for him to clue her in.

'So?' she said.

'Right,' Burnett replied. He told her everything that had happened. She hadn't even seen the storm, instead trying to work on tomorrow's sentry deployment, so it came as a shock.

'Let me get this right,' she said, once Burnett had finished. 'You want to transport every single person we have living here in Birmingham down to London, a place we know is basically hell on earth. We're going to somehow magically break into a nuclear bunker – sorry, a *top secret* military bunker, because a dying Swiss physicist who could have been a bandit having a laugh told you there was a mega apocalypse on the way. On top of that, you want to broadcast our intentions to the whole world, so every single scumbag out there can come and ambush us on the way?'

'At some point,' Burnett said, pulling up, 'we're going to have to come back together as a species. Who knows, maybe this is exactly the kick up the arse humanity needs to get together and reclaim our sense of purpose.'

'You're a crazy person, you know that, right?'

'Quite possibly.'

They loaded the radios and the generator into the van, Burnett glad to find nobody had pinched it in the intervening hour or so.

Tyler climbed into the driver's seat and turned to him. 'Say I'm with you. How do we get everyone down to London?'

'Same way most of us got here in the first place. We load up the coaches. We take as much food and supplies as we can, and we protect the convey any way we can. We've got enough military jeeps kicking about.'

'And if the coaches don't work? They've been out of action for months.'

'We work something else out.'

'When do you make the broadcast?'

'I'm not sure I will, yet,' he replied. 'You do have a point.'

'So do you, though.'

'And there's the rub.'

Back at the Bullring, they split up. Tyler went to start the process of organising the logistics of what would be the biggest operation they could possibly mount. It could take them months to get mobilised, but the Swiss man had said they might not even have days. They needed to get moving. It was too late to gather people together, but Burnett was too wired to sleep. He walked back to the council building, empty and dark. He went to the office, lit a candle, and started to work on a speech.

Burnett woke face down on several scraps of paper some hours later, the sunlight of the new day streaming through the windows. He bolted up, gathered together the papers and headed back to the Bullring.

People started to congregate for breakfast. The way it usually worked, breakfast happened in shifts. The essential workers or those who had to travel a distance came in first, and the last service was for those not working. He thought back to the previous night, to the indignation of the elderly woman at dinner, and realised his meritocratic system was hideously imbalanced, with the least fortunate survivors, the old and infirm, feeding on the scraps left over from the rest of them. He made a mental note to redress that balance, somehow, should he ever get the chance.

Tyler had already passed word around to the early eaters — nobody goes to work today. The flutters of gossip and rumour had already circulated the camp, and people abandoned the usual system to try to glean some snippet of information. He tried to avoid the clamour for news and hid away, letting Tyler deal with it.

Once breakfast was over, they gathered together, hundreds of people, before the steps of the council building, the only place Burnett thought big enough to address people.

Thank fuck it's not raining.

When the injured and elderly arrived, the crowd parted for them, so they could be front and centre. He knew they'd be the biggest challenge to win round, so he wanted them close enough to answer directly.

His hands started to sweat as he stood alone, a few steps up. Back before coming here at the barrel of a gun, Burnett would never have imagined he'd ever be in this situation. Since the storm he'd had someone else happy to take the platform – be it Father Leonard, or Tom, there was always someone else to do this kind of thing. He was not one for public speaking.

And yet here we are.

He coughed. A hush fell over the crowd.

'Good morning,' he said, his voice small and wispy in the open air. 'I'm sure you're keen to know why you're not out on your work details yet.'

'We're not complaining,' someone called out.

A ripple of nervous laughter went through the audience.

Burnett cleared his throat again, wanting a glass of water more than anything in the world.

'There are more storms coming. We think. Storms worse than the one that led us here. But we have a solution. We're going to have to leave. To London.'

He stopped to let that sink in. The crowd before him stared back in complete befuddlement.

'What the hell are you talking about?' a woman called out. Burnett was not remotely surprised to see it was the woman from the night before, front and centre before him.

'Sorry,' he said. 'That came out a bit... haphazard.'

'Take your time, lad,' the woman said.

He took a breath, and remembered the crumpled notes. He took them out, but they were a mess of jumbled thoughts. He stuffed them back in his pockets.

'I take it everyone here has heard the prevailing view of what caused all this shit?'

He talked. First about the scientists in Geneva and about the storms. He talked about the radios, and about the mission he'd sent Greg and Lydia on. With every point he grew in confidence, and the crowd seemed to turn his way. He spoke without interruption, while the faces in front of him changed from confusion to incredulity, to a growing acceptance.

When he finished, a hush fell over the crowd.

'I think that about covers it,' he said, finally.

'What about the people who can't travel?' the woman asked, but the anger was gone from her voice.

'We need to assess that, and see how we can get *everyone* fit for travel. If needs be we'll put wheels on a hospital. Don't get me wrong — nobody is going to be forced to go anywhere. But if we believe the men from CERN — and I think we should — staying here is an almost certain death. We need to get underground. If anyone thinks they have a better way, I'm all ears. But as of *right now*, we're mobilising. We need every single person thinking about getting out of here. I want to be on the road first thing tomorrow morning.'

Tyler stepped up beside him.

'Right,' she said, in a much more commanding voice than Burnett had managed. 'Anyone have a problem with this plan?'

A smattering of hands went up.

'Anyone not understand the plan?' she shouted.

The raised hands went down.

'Any questions, come and see me,' Burnett said. 'But I'm not spending the day talking about this. You're with us, or you're not.'

He walked up the steps. Behind him, the crowd fell into deep conversation.

'Good job,' someone called out behind him. He turned and offered them a smile, but he couldn't work out where it had come from, so he turned back and headed into the council building.

Inside, he walked up the wide ornate staircase, still showing fire damage from the first storm, and the bullets from the battle to take back the city. He carried on through to the office. From the window he could see the crowd, thinner but still there. People milled about, talking in small groups. No doubt debating the validity of his claims and the sanity of his plans.

He rubbed his eyes. Whatever little sleep he'd managed to get here last night, it wasn't enough.

'Went better than I thought it would,' Tyler said, entering the office.

'Thanks.'

'You left out one part though.'

She sat down in the chair across from him, and picked up a paperweight. 'You know, the part where you're going to make it impossible to get to London.'

He sighed. 'I get what you're saying, Ty. But I have a responsibility. *We* have a responsibility.'

'Our responsibility is to the people you talked to back there,' she replied. 'Not anybody else.'

'You think we're the only good people left? The only ones who deserve a fighting chance to survive?'

'So this is about your friends?'

'No,' Burnett replied, affronted despite the truth of her statement. 'This is about the future of our species. Say we make it to the bunker and everyone else dies. The whole of humanity, wiped from the face of the earth. How long will we survive on our own? Three hundred people? It might be nobody hears the broadcast, and it's all for nothing. It might be the people who hear it are bad people, who will try and get to the bunker first. But I won't be responsible for knowing thousands, *tens of thousands*, died, because I didn't share the information that could have saved their lives.'

She nodded, and put the paperweight down. 'I get it,' she said, standing up. 'I do. But I still think you're wrong.'

'I guess we'll find out, soon enough.'

'Guess so.'

She left. Burnett sank back into his chair. Maybe she had a point. Maybe this was all about giving his friends a chance. Yet who was to say any of them had made it?

The radio rig had been wheeled up, as per his instructions. He fired up the generator, and the board came to life. He flicked the switch marked 'record' and picked up the handset.

He hit the button.

'This message goes out to anyone and everyone that can hear it,' he began.

He looked out of the window at the crowd below.

'The storm is coming again.'

CHAPTER FOURTEEN

SETTLE FOR NOTHING

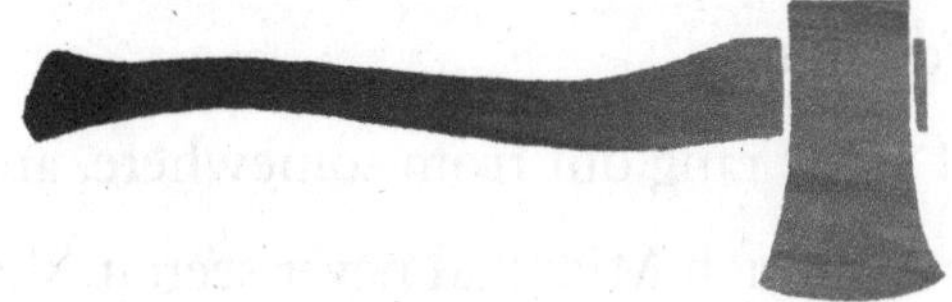

The campfire was warm, but other than that, Mira could find nothing to enjoy about it. She sat on a long log, Susan at her side, the two women from the truck on the other. There were four other women, too. Each of them sat with their hands bound, mouths gagged with tape.

Across from them, grinning as they ate their dinners of tinned beans and sausages served in bowls which looked like they hadn't been washed since the apocalypse, sat their captors, including Bill, who whistled a jaunty little tune between mouthfuls.

One of the men smiled at Mira, showing yellowing, rotten teeth. She turned her gaze away in disgust. Since Bill and his men took them, they had been through another electrical storm, during which Mira had actively prayed her life would be taken. It had turned out to be a normal storm. Nothing happened to her, or to the men holding them.

Since then they'd been on the road. It had become clear their captors didn't have a clue what to do with their new prizes. They were traders, and women made as much sense as commodities to these arseholes as the beans they ate. So far, the fact they were merchandise meant the men had kept their hands to themselves, but she'd not heard an explicit declaration they were out of bounds, so how long would that situation last?

Her stomach turned at the thought of any of these men touching her, the churn in turn reminding her how long it had been since she'd eaten.

A squawk of static rang out from somewhere, and Bill got up to go check it. Although Mira had never seen it, she was sure he had some kind of CB radio in his truck. There were little electrical noises from time to time, and Bill would disappear, coming back with new instructions for the group. Whether this little gang was part of a larger whole, or if he monitored the activities of others, she couldn't be sure. Either way, she dreaded the time they finally got in a position to trade with another group. That would be the point they'd truly be in trouble.

She closed her eyes, and let the weariness in her bones spread over her. The sun had been down twice since she'd had food or sleep.

'Listen to this,' Bill said, returning.

Mira forced her eyes open again, a harder task than she'd imagined. The thin man struggled with a large, antique looking radio, hooked up to a car battery. He set it on the ground, and switched it on.

'...may or may not know that the storm that wiped out so much of our world six months ago...'

Mira sat up, and turned to Susan, whose eyes went wide.

Burnett.

He was alive. Mira was so distracted she almost forgot to listen.

'...these storms might not hit us, or they might have no impact, like the ones we have just seen. From what the scientists at CERN said, however, we have to consider they might be even more severe than the first storm. But there are measures you can take. The EMP will not impact below the surface; although we don't know exactly how deep you'll need to be. If you know of deep tunnels, or caves, these might represent your best chance of survival. We do not know when these storms will arrive, but we believe it will be a matter of days, not we eks.'

There was a pause. The men across the campfire wore expressions of worry and intense concentration, except the man with the yellow teeth, who eyed the sky distrustfully.

'For anyone listening in the United Kingdom,' Burnett's voice continued, *'this message is coming to you from the settlement in the city of Birmingham. By the time you hear this message, we will likely already be on our way to London, with a view to using military bunkers under the capital. If you wish to join us, head to Whitehall.'*

Another pause, and Burnett's voice deepened.

'If anyone listening has ideas about getting in our way, remember this: we are all the same under the storm. That, and we're armed to the teeth. Good luck, everyone.'

The message signed off with a beep, followed by silence. After ten seconds, another beep sounded. Burnett's voice returned.

'This message goes out to anyone...'

Bill flicked a switch, and the voice went dead.

'Fuck me,' the yellow-toothed man said.

'Load of bollocks,' another man said, throwing up arms displaying terrible tattoos of his no doubt dead family to emphasise his point.

'I don't know about that,' Bill said. 'I heard about what happened in Birmingham. This guy manages to overthrow the government what's restarted. Killed a lot of people. But he's been rebuilding. Anyone's likely to hear about this shit, it'd be him.'

'What do we do?' the yellow-toothed man asked.

Mira looked at Susan. If they could get back to Burnett, they had a shot.

'Let's see what everyone else is saying,' Bill said, and turned the radio back on. He turned the dial and Burnett's message turned to static, then a chatter of conversation.

'*...fucking storm gonna knock me out. Survived the first one, gonna survive this one.*'

'*I say we get down to the bunker before they do, keep it for ourselves.*'

'*It's fucking bollocks, mate.*'

The man with the tattoos motioned to the radio at that confirmation of his theory.

The babble continued, and it dawned on Mira what was going on. This was the black market, alive and well. In the months since the storm, bandits like the men sat opposite had made the roads increasingly treacherous, but never seemed to run afoul of each other. At some point someone must have discovered the CB network was still there, and that knowledge had spread as they crossed each other's paths. After all, looting and pillaging only worked if you could do something with the goods you looted. The disparate groups developed a black market, and in turn, a rogue's creed. They didn't compete with each other, and they didn't mess with each other.

One big, happy, psychotic family.

'I tell you what we should do,' a voice rang through. Deep, Mancunian. *'We should get between that cunt and London, and stop him. I reckon he's got more food and guns and fuel than the rest of us put together. I say we band together, take it from him, and go take his fucking bunker, too.'*

Silence greeted the suggestion at first. Bill looked at his men, who shrugged in turn. He picked up the radio.

'Sounds like a capital idea to me,' he said.

'Yeah,' a woman's Brummie voice replied. *'I owe that smug cunt.'*

There were more and more murmurs of assent.

'That settles it,' the Mancunian said. *'Where do we meet?'*

Bill picked up a map he'd been perusing earlier. 'How about we wait on the North Circular?' he asked. 'They'll either be coming down the M1 or the M40. We can have scouts tell us which one and move.'

'Nice one, Bill,' someone replied.

'Oh, and lads,' Bill said, looking across to the log. 'If we get down there quick enough, I've got the entertainment sorted.'

He gave the girls a wide smile, while a cacophony of jeers and cheers came from the speakers. One of the women along the bench gave a low moan.

Bill turned the radio off, and the camp fell silent, save for the crackle of the fire between them.

'Right then,' Bill said. 'Back on the road.'

'Hang on, Bill,' the man with the yellow teeth said. 'Don't you think we should talk about this?'

'What's to talk about?'

'Well, how 'bout if this is a good idea? What if people find out what we did to that biker crew?'

'How the fuck would anyone know about that?'

'Someone could have found 'em. And what if this fella is right? Maybe we should be finding our own bunker somewhere.'

'Don't be a cunt,' Bill said. 'We're going.'

'Well I'm not,' the yellow-toothed man said, standing up.

Bill drew out his pistol and shot the man in the face, sending his body crashing into the campfire, which spilled everywhere. 'Anyone else not fancy going?' he asked of the rest of his men.

Nobody did.

Bill's men herded them back into the truck, mouths still gagged, hands bound behind their backs. As one helped Mira into the vehicle, a firm hand grabbed her buttock, squeezing it hard enough to make her wince.

'Don't worry, darling,' a voice said in her ear, rancid breath on her neck. 'You're going to a party.'

The door to the back of the truck closed, plunging the eight women into darkness. They hadn't been strung up, and there were no seats in the back of the van, so when the engine started and the van pulled away, all eight of them toppled over and into each other. Mira fell backwards, head smacking against the raised metal of the wheel cover. One of the other women fell against her. She rolled off, and Mira realised the tape covering her mouth had come loose.

'Susan,' she said. 'Where are you?'

A muffle came from nearby. They scrambled about, trying to get a purchase on their position. Mira's face whacked into someone's hip, pulling the rest of the gag off. Her hand brushed against hair.

'Don't move,' she said to whoever it was. She inched her fingers over the woman's face, careful not to gouge the woman's eyes. She found the edge of the gag, and pulled it slowly away.

'Thanks,' the woman said. 'Everyone, let's work together to get these fucking gags off.'

It took a while, but soon there were eight voices, free of their gags. Susan was the last to be able to lend her voice to the group.

'Those fucks,' she spat. 'I'm going to kill every one of those fucks.'

'How exactly do you plan to do that?' one of the other women asked.

Mira's eyes had adjusted to the pitiful amount of light permeating the crack in the back door of the van, and they could barely make out their distance from each other.

'We should try and get our hands free,' one of the women said.

They tried, but to no avail. They wasted an hour at least, trying and failing, scrabbling with tooth and nails against knots that were just too tight, too rigid.

'What the fuck do we do?' Mira asked.

'Kick the back door.'

'What, and try jumping from a moving truck?'

'We could try and roll the truck,' Susan suggested.

'We could die trying.'

'I'm okay with that,' Mira said.

A woman snorted. 'Well, I'm not. If it doesn't work, you know they're going to come back here and make us pay for it?'

'Pay now, or pay later,' Susan said. 'I'd rather have tried. You got any better ideas?'

Nobody did.

'Fuck it,' one of the other women said. 'Let's give it a go.'

'How exactly do we do this?' Mira asked.

'Start off on one side and throw ourselves at the other,' Susan said.

They moved to the left hand side of the truck, and a fit of giggles passed across the eight of them as the stupidity of their plan dawned on them.

'Ready?' Susan asked, and the laughter stopped.

'It's been the opposite of a pleasure meeting you all,' a woman said.

'Three.'

'Two.'

'One.'

They charged, and for one glorious second it looked like it might work. The van tipped, rising onto one set of wheels before tipping back down onto four. The driver, not having expected the sudden shift, over compensated, and the truck careened and swerved across the road. He managed to get it under control, but didn't seem to be slowing down.

'Again,' Susan cried. 'Harder!'

The second attempt came closer, and the truck again teetered, before slamming back down onto its wheels. The driver struggled again, and this time seemed to slow down.

'Again!'

This time Mira threw herself with every ounce of strength she had, and the van teetered, hung on the balancing point for a second, and finally went over.

The side of the van crashed into the road, slamming them to this new floor, the side screeching against the tarmac in a squall of angry metal.

The van came to a stop.

'Let's go,' Susan said, jumping to her feet.

They stood, woozily, leaning on each other for support, and kicked the rear doors, which swung open, bathing them in cool evening light and a gust of fresh air. Mira felt a swell of pride, until she saw what lay beyond the doors.

Outside, a line of cars, trucks and lorries spread out across the lanes of a wide road. Hundreds of men, all armed, stared back at them.

One of the men laughed, and the others followed suit.

'Fucking hell, Bill,' one of them shouted. When you said you were bringing us entertainment, I didn't realise you meant there'd be a fucking show.'

A round of applause rippled around the crowd, and Bill appeared, a large cut down his face.

'You bitches are gonna pay for that,' he said.

Chapter Fifteen
The Old Wind

Tom woke, still at the table, the empty glass in his hand, the empty bottle flat on the table. His eyes, heavy-lidded and aching, opened and tried to focus. It was a few seconds before he computed that across from him Tana and Chen sat with looks of utter revulsion on their faces.

'Morning,' he said, his voice cracked and broken.

Tana stood. Without a word he left the table.

Tom's cheeks flushed red.

'Mate,' Chen said. 'You need to sort yourself the fuck out, yeah?'

He, too, stood, leaving Tom alone with his shame.

Tom picked up the empty bottle. How much had he drunk last night? His churning stomach and thumping headache told him it was a considerable amount.

Groggily, he climbed the stairs to the bathroom, and threw up in the toilet. He brushed his teeth with a dead man's toothbrush and rummaged through the medicine cabinet until he found some cold and flu remedy with paracetamol in, and some rehydration sachets, which he mixed with the rust-flavoured water that spurted from the pipes.

The face which greeted him in the mirror when he finally readied himself to face his friends was not a pretty one. He still bore a deep red scar on one cheek, around which a curly mess of beard had grown. His hairline had receded; what remained of his hair was matted and greasy. Worst were his eyes, sunken, shallow things. His skin was grey. He looked to have aged over a decade in less than a year.

He found some electric clippers, but the battery was dead, so he fished out a pair of nail scissors, and started to hack away at the matted hair and beard. A fierce need to cleanse himself of the person staring back from the mirror seized him, so much he barely heard the knocking at the bathroom door.

'So fucking help me, Tom, if you don't get out of there in the next minute we're going to fucking well leave you here to rot.'

Tom opened the door, letting it swing open behind him whilst he continued to work the scissors. Tears streamed down his face, snot dripping into what remained of his moustache.

Tana's rage evaporated the moment he saw Tom. Behind him, Chen came up the stairs.

'Holy shit,' Chen said.

'I second that,' Tana said.

'I need to sort myself out,' Tom said, with a finality which suggested it should serve as sufficient explanation.

'Here,' Tana said, moving forward. 'Let me have them.' He took the scissors from Tom. 'Three sisters, so I'm pretty good with hair. Chen, go see if there's better scissors in the kitchen. I'm not going out in the streets with him looking like he's escaped a lobotomy lab.'

'Thanks,' Tom said, wiping the tears from his eyes.

'It's alright,' Tana said. 'But you're not wrong, mate. You need to sort shit out.'

'I know.'

Tana placed a hand on Tom's shoulder. Tom reached up and clasped it in appreciation.

'What the fuck have I done to my hair?'

The sun had not yet fully risen as they left the house. Tom's newfound determination towards sobriety joined with their determination to track down Mira and Susan. They walked through the old town, past the fresh corpses, past the last house, and found themselves back on the open country road.

It was a bright spring morning, with the birds in full song. The cheerfulness of the general scene butted against their reality, as Tom scratched the itchy stubble which remained from his impromptu restyling. The breeze felt cool on his head and face though, and he wasn't sorry for that.

They needed a car. Every time they came across a new prospect, they engaged the same ritual to try to coax it into life, before abandoning it.

Something glinted, at the corner of Tom's vision. He stopped. In the field beside them, its long grass swaying in the breeze, a man stood staring at them.

'Holy fuck!' Tom shouted.

The words weren't even out of his mouth before his eyes adjusted. It was a scarecrow, its flannel shirt and straw body obvious a split second after he'd seen them.

Tana and Chen wheeled around. When they both saw what had spooked Tom, they burst into laughter.

'Funny,' Tom said. 'Like it wouldn't have shit either of you up to see someone standing in the middle of a field, staring at us.'

'You're right, Tom,' Chen said. 'It's a terrifying scarecrow.'

Tom shook his head, embarrassed to be the butt of the joke but glad to hear laughter once more, when the glint caught his eye again. 'Guys,' he said. 'Hang on.'

'Don't tell me,' Tana replied. 'It's come to life and wants to find its courage?'

'Brain,' Chen said. 'Lion was the one who wanted courage. Scarecrow wanted a brain.'

'Are we really going to argue about this?'

'Well if you're going to quote the Wizard of Oz incorrectly...'

'Guys,' Tom said again. 'Follow me.'

He jumped the fence and started to trudge through the long grass. He went past the scarecrow, resisting the urge to punch its stupid sack cloth face, to the tractor beyond.

'You think it'll work?' Chen asked.

'Beats me,' Tom said. 'I'd guess these things are meant to be pretty hardy.'

He climbed into the cab and searched for the ignition. After many random jabs, he found the right button, and the huge engine spluttered into life.

'Woah,' Tana said, standing back.

It was an impressive machine, its rear tyres nearly as tall as the big Samoan.

'How do you drive it?' Tana called, over the din of the engine.

'Fucked if I know,' Tom shouted back.

Tana and Chen climbed aboard, and together they tried to fathom out the levers, gears, and button combination they needed to get it moving. It lurched forward once, and stalled, but soon they moved through the grass, Tom at the wheel.

'Doesn't go very fast, does it?' Tana shouted.

Tom fiddled with some more levers, and the speed started to creep up. He drove through the long grass, leaving a deep scar through the field, and headed back onto the road, where the speed picked up again. It wasn't much faster than they'd been walking, and there wasn't much room in the cab, so Chen and Tana hung off the side. It was also bloody noisy, so there'd be no element of surprise, and they had no idea how far the diesel in the tank would take them. Still, it beat walking.

They approached another village, and Tom slowed down. There were no signs of activity, but Tom slowed to an almost glacial pace, not wanting to miss signs of their quarry. The place looked to have been well ransacked – doors kicked in, windows broken, rubbish strewn about. Whoever was responsible hadn't gone so far as to make the place inhabitable; bodies still lay exposed from the storm.

'Funny how you don't even register the bodies anymore,' Chen said.

A shot rang out. The bullet pinged off the tractor's frame. Both Tana and Chen ducked down, pressing themselves into the cab as best they could.

'Go!' Tana shouted.

Tom obliged, moving through the gears, picking up speed. A second volley of bullets came, from Chen's side this time, and someone stepped out in front of the tractor, rifle in hand. Bullets rebounded off the metal, or bounced off the giant tyres.

The man who had stepped out in front of them realised his error immediately. He fired off two wild shots, which Tom ducked down to avoid. The man was right in front of them. Tom swerved.

The front of the tractor clipped the gunman, who fell under the huge right tyre. The tractor barely even registered the impact, but the sound of cracking bones was clear enough.

Tana jumped down and grabbed the man's discarded rifle as two other gunmen, incensed at the death of their comrade, burst into the open ground behind them. Tana jumped back up, their bullets rebounding off the tractor's wide rear.

'Down there,' Tana called to Tom, motioning down a side street.

Tom spun the wheel, but underestimated the turning circle of the huge vehicle. He avoided the buildings on either side, but ploughed straight into the cars parked at the edge of the road. They came to a sudden halt, Tom's face slamming into one of the support poles. Chen was flung from the side, landing roughly on the street.

Tana climbed onto the roof, which immediately strained against the weight of him. The two gunmen were not far behind them, but he managed to lie down flat, with the rifle out, before they could open fire again.

Tom jumped down from the cab, but landed on his bad knee and let out a yelp. A bullet pinged near him. His head bled from the impact with the car. He scrabbled back toward the cover of the tractor, the pain in his leg having other ideas.

Chen jumped out from behind the smashed car. He grabbed Tom, dragging him to safety.

Another shot from Tana's rifle. Both gunmen opened fire in response. Tana ducked down to get out of the line of fire.

'They've found cover,' Chen said, peering round as Tom tried to coax his knee to move again. 'We need to help Tana, he's got no chance.'

'What the hell are we going to do?' Tom replied. 'We don't even have weapons.'

Chen took off his shirt and picked up a large shard of broken glass. He wrapped the shirt around his hand to protect it, and grasped the glass.

'You can't be fucking serious,' Tom asked.

'You got a better idea?'

'Fuck,' Tom replied. He took off his own shirt, mumbling that at least Chen still had a vest on, and picked up a shard.

Chen's blinked in disbelief at the sight of Tom's scars, until another bullet refocused his attention. 'You go that way,' he said, motioning to go round the tractor.

Tom waited until Tana started to shoot again and hobbled across the street. He ducked into an alleyway.

Another shot, followed by a yelp. Either Tana had improved the odds, or the balance had tipped the other way.

Tom moved around to a back street and doubled back, trying to come out behind the gunmen. He peered round the brickwork, the improvised knife clutched in his hand.

'Put it down!' Tana shouted.

Across from him, in the street, lay one of the gunmen. Alive, but writhing in agony at the bullet in his stomach. The other gunman stood in the open, his pistol held against Chen's temple. Chen was on his knees, hands held outward, the glass shard discarded on the floor.

Tom started to creep forward.

'You put it down or I'll put a bullet in your friend's head,' the gunman shouted.

Tom's knee popped. He froze, but the gunman didn't turn.

'Put it down!' Tana bellowed back from the tractor's roof.

Tom was a few metres away when the second gunman noticed him. He stopped writhing and moaning for a second.

'Ted!' he shouted.

The gunman turned, but to his friend, not Tom.

Tom burst forward, closing the gap, and lashed out with the glass shard in his hand. The man swung his pistol round to Tom, but too late. The glass sliced through his throat, spraying Tom with blood. It cut deep into Tom's hand, and pain rushed up his arm.

The gunman fell to the floor, eyes wide, his hands going uselessly to his throat, trying to hold back the red tide. He gargled and fell forward.

'You fuck!' the other man said, struggling to get away. A smear of red trailed in his wake. Tears ran down his cheeks. He inched towards his own gun, which lay an impossible distance from him.

Chen stood. 'Thanks,' he said, and embraced Tom.

'It's okay,' Tom replied. His hands were shaking, one of them dripping with blood.

'Here,' Chen said, and took the shirt from Tom's hand, rewrapping it around the wound. 'Keep pressure on it. We'll sort it out later, yeah?'

Tom nodded. Behind them, Tana jumped down from the tractor and headed over to the last man, kicking his gun well out of reach. The man stopped, and gave a moan of despair. Tana kicked him onto his back.

'Stop moving,' he said.

'Fuck you.'

Tom and Chen joined Tana. The man looked up at the three of them with hatred and panic.

'Why were you shooting at us?' Tana asked.

'This is our town,' the man replied. 'You come through here, you got to pay tax.'

'You never asked for tax. How's your plan working out for you?'

'Fuck you.'

A thin red bubble came from the man's nose, and popped.

'It's safe to say things have not gone your way,' Tom said, kneeling. 'Tell us what we want to know and we'll help you.'

'Fuck. You.'

'Fine,' Tom said, getting back up. 'Chen, pass me that glass.'

'Wait,' the man said. 'What do you want to know?'

'Two friends of ours were kidnapped. Two days ago,' Tana said. 'We want to know who by, and how we can find them.'

'It wasn't us,' the man said.

'We'd worked that one out,' Chen said. 'You aren't dressed like a third-rate biker gang.'

'Bikers? That's Sayles's crew. I don't know where they are, but they came through here. Traded some fuel for food. Didn't say where they were going.'

'How do we find them?' Tana asked.

'I don't know.'

'Fine,' Tom said. 'Chen, I've changed my mind. Hand me the pistol.'

Chen hesitated, and picked up the pistol, handing it to Tom.

Tom levelled it at the man, whose eyes went wide.

'Say "good night".'

'Wait! The blockade! Maybe he's headed for the blockade!'

'The what?' Tana asked.

'There's a message, on the radio. CB. Says a group from Birmingham are going to London. Something to do with the storms. Anyway, the gangs, they decided to go try and stop them. Raid the convoy.'

'Where's the radio?' Tana asked.

'Fred had it.'

'Which one's Fred?'

The man pointed back down the road at the angry smear of red which had once, apparently, been Fred.

'Thanks,' Tom said.

'So,' the man said. 'You'll help me? Get me to a doctor? I'm sorry for...'

Tom raised the pistol, and fired it at the man's head, cutting him off.

'Fuck,' Chen said.

'Fuck him,' Tom replied. 'Let's go see if we can find this radio.'

Chapter Sixteen

Condor And River

Getting everyone ready to leave the house that had been their home these last months was harder than Max had thought it'd be. The small bag he'd packed had nothing of real value — his house had been completely taken by the storm, so the bag itself took its own significance, a sign of how little remained he could truly call his own. Five pairs of underpants and a few T-shirts did not an existence make.

They emerged onto the street, blinking. Some of them hadn't seen sunlight for weeks. Max felt sure they'd made the right choice. They knew they'd have to leave the house some time. In the weeks after the storm they'd imagined it would be when the government swooped in to rescue them. When that didn't happen it became when the Kurgan was no longer a threat. Now, it was looming starvation.

Out in the daylight of a warm spring morning, he saw how close they'd come. All six of them were not much more than skin and bone, Darren excepted. Darren never seemed to lose his heft.

Max took Nana's elbow, as she picked her way through the rubble strewn streets. They set off southwards, each of them casting the house a solemn backwards glance.

'Which way?' Ava asked.

Max motioned past the swinging body, ripening in the morning sun. He and Ava had patched things up last night, once everyone had gone back to their rooms. Or, at least, she had crept into his bed during the night. They hadn't spoken much, but the ice had thawed this morning.

They picked their way through the adjacent building as Max had done the previous day. Darren carried Nana the whole way, even through the rubble.

'Thank you, dear,' she said, as he placed her carefully back onto her feet.

'It's even worse than I remember,' Jess said. She stared at the desolation around her. Max was so used to seeing it he barely registered the warped glass, blackened structures, and rubble piles which had once been buildings.

'Come on,' Max said, and they trudged onwards.

As they approached the river, Max motioned for them to stop. Noises came from the area ahead of them: clangs, shouts, distant calls. Max's heart sank.

He's still trying to get in.

If the Kurgan was still there it meant they'd have to come face to face with him if they wanted into the bunker, but it also meant the bunker itself was proving impregnable.

They moved, low and slow, around the wall of what had once been a swanky five-star hotel, keeping out of sight while trying to get a better view of what lay ahead. Finally, Max brought them to a stop.

'I need to sit,' Nana whispered. 'Sorry.'

Darren picked up two large blocks of masonry and arranged them into a chair for her, before hiding behind the wall and putting his hands over his ears.

'It's okay, fella,' Max said, taking Darren's shoulders and staring deep into his eyes. 'Everything is fine, okay? We're not going to move from here, and they're not going to come from over there.'

Darren nodded, his lips tight, his eyes darting to the broken window pane through which Max and Ava were able to take in the scene before them.

'What do we do?' Mouse asked.

I wish I had an answer.

Max peered over. The Kurgan stood in the middle of what had to be over a dozen men, ordering them about. The men hammered away at the door, the frame, the wall around it. It looked like they'd removed the brickwork, to find thick cement beneath. They hammered away at the concrete, to no avail.

'Hmm,' Ava hummed, staring intently at the attempted break in.

'What?' Max asked.

'That's the entrance right? Except it can't be the only one. The bunker isn't going to be one big room; it'd be a whole complex. I mean, this was Whitehall, right?'

'Yeah?'

'Whitehall was what? Ministry of Defence, Army, Foreign Office, that stuff?'

'I dunno,' Max replied. 'Can't say I ever paid much attention.'

'Okay, but that's a lot of people you'd need to save in the event of a crisis. But there's a big something missing.'

'Prime Minister?'

'Prime Minister, the cabinet, ministers. Parliament is across the way, or it was. There's no way they didn't plan to be able to save the PM in the event of an attack.'

'So there must be an entrance there, too?'

'Right.'

They looked over to the tall spire of Big Ben, burned out but still standing. Next to it, little remained of the Palace of Westminster, once the seat of power, reduced to a dusty collection of broken limestone and iron.

'Or,' Ava said, 'there would have been.'

'Doesn't hurt to check it out,' Max said.

Max told the others to stay out of sight, and he, Mouse, and Ava moved away as quietly as they could, picking through the rubble and staying as hidden from the Kurgan as possible.

The closer they got to the old parliament building, the more desperate it seemed. The ground was completely covered in debris, and even if they could find the way, it would need a serious effort to get inside. They'd need men, diggers, the works. What they had were three skinny people who hadn't eaten since the night before.

'This is pointless,' Mouse said. 'We could dig for days and find nothing.'

'What about this?' Mouse said, pointing behind them.

They'd used the one remaining structure as cover from the Kurgan's men, but hadn't thought to give it a second glance. Max hadn't even taken in what it was, until he saw the soot-smudged red circle of a London Underground sign.

'Could be worth a look,' Max said.

'Could be a complete death trap,' Ava said.

The huge concrete archway had collapsed, but some gap remained. Max sidled through, into the darkness beyond.

The air was stale and dusty. The entrance might have collapsed, but the stairwell down into the station was still there. The fires must have raged intensely here – even in the low light, the walls, the ceilings, the stairs themselves looked scorched and blackened. More than a few feet down was total darkness.

Ava and Mouse squeezed through the gap and joined him at the top of the steps.

'This isn't going to work,' Ava said, her voice trembling.

Ava was not a fan of enclosed spaces. To her, this must be like walking into a coffin.

'If you want to wait outside–' Max began.

'I'm fine,' Ava replied, cutting him off.

Max grasped to find the handrail, but it was no longer there. The steps were warped and cracked. There was no way to get down.

'You're right,' Max said. 'We should go back.'

'We should...' Mouse said.

There was a yelp, a crash, and the sound of Mouse tumbling.

'Mouse!' Ava shouted.

Silence greeted her.

Max groped around, staring into the darkness. 'Mouse?' he called.

'I'm okay,' Mouse called back, his voice echoing up from far away. He didn't sound convinced by his own statement.

'We're coming down,' Max said.

They inched their way down, feeling their way. Max could hear his own increasingly frantic breath, and the hammering in his chest. He kept waiting for his eyes to adjust to the darkness, but there was no light to adjust to. The total absence of sensory data beyond the stale smoky smell in the air started to overwhelm him. His breaths became shallow, small rapid intakes of stale, burnt air.

'Down here,' Mouse said, brightly, still sounding a million miles away.

'Are you at the bottom?' Max called out.

'Sort of,' Mouse called back. 'I can see a light.'

That spurred Max forward. Behind him, Ava kept pace, her feet stumbling over the same debris as his own.

The slope stopped. He was finally able to put one foot in front of the other.

'Mouse?'

'Over here,' he replied. He was still ahead of them.

A hand slipped into Max's, sweaty and cold. He and Ava moved forward together. They only had to go a few metres before they, too, could see the light. It wasn't so much a light as a vague lessening of the gloom. There was a hole in the floor, and a tunnel beneath it. The light came from somewhere along the tunnel.

Mouse's head popped out of the hole. 'You're never going to fucking believe this,' he said, grinning.

They eased down into the tunnel. Max dropped to the floor and dusted himself down. It was a long tunnel, barely touched by the fire. They were no longer in the London Underground system.

There were no signs, or ads here. Along the corridor, back along the way, was a door. It was solid metal, with a small glass plate in the middle. As they approached, Max could see the glass was inches thick.

'This is it,' Max said.

He peered through the glass, but its thickness meant he couldn't make out much beyond, except the light.

The door had no handle, and it dawned on Max that finding the door was less than half the battle. There was no way in.

The elation of finding it seeped away, replaced with anger.

He hammered on the door with both fists, making no discernible noise on their side of the steel.

'Do you think there are people inside?' Mouse asked.

Max stared through the window. He'd thought there was no way the bunker would be occupied, but there it was – a little electric light. Would that be on all the time? Or did it signal occupancy? Either way, it didn't much help them.

The door made a thudding sound, and moved slightly.

'What was that?' Mouse asked.

'I think they might be letting us in,' Max said, wanting rather than believing it to be true.

He ran his fingers across the surface of the door, until he found the edge of the cold steel. There was a slight raised lip. He pulled at it, and the door shifted again.

'Give me a hand,' he said.

Together, the three of them inched open the door. The weight of it was huge. With muscles straining, their fingertips howling with pain, it swung open.

Light flooded them from the corridor beyond.

They stood in front of the open doorway. Max stepped through, the others falling in tight behind him.

'Stop right there,' a voice called.

They froze. Behind them the door swung shut. Max looked around.

Another door. At the end of the corridor.

Of course.

Another slab of steel, above which sat a small speaker.

'Identify yourselves.'

'I'm Max, this is Ava, and Mouse. Who are you?'

No answer.

We're going to get fucking shot.

The next doorway didn't have a glass panel, and looked to be every bit as impregnable as the first. To the side was a small keypad, while next to the speaker sat what looked to Max like an old-fashioned webcam. He moved forwards. He hadn't heard the hum of an electric light for so long it sounded like it came from another planet.

'We're not here to hurt you,' Ava said. 'We're here because we're hungry.'

'Are you with the others?' the speaker asked.

'What others?' Ava asked.

Max knew who they meant. The Kurgan. 'No,' he said. 'We're not with him. We're trying to get away from him. There are six of us in total. Three here, two other women and a man. We're hungry, and we're tired. Please, if you let us in, we won't be trouble.'

Silence.

Max stared into the camera, trying to stare into the eyes of the man on the other end of the speaker, who was hopefully trying to work out what to do next.

'I'm sorry, there's too much of a contamination risk,' a second voice said, deeper than the first.

'There's no contamination,' Ava said, confused. 'There was no nuclear explosion. It was an electrical storm.'

'Can I ask who we're speaking to?' Max asked.

Silence. Max looked at Ava, who shrugged.

What the fuck do we do?

'This is the Chief of the Defence Staff,' the second voice said.

'Okay,' Max said. 'What does that mean?'

'Means he's the head of the Army,' Ava said, in a low voice.

'That's right,' the voice said.

'Oh,' Max said.

'Hang on,' Ava said. 'Are you the CDS because it was your actual job, or did you take the job because the people above you died?'

'Everyone in here has earned their positions, Miss.'

'Have you got a name?' Max asked.

'General Coles.'

'Okay, Coles. You going to let us in?'

'Do you have weapons?'

'No,' Max replied.

'And you expect me to believe you?'

'If you didn't believe him, why would you ask?' Ava asked.

There was a pause, and a clunk. The door swung open.

They stepped through, and found themselves in yet another corridor. Unlike the other corridors, this came replete with armed soldiers at either end, their guns aimed at the new arrivals. The men and women wore army khakis.

'Hi,' Mouse said, waving gingerly.

'This way,' a woman said, and beckoned them toward one of the two flanks.

'Sure,' Max said.

Soldiers searched them. They led them out of the corridor, into the bunker complex. As Ava had said, the place was enormous, and they walked past several huge empty rooms before they reached their destinations.

So much space.

There were bunk areas, mess halls, even a hospital. Well, it was either a hospital, or the staging area for the alien autopsy videos Max had seen on YouTube.

Ava stared into each one, open mouthed, and shook her head. Everything was clean, well-stocked, and electrically powered. The lights were so bright, so stark, they burned Max's eyes.

They moved forward, gun barrels urging them on until they came to a control room. One of the soldiers held open the door and ushered the three of them in. Even more armed men and women stood inside. Banks of desks filled the outside of the room, staffed by people staring at computer screens. Max noted on one screen the grinning face of the Kurgan as he directed his men.

In the centre of the room stood a huge oak table, around which were seven serious looking people, at least three of whom Max recognised from off the telly. Or did he? Was it that the whole thing looked like the deck of the Starship Enterprise?

'Holy shit,' Mouse said, pointing. 'That's the fucking Prime Minister.'

That'll be where I recognise him from.

The middle-aged man with immaculate hair and a pressed shirt stood. He appraised the three new arrivals with a sneer. 'Charming,' he said, peering over the top of his glasses. He turned to one of the uniformed men. 'And the others?'

'They're...' the man started, staring at his screen.

'Well?'

'They're breaking in, sir.'

Somewhere, far away in the complex, gunfire rattled, and a distant scream rang out.

Chapter Seventeen

No Rest For The Weary

'It's fucked,' Tom said, cradling the shattered remains of the CB radio in his hands. He sat in the back seat of a Range Rover, which Tana was driving at great speed down one of the country's arterial roads, weaving in and out of months-old car wrecks and decomposed bodies, which burst into clouds of dust under the wheels.

'You sure?' Chen asked, from the passenger seat.

'I'm no expert,' he said, holding out the broken parts to Chen. 'But yeah.'

Chen took the parts from him, and started trying to do the same magical re-assembly job Tom had spent the last hour trying to achieve.

'Doesn't matter,' Tana said, his eyes fixed on the road. 'Somewhere between Birmingham and London, there's going to be an ambush, and that's where it's most likely Mira and Susan are going to be. So that's where we're going.'

'Would be nice to have something a bit more specific,' Chen said, somewhat forlornly, still trying to put the pieces back together.

They'd found the Range Rover round the corner from the bodies. The bandits had quite a collection of useful shit, which they'd duly plundered. Now, the large family car pretending to be an off-road vehicle was laden with three spare tanks of petrol, bottled water, food, and even some spare clothes. Tom had new garments for the first time in weeks. He also had a hip flask secreted in his jacket pocket, its cold weight a reassuring presence against his breast.

Now he didn't have the radio to fiddle with, it took all his energy not to reach into the pocket, remove the flask and down it in one. Of course, if he tried, Tana or Chen would have it out of his hands before a drop touched his lips.

Fuck them, though.

They didn't know what he was going through, the memories haunting him. Not for the first time, he'd had to execute a man. He'd done it to Baxter, spilling the man's guts over his shoes. On a beach in Scarborough, he'd shot an unarmed man. And there was Jen. Now, there were two more bodies to add to his tally.

He'd had to kill them, of course. Had to open the throat of the first man and execute the other. The first man would have killed Chen, no doubt about it, and he'd saved the other man a slow, painful death, but none of that changed the fact Tom had a kill count which at one time would have guaranteed him his own lurid Channel 5 documentary.

When he'd found the flask, he'd put it into his new coat pocket as a kind of security blanket. He wouldn't *need* it, of course. But that was bullshit. After an hour of feeling its weight against his heart, feeling the mystery liquid inside sloshing about with every jolt of the car, he knew full well the first chance he got, he'd be finding out exactly what glorious nectar it held.

A burst of electrical crackle came from Chen's lap.

'Fuck!' Chen said, and promptly dropped the components. 'Piss. Tana, pull over, I think I can get this working.'

Tana frowned but complied, pulling over to the side of the road, tyres scratching over the gravel.

'Thanks,' Chen said. 'I can't work while everything is moving.'

'I need a piss,' Tom said, and opened the door.

They'd pulled up alongside a stretch of nothing. Fields stretched out behind them, in front and at the sides. There was nothing more than one small clump of trees.

Perfect.

He walked around the back of the car and, checking the road, crossed over. How long would it be before he unlearned that particular behavioural habit? They hadn't seen another car on the road for nigh on a month, and yet he still checked both ways before crossing a road.

He went into the trees. Not as much cover as he'd like, but it'd do. He took care of nature's call first, wiped his hands on his new coat, and reached inside.

The flask was gloriously weighted, and cold. It was halfway out of the pocket when the doubts started to gnaw at him. What would Tana say if he could see Tom?

What would Jen think? What would Leon?

The flask fell back into his pocket. It stayed there another second, until his hand reached back in, and pulled the flask back out. Before reason could protest further, he grappled with the screw top, and raised it to his lips.

The whisky inside stung his lips first, a rush of sensation topped by the hit of the burning liquid at the back of his throat a moment later. He took a deep swig and closed his eyes, enjoying the surge of heat spreading through his torso, and the murkiness flooding his brain. He took another sip, a smaller one this time, more to savour the taste. It was shitty whisky, but it felt too good for him to care.

He put the top back on, and placed the flask back in his pocket. The thought hit him he'd need to do something about his breath before he got to the car.

The car.

A wave of embarrassment flooded over him. If he forced himself to throw up, he could purge it.

He turned around, and found Tana stood behind him. Tana's huge hand curled into a fist. He punched Tom in the face so hard Tom flew backwards, his hip smacking into a tree root as he landed.

'You fucking arsehole,' Tana bellowed at him. 'What the fuck do you think you're doing?'

'Tana, I...'

'No, fuck you. Don't you dare talk. It's time for you to listen. I'm sick of this shit. You remember when we used to follow you? Look what you've become! You think I didn't see you pocket the flask? I used to be a beat bobby, for fuck's sake. I let you have it, because I had hoped you wouldn't need it. But here you are. You're pathetic, Tom. You're a fucking drunk.'

'Fuck you, Tana,' Tom said. His cheeks were wet with tears and hot with shame. 'Are you fucking surprised I need to drink? What haven't I lost? Everything! Every friend I had.' He paced, no longer looking at Tana. 'I lost my leg. I lost my face. And I carry around this shit with me. Every. Fucking. Day. So, who fucking cares if I need a drink to get through this pitiful excuse for what used to be a life? I have nothing to live for.'

He spat blood and whisky onto the leaves at his feet.

'Oh yeah, Tom,' Tana said, sarcastically. 'Yeah, you're the only one who's suffered so far. You're the only one who's lost people.'

'Fuck you,' Tom said.

'No, Tom. Fuck you. I'm done carrying you around in this state. You're no help to anyone.'

'No help?' Tom shouted, his own fists balled at his side. 'Who was it, Tana, who took down those bandits back in that town? I had to cut the throat of a man I'd never met, and put another out of his misery. Why was that, again? Oh yeah, because you couldn't fucking kill him with your first shot.'

'If I'd killed him,' Tana shot back, 'we wouldn't know where the girls are.'

'Do we know? Really? Because all I've heard so far is a whole lot of maybes. But you know what, don't leave me here. Do me a favour and fucking kill me.' He moved in closer to Tana. 'You want to know why I drink? Because I can't fucking live with myself, but I'm too much of a fucking coward to do anything about it. So, please, do me a favour.'

He started to sob. The strength left his legs. Tana caught him, and pulled him into an embrace.

'I killed her, Tana,' Tom sobbed. 'I can't do this anymore.'

'I'm sorry,' Tana said, the anger gone from his voice. 'But we're here for you, okay? Chen is your friend. I'm your friend. And we've got to go help our other friends. We do need you. I need you.'

Tom nodded, pulling away from the embrace. He wiped his eyes, reached into his coat, and pulled out the flask. He undid the top and poured the whisky out, soaking the leaves by his feet, before taking the empty flask and throwing it as far as he could.

Tana smiled at him, and put an arm around his shoulder.

'Guys!' Chen said, running into the tree-line. 'You've got to hear this.'

'What is it?' Tana asked.

'You're never going to fucking believe this. It's Burnett.'

The message played three times before Tana switched the radio off. His face betrayed little of his thoughts. Tom watched him closely. Tana had been the closest to Burnett, both as a friend and a comrade. They had tracked down Ewen together. If it hadn't been for the pair of them, Tom would be dead.

When Burnett had disappeared before their camp came under attack, it had weighed heavily on Tana, who felt he'd given up too easily on his fellow officer. The rest of them had quietly assumed Burnett had met some terrible fate out there on the roads.

'Sounds like he's okay, at any rate,' Chen said.

'Yeah,' Tana said.

'This changes everything,' Tom said.

'How?' Tana asked, fixing Tom with an implacable stare.

'Because we know he's walking into an ambush.'

'Sounds to me like he can take care of himself,' Tana said. 'We should focus on the girls.'

'Either way,' Chen said. 'We're heading to the same place. We just need to know where to go.'

He turned the radio on, and started to fiddle with it, trying to pick up some other signals.

'You okay?' Tom asked Tana.

'Fine.'

'We'll find him, okay? He'll be able to explain what happened. It's a good thing he's alive, right?'

'Of course, it's just...'

'I know. You mourned him. You're wondering how he could turn his back on us, but we don't know what happened. He could have got back to the camp ten minutes after we left, or been kidnapped by bandits. We don't know. Think of it this way — how would you feel if you knew Jen was alive? It was crazy back then, and we had to walk away from the camp. It's not your fault, and it's probably not his, either.'

'Yeah,' Tana said, with a heavy sigh. 'But you know what he was like. Always skulking off. All this time I wanted was to know he was okay, but I feel...'

'Abandoned?'

He sighed again. 'If he'd have been there, maybe Jen would still be alive.'

'Yeah,' Chen said. 'And if a frog had wings it wouldn't bump its ass when it hopped.'

Tana laughed. 'Did you really just quote *Wayne's World*?'

'Made you laugh, didn't it? Listen, I can't find anything else on the radio. There's something there, but this piece-of-shit radio is too knackered to pick it up. Let's get on the road, see what we can find.'

They got back in the car. The day was almost gone. Chen took the driving seat, with Tom beside him.

'You know what, I could do with a drink,' Tana said.

'Tell me about it,' Tom said, staring out the window at the trees outside.

Chapter Eighteen

The Wolf Is Loose

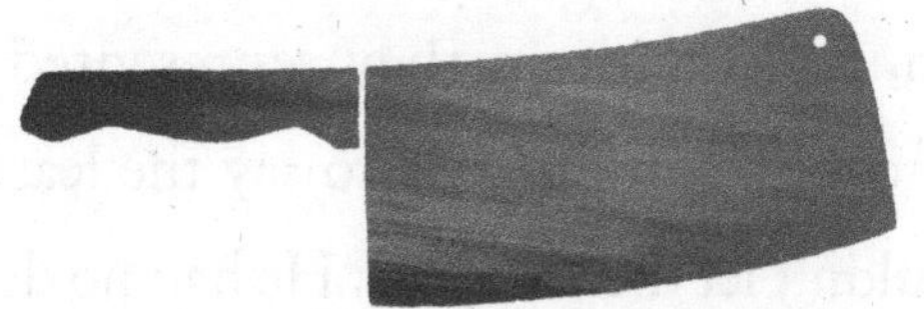

Burnett walked into the prison wing with a certain amount of trepidation. The men locked up here were one of several headaches competing for his attention, but a significant one he couldn't leave without dealing with. Couldn't let them out, couldn't invite them to join him, but leaving them here to die didn't fill him with good feelings, either, no matter their crimes.

Most of those involved in Grayling's nefarious scheme to turn post-apocalyptic Britain into a neo-fascist state had fled Birmingham as soon as they realised the tables had turned. A handful had remained, despite the capture of their leader and the death of their military head. Burnett and the other survivors of their regime had been far more merciful, imprisoning them in the same prison Grayling's hoodlum army had turned into a virtual concentration camp, except with the rights and good treatment Burnett and the others hadn't been afforded.

Those first weeks after Burnett had toppled this so-called government had been chaos. Of the survivors, barely half had stayed, stripping Birmingham of much needed supplies on their way out the door. What had happened to them, Burnett didn't know, but he suspected he'd see some of them again.

Grayling, the former city councillor with a penchant for bad decisions, had been the first locked up, but they had around twenty people banged up here. They were fed, watered, given exercise and generally kept comfortable, but there could be no trial for them, and the drain they represented on the city's resources was counterproductive, to say the least. For all that, though, he couldn't let them go free. He had no doubt they'd get as far as the edge of the city before turning straight back round to attack his people again. No matter how well they'd been treated, the resentment he felt every time he walked in was palpable.

The cells were empty, which filled Burnett with a momentary panic, until he realised it would be exercise time for the inmates.

He strolled past the few guards left, out into the yard. The prisoners split into two sides – the petty criminals, drug dealers, and malcontents Grayling had used for muscle, and the former leader himself, who sat alone at the far end of the yard, a purple welt under one eye of his age-ravaged face.

'Oi,' one of the criminal gang shouted, as he saw Burnett enter. 'What's this about you fucking off?'

'You've heard?'

'One of the guards told us. You can't fucking leave us here to die, you pig fuck.'

'What do you propose I do?'

'Let us the fuck out of here,' another man said.

Burnett sensed they were trying to surround him and backed away. Two of the armed guards moved into the yard, too, and the men backed off.

'I can't do that,' Burnett said. 'You know why.'

'Fuck you,' the man said, and spat towards Burnett's feet.

'I tell you what I am going to do. Your friends out there have spent the last few months trying to take back the city. As soon as we're gone, they'll be moving back in. We're going to lock you in the prison, but leave the keys in the door, so to speak. When they get back, you'll be free in no time. I have no doubt about it.'

'And if they don't come for us?'

'You'll work something out.'

The man shook his head, but put up no further protests. It was as good a deal as he was going to get, and he knew it. He was probably already thinking about getting out of here.

Burnett headed back to the door. He thought about wishing them luck, but he didn't wish them anything of the sort.

Grayling, who had watched from across the yard, shuffled over to Burnett. He grasped the detective's sleeve. 'Please,' he said, half whispered, half hissed. 'You can't leave me here. The minute those guards are gone, they'll kill me.'

Burnett looked into the eyes of the old man and remembered his friend, Phil. Another old man who'd died right here in this prison. Because of this man.

'You made your bed,' Burnett said.

He pulled free of Grayling's grasp and turned away, walking out of the prison yard.

When they finally got it going, the convoy was immense. Seven coaches, flanked by four army trucks, three Land Rovers and two Jeeps. Between them they carried three hundred and seventy-five people, twenty of them armed. There were three shotguns, twelve rifles, three machine guns, nine grenades, and thirteen pistols between them, but by Burnett's estimation they'd run out of ammunition roughly five minutes into a firefight. Still, he was glad Grayling and his men had left so much army equipment lying about.

They filled the army trucks with food, medicine, water, and anything they thought they might be able to barter with, except for one truck which was set up as a mobile ward for the already infirm. If things went wrong there wouldn't be room for the injured in there, so they also had a battered old van — about the only other working vehicle in Birmingham they could find, which would be their field hospital.

Four hours after they set off, they were halfway to London. Burnett still hadn't heard from Lydia and Greg. He'd hoped for at least a status report, but the last thing he wanted to do was to contact them at the wrong moment and give away their positions. He would have to wait.

They'd set off far later than he'd wanted to, courtesy of his trip to the prison, and as a result the sun had already started to wane. He'd hoped to get to the bunker before nightfall, but that would have been a pipe dream even if they'd set off at the crack of dawn.

When they were still packing up the coaches after lunchtime, he'd had to face the decision to delay another day or throw caution to the wind and hit the road. He chose the latter, figuring there wouldn't be much point being in Birmingham when the storm hit.

'How long?' he asked Tyler, who drove the Jeep at the head of the convoy.

'No idea,' she said, weary of his asking. 'We're making better time than I thought we would.'

She swerved between dead vehicles and slowed to allow the coaches time to manoeuvre through the wreckage and catch up. Once they were clear, the Land Rover bringing up the rear honked its horn to signal to move forward.

Burnett watched the countryside scroll by, slowing down and speeding up again. He'd started to zone out when movement caught his eye. 'What's that?'

'Shit,' Tyler replied. 'Looks like a bus, or something.'

Careening toward them from a side road — going fast enough to intercept them at the next junction — a minibus, dirty and knackered-looking.

'It's going a fair old pace,' Burnett said.

'I'm going up,' Tyler said. 'Take the wheel.'

'Fuck's sake, Ty,' Burnett said, shuffling over to the front seat as she climbed over him, reaching to the back of the jeep to pull out a machine gun.

The top of the Jeep was canvas, and she popped the buttons, flooding the car with cool wind. She steadied herself in the passenger seat and rested the barrel of the gun on the top of the windshield.

'Hold it fucking steady,' she shouted over the wind.

'Doing my bloody best here,' he shouted back, trying to move his legs into a comfortable position.

The bus kept going. Once it came to the junction, it turned toward them, flashing its high beams at the convoy. Tyler let rip with a short burst of gunfire high over them, enough to spook the driver. The minibus swerved and screeched to a halt, a hundred metres in front of them. Burnett eased down on the brakes and hit the hazard lights to warn the rest of the convoy.

'What do we do?' he called.

'Keep going,' she replied, not taking her eyes off the gun barrel off the minibus.

'What if they need help?'

'What if they don't?'

He slowed.

'I can't fucking go through them,' Burnett said. 'Let's hear them out.'

Tyler shrugged. She turned around in the jeep and gesticulated wildly to the drivers behind them. Burnett had no idea what she was trying to convey, but at least one of the drivers did — a Land Rover sped past them, blew past the minibus and came to a halt twenty metres beyond it. Two figures jumped out, their weapons scanning for an ambush.

The convoy came to a halt twenty metres from the minibus. Tyler jumped out and started to approach, her weapon pointed at the new arrivals.

'Out, with your hands in the air,' she shouted.

Both front doors opened. Two sets of hands came out, followed by their owners, a man and a woman. He was black, with a thick white beard. She was white, her face deeply lined and clearly terrified.

'You're heading into a trap,' the man said.

'Oh yeah?' Tyler shouted back. 'And you two would be the bait?'

Both shook their heads.

'Ty,' Burnett called, getting out of the Jeep. He kept his pistol in his waistband. The rest of the convoy remained in their vehicles, engines running. The man and woman turned their attention to him, their hands still raised. He noted the bulge in the man's waistband.

'You're heading into a trap,' the woman reaffirmed.

'What makes you say that?' he shouted back.

'We heard your message. Started to head to London. Outside the city, where it turns to rubble, we came across them.'

'Them?' Tyler asked.

'Hundreds of them,' the man said. 'Bandits. Highwaymen. Whatever the hell you want to call them. Every motherfucker still walking the earth, by the looks of it. And more comin' all the time. They heard your message. They're waiting for you.'

'How'd you get away?' Tyler asked.

'Not all of us did,' the woman replied.

'We have wounded,' the man said. 'We could use your help.'

'Ty, go get the doc.'

'Sir...'

'Do it.'

She scowled, and headed back into the convoy.

'We'll help you,' Burnett said.

The man nodded. 'Thank you. Can I open the side door, let the others out?'

Burnett nodded, but his hand went instinctively to his waistband, a gesture which didn't go unnoticed by the man.

The door slid open. Inside, a dozen people sat crammed in amongst what was presumably their entire worldly goods, which by the looks of it included a few crates of live chickens. The animals started clucking angrily at the sudden intrusion into their world.

Of the people, some looked in a bad way. Tyler returned with the doc, a woman who Burnett had never seen as anything other than the harassed doctor of the apocalypse, waging her perpetual battle against the death and mayhem surrounding her. Burnett wasn't sure he'd ever had a normal conversation with her. She, Tyler, and the man from the minibus took a patient each, carrying them back into the midst of the convoy.

'Thanks,' the woman said, watching her people being led away.

'Not a problem,' Burnett said. 'How far away is the ambush?'

'A few miles.'

'Can we go round it?'

'Not if you want to get into London. Even then...'

'What?'

'I don't like your chances of finding this bunker,' she said. 'London's... gone.'

Burnett looked down the road. It seemed quiet, but he had no reason not to trust her word. She even had the wounded evidence to back it up.

The sun was almost down. Were they better heading towards an ambush at night, or during the day? If he wanted to wait, he'd have to find somewhere to house three hundred people.

He didn't have anything approaching a plan B. Either they made it to the bunker, or they didn't. Everything else was death.

'We have to try,' he said. 'You're more than welcome to join us.'

'Thanks,' she said. 'But I'd rather not drive headlong to my death.'

'You'll still need to get underground.'

'We'll think of something,' she said. She turned back to the minibus, and climbed into the driver's seat. In the back, one of the remaining passengers pulled the door shut.

The engine started.

'Hey,' Burnett shouted through the passenger window. 'Where are you going?'

The woman ignored him and drove across the lanes before hitting the accelerator hard, speeding on past the convoy.

The black man appeared out of the hospital truck, his hand red with blood. 'Hey!' he screamed after the retreating taillights. He turned to Burnett. 'That fucking bitch,' he said. 'She stole my fucking chickens.'

'Looks like you're with us,' Burnett said to him.

He nodded, and headed back to the hospital truck.

Tyler returned. 'So?' she asked.

'So, we're heading for trouble.'

'Sounds like it. We gonna turn away from it?'

'No.'

'Didn't think so. I'd best go talk to the other drivers.'

She left. Burnett climbed back into the passenger seat of the Jeep and breathed a deep breath. He stared at the retreating light for a moment, and got back out. While Tyler went to each of the army trucks, he climbed into each coach to warn them what was coming. Nobody looked happy at the news.

When they climbed back into the Jeep, the light was gone.

'What do you think?' Tyler asked, starting the engine.

'Fuck it,' he said. 'Let's take the fight to them.'

Chapter Nineteen
Grey Room

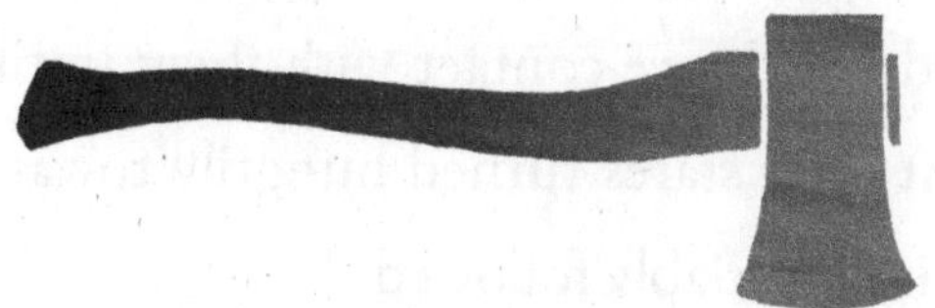

Bill, it turned out, had only marginally more standing in this world of rogues than his captives did. After the crash, with the women in his captivity staggering out of the broken frying pan of the truck into the world's biggest fire of circumstance, he was relieved of his precious cargo with about as much consideration as one might pay the paperboy.

Tattooed men led the women away from Bill, whose protests fell on the deaf ears of a wall of the burliest men Mira had ever seen. Bill's own men sank away into the crowd, leaving him alone. Mira didn't get to gloat. She was too terrified about what came next.

Susan limped along beside her, a red gash across her forehead, clutching her arm. Mira had gotten out of the crash relatively unscathed, save for a sore nose and a scraped knee that mottled her jeans with blood.

'This way, ladies,' a terrifying man said. He had a face full of tattoos. Terribly rendered images of the sun. The other men with him bore the same ugly adornments.

The ambush was made up of a motley group of different tribes. There were trucks and lorries and bikes of all shapes and sizes. Clustered around them, eyeing each other nervously, were disparate groups of survivors. They had tried to mark themselves out, somehow, with varying degrees of success. The inked men leading them away from Bill were top of the pile, judging by the way nobody made eye contact with them until they passed, at which point their stares turned hungrily toward the captive women. A smirk invariably followed.

The men led their captives right to the heart of the line. A petrol tanker stood, sprayed in camouflage colours, and daubed in red letters, six feet high: Sun Warriors.

The same symbol which adorned the men's faces bookended the letters at either side. A huge snow plough sat attached to the tanker's front, rusted and scorched with fire. Two other trucks also bore the symbols of their gang. One carried a trailer, stocked full of plunder, while the other trailed a jerry-rigged set of caravans. Around the trucks were a series of barrel fires. Men sat around in large moth-eaten armchairs, drinking beers and messing around like this was a Saturday night session.

'Look out, lads,' the man leading them in called to his brethren. 'Look what we got here.'

Cheers and catcalls came from the other men, who staggered to their feet to drunkenly leer at the women. One man grabbed his crotch and started thrusting it at them.

'What the fuck's going on here?' a woman called out from behind the rig. She stepped out into the firelight. A gnarled looking middle-aged blonde woman, with leathery skin and matted hair, she was as imposing as the men, albeit entirely outnumbered.

'Oh fuck off, Luce,' one of the men shouted.

The woman looked each of the men up and down, weighing up her options. She had a large knife strapped to her side, but no gun Mira could see. She shrugged, spat on the floor, and turned away.

'You ladies look tired,' the leader of the Sun Warriors said. At least, Mira assumed he was the leader. He was the oldest of the men, and the biggest. He was bald, stacked, and wore a thick handlebar moustache between his two tattoos, much better quality than those on the rest of the men. 'Let's have you go and take a lie down, shall we?'

They shuffled forward to the caravans. Mira's breath started to quicken. Everything she'd been dreading, anticipating, was metres away. She looked around, desperate for an exit.

There was nowhere to go.

Outside the Warriors' camp, men peered in, hoping for a glimpse of flesh.

There were no women, Mira realised. Aside from the mysterious Luce, who'd completely vanished, there was not a woman amongst them.

These were men who had learned to kill, to cross every boundary society had put on them. The kind of men who heard about a convoy of desperate people and thought first of how best to exploit it, inflict misery on it. These were dangerous men.

They reached the first caravan, and one of the men grabbed two women, whimpering, terrified. He led them inside, and the door closed. Mira felt the same loss of control. Her cheeks stung wet with tears, and her knees threatened to give way underneath her. They went to the next caravan, a man pushing Mira forward next to another woman. This woman's pose remained resolute, unwavering. She stared forward, eyes not meeting anyone. Mira wished she could be as brave.

'No!' Susan called. 'She stays with me.'

'Like fuck,' their guide said.

'She stays with me, or so help me God, I'll bite your tiny cock off. She stays with me; I'll make sure you don't regret it.' She looked the man up and down, salaciously.

'Fine,' the man said, pushing Mira and Susan into the caravan. The door slammed shut behind them.

It stank. Feet, sweat, food, and faeces mixed together into an abominable stench. Mira gagged.

'Are you okay?' Susan asked, grabbing Mira in close.

Mira nodded, her lip trembling. 'Why did you have to say that to him?' she asked. 'He's going to expect...'

She looked over at the bed, its sheets filthy.

'You're not doing anything,' Susan said.

'What do you mean?'

'You're leaving.'

'What? How?'

There was a small window at the back of the caravan. Susan strode over, and flipped it open. Luce's head appeared in the crack.

'She ready?'

'How did you...?' Mira asked.

'Less talk, more escape,' Luce said. 'Your friend here motioned me to save you, so here I am. Don't fuck about. You're a skinny little one, I'll grant you. Might be you'll actually fit through here.'

Laughter, booming and awful, sounded outside the front door.

'No,' Mira said. 'No, Susan. I'm not leaving you here.'

Susan grabbed her face, her eyes full of fury. 'Yes, Mira, you fucking well will, because whatever comes through the door, I can deal with if I know you're safe. Get out of here. Get to Burnett if you can. Go.'

'No,' Mira whimpered.

'You can get her clear?' Susan asked Luce.

'I can try. Come on, sweetheart, let's get moving.'

Mira squeezed Susan's hand. She started to sob.

'Go,' Susan urged, and pulled her hand away.

Mira climbed through the window, her skin scraping on the sharp plastic as she hoisted herself through. Once she was halfway there, Luce hooked her strong arms under Mira's armpits, and lifted the rest of her out. Mira's muddy boots had scarcely cleared the window when they heard someone opening the door on the other side of the caravan. Luce closed the window, and the pair of them ducked through the darkness.

Luce seemed to know the encampment well and was well versed in being able to move about unseen. The ambush line was long, but thin. They were soon clear of it, retreating from the line.

'How can you bear it?' Mira asked, once they stopped moving.

'Ain't got no choice,' she said, her accent definably Australian.

Mira considered her eyes, reflected in the moonlight, and saw nothing but sorrow and pain.

'My friends are coming,' she said. 'They can help.'

'The convoy?' Luce snorted. 'More likely they end up dead.'

A scream came from one of the caravans. Mira instinctively went to stand, wanting to run back, but Luce pulled her down.

'We need to get you out of here,' she said. 'Before they notice you're gone.'

She turned away and moved further from the convoy.

'Wait,' Mira said. 'I need to get to the others, warn them.'

'You can't,' Luce hissed. 'You want to try and go through the line, and wander out where they're looking? No fucking way you'll make it.'

'I have to do... something.'

'Bullshit,' Luce sneered. 'Your friend made a hell of a sacrifice to get you out of there; you best make sure it was worth it, miss.'

'I can't run,' Mira said. 'I have a friend in there, and more coming. They're going to die, unless I help them.'

Luce laughed. 'Right. What exactly do you plan to do, Miss Skinny Ribs? You're a little girl. You going to take on all these?' She gestured at the long line.

'You could help me.'

'I don't see it evens the odds up, much.'

'I mean it. What the hell are you doing here, anyway? You don't belong with these arseholes.'

Luce crossed the gap between them in a second, her hand coming up to Mira's throat. 'You don't know a fucking thing about me, okay?'

'Maybe not,' Mira said, struggling not to show the woman her fear. 'But I'm guessing you don't want anything to do with the slaughter of hundreds of innocent people?'

Luce sighed, and pulled her hand away from Mira's throat. Raucous laughter rose from one of the groups, making Mira's stomach turn.

'Some of them aren't bad people,' Luce said, sounding weary. 'They're desperate. They've had to do desperate things to get this far. Look, we still need to get away from here; they're going to notice you're gone soon. I'm not saying no. Let's get off the street.'

They moved across the next road, into the back streets. The broken and burned buildings here at least offered cover from the road. They ducked into the remains of an old betting shop, their feet crunching over shattered glass.

A kicked-in door at the shop's rear revealed steps leading upstairs. The first floor was an office. Looted or gone to seed, it was hard to tell. Either way, it was hardly inviting. Chairs lay strewn about next to cracked and shattered computer screens. If this was looting it was doubtful the thieves had found much of real value. The tiny staff kitchen held a single pint of congealed milk and a dozen smashed mugs. In the scant night time light streaming through the broken windows, the whole scene had a distinctly terrifying vibe.

'They're looking for you,' Luce said. She stood by the window, peering round to look back at the ambush line.

Mira joined her. The window offered a panoramic view of the whole scene awaiting Burnett. The line stretched across six lanes of the junction, across the adjoining dual carriageway, blocking off whatever route Burnett chose to take. Away from the group, three torches moved their way, scouring the area for signs of their escaped prisoner.

'You're not going to run, are you?' Luce asked.

'No.'

'What are you going to do?'

Mira shrugged. 'I have no idea.'

A loud whistle rang out from the line of trucks, and the three torches stopped, heading back. The various vehicles blocking off the dual carriageway started their engines, and moved, joining the group across the junction.

Down the road, Mira saw why. The convoy approached. Their lights were on full, making it hard to see how many there were, but Mira guessed it was a lot.

'We're going to need some weapons, whatever we do,' Luce said. 'I don't think I'll be able to take the lot of them with just Sally here.' She patted the knife hanging from her belt.

Mira turned to her. 'You mean?'

'I can't let you take on the bloody lot of them on your own, can I?'

Mira hugged her. 'Thanks.'

'Don't thank me yet.'

'Wait...' Mira said. 'You named your knife Sally?'

Luce didn't answer. She stared out the window at the approaching convoy.

Mira joined her, weighing up their options.

'Hey, Luce,' she said. 'Is there actually petrol in that tanker?'

Chapter Twenty

Dirty Boots

The ground underfoot became increasingly difficult to traverse the closer Lydia got to the centre of the city. She'd crossed into London on a push bike, which she'd been cycling for five straight hours in the dark. Now it was day and she was back on foot. She'd discarded the bike not long after she'd crossed the north circular. It had gotten a puncture, and her sore arse had been bloody glad to get rid of it.

She hadn't eaten or drunk anything since the previous day, sustained instead by a pure hatred for the men who had killed Greg, something more calorific than she'd have imagined.

She'd not seen a single person since the accident. She'd seen dogs, and cats, each one eyeing her warily. Since crossing into London she'd not seen so much as a pigeon. Clearly the fires which ravaged the city had driven the life from it too.

The extent of the devastation took her by surprise. They'd heard tales in Birmingham of fires sweeping the capital in the wake of the first storm, but she'd assumed they meant London in the way Hollywood meant London: Big Ben, the Palace, the centre of the city. She hadn't realised it was the entire sprawling metropolis. The intensity of the fires must have been something to behold, leaving the roads buckled underfoot and whole streets demolished. Some buildings were relatively unscathed, but most were burned-out shells or reduced to rubble. It brought to mind footage of the Blitz. This was the same, but on an epic scale. Most of the city was gone.

Her feet were swollen and sore. She'd already tapped the last reserves of her strength and will. She was still on the outskirts of the city and had a long way to go, especially on foot. Rest would be required, and soon. She was better off moving at night, at any rate. The pistol in her waistband might help her if she came across one, maybe two people, but if she came across a group, pulling a gun would get her killed faster. Better to move at night, unseen.

One of the side streets looked intact, so she made a turn, and headed toward the least damaged house. These were impressive terraced buildings, no doubt each would have been worth north of a million quid before. Even the most committed estate agent would struggle to shift them now.

The door was busted open, so she didn't have to worry about the noise of breaking in; although that meant there'd be nothing to eat inside. The fires hadn't damaged the house, but there was still an earthy, smoky smell. She chose the sofa which didn't have a skeleton fused to it, and fell onto it. Her eyes started to droop, and she drifted into sleep.

Her dreams filled with smoke, fire, and Greg. She dreamt of sleeping with him, but every time she looked in his eyes they stared back empty, vacant. There was a scratching sound in the dream, like something trying to claw its way into her consciousness.

She woke with a start.

She wasn't alone.

Sitting across from her, its expression one of puzzlement, was a dog. Its fur was dirty and it was skinny, but it looked happy and healthy.

She bolted up from the sofa, which made the dog jump, too.

'Hey,' she said, holding out her hands. 'It's okay.'

The dog cocked its head.

It didn't take long to establish it wasn't going to rip her throat out. He nuzzled into her, and showed her his belly. She took him through to the kitchen, to see if there was anything for either of them to eat. The kitchen had been predictably stripped bare, but there was a dog bowl, so Lydia kept searching until she found the bag of dried dog food that went along with it.

'This your place, fella?' she asked, pouring out a generous bowlful.

The dog got stuck in, and she went back to the cupboards. There was an unopened packet of Ryvita, which she tore into and munched through. She needed water, but the taps just juddered when she tried them.

She patted the dog, who had finished the bowl. 'I have to go,' she said, stroking behind his ears. 'I'll leave the food out where you can tear into it. It should keep you going a little while.'

The back door led into a garden. It was night, but under the full moon everything was clear enough. The gate beyond was open, so out she went.

Five minutes later, as she started to get into a rhythm once more, something moved behind her. Her hand went to her gun. Whipping round, she had it cocked and in her hand.

It was the dog, cocking its head at her again.

'You want to come with me?' she asked.

The dog moved to her side and sat, peering up at her.

'Okay. But I need to give you a name.'

She knelt and felt for the collar buried under his matted fur, which made him flinch. She twisted the collar a little, and found the name badge hanging from it.

'Greggles,' she said, reading the name. 'Of course. Okay, well, Greg, I guess it's you and me again.'

They set off down the street, the dog padding alongside her. They moved through devastated streets, to the point where it became difficult to know where in London they were going. Only once they passed Camden Lock did Lydia have any idea where they were.

She turned a corner, and stopped. At the far end of the street, a body hung from a rope. There were no signs of anyone in the area — she'd started to think the whole city abandoned save for plucky Greggles, but here was proof to the contrary.

The body was a few days old, judging by its lack of decomposition. It had a pistol tucked into its waistband, which meant whoever had done the hanging didn't need or fear the guns. Quite aside from the hanging, that seemed to Lydia like reason enough to fear them.

Greggles barked. Lydia looked around, but there was no sign of anyone. She walked underneath the body, looking up at it.

She was so busy looking up, she failed to notice the wire across the path. Her foot caught and a rope snaked around it, whisking her into the air with a scream.

Greggles started to bark again, and Lydia wondered for a second if he wasn't a cunning accomplice, summoning his masters to their captured prey. Or he was chastising her for failing to spot the trap he'd tried to warn her about with his bark.

She dangled there, swaying back and forth in the breeze. The dog sat below, staring up, perhaps trying to fathom what kind of a game this new human of his was playing.

The pistol slipped, clattering to the street below before she could react.

'Fuck!'

Fuck.

She tried to pull herself up to look at the knot, but wasn't limber enough for the task. She might have lost the extra pounds she'd carried around since motherhood in the months since the storm, but it didn't mean she was fitter than before.

The dog barked below.

'Hey, boy,' she called down to him. 'If you can work out how to get me out of this, I'll love you forever.'

The dog panted, but made no move to magically free her.

You're going to have to get yourself out of this one.

The bait for the booby trap was almost within touching distance, the gun in its waistband too, if she could get to it. She strained to get a good look at the knot around her feet. It looked solid. The rope ran up to a wooden beam, blackened by the fire but still intact. If she could get the gun, she could shoot the beam, loosen the rope. A long shot, but the only option she could see.

She swayed, back and forth, side to side, trying to generate enough motion for it to sustain her arc, using her arse like she was a kid back on the swings in some park in Leeds, trying to impress some boy in oversized baggy trousers.

As she swung closer, she could smell the decay of the hanging man. His face had bloated and swelled in the sun. She reached out, but missed the gun, her hand grazing his. For a second her heart pounded at the thought he might reach out and grab her, pull her in close to him, leering, but he stayed dead.

On the next pass she got her fingers on the butt of the pistol, loosening it from the waistband. On the one after that, she pulled it out, nearly letting it slip. She managed to wrestle it into her hand, and swung back, letting the motion die out.

She took aim. She was basically aiming for her foot. She was hardly a master marksman, and if she got this wrong she'd likely take her toes clean off. She took a deep breath and lined up the beam with the sight on the pistol, her stomach muscles screaming at her as she tried to hold herself up. She closed her eyes, focused, and opened them again. She squeezed the trigger.

Nothing happened.

She checked the safety, and tried again. Nothing. She took out the magazine, and found it empty.

Of course.

The gun was bait. Worm on the hook to draw the fish in. There was no way whoever set the trap was going to leave their prey with a working gun for when they came to collect their winnings.

Rage and frustration swelled within her, and she screamed.

The dog ran off, terrified. Swinging there, she started to cry.

She stopped herself.

No. Everyone is counting on you.

With every ounce of strength she could muster she drew herself up and wrapped the rope around her hand. She tried to work the knot with her other one, her abs screaming in protest. The knot was too tight, so she looked to the beam holding her in the air.

A crack ran along the woodwork. She chanced a look down. It was higher than she'd realised. A fall from here could do significant damage, especially with the bits of brickwork and debris scattered around her potential landing zone. Not to mention she'd likely be coming down on her head.

Don't see many other options.

Hoisting herself up further, she gathered the rope in her hands, and let go.

She dropped down. As the rope went taut again, pain barrelled through her tied ankle. She cried out, the splintering of wood above almost as loud as her.

The beam had buckled, but not broken. The rope looked far more precarious. Forcing herself into a sitting position again, she grabbed it, and started to climb. Her arms burned with the effort, and her ankle protested every movement.

She let go.

Something snapped in her ankle at the same time the beam split in two and fell apart. She fell, headfirst, the ground coming up on her in a flash. She brought her arms up to brace the fall and felt something else snap as she connected with the hard concrete. She didn't even have time to register the pain before the shattered beam came down on top of her.

Chapter Twenty-one

Shuddering Earth

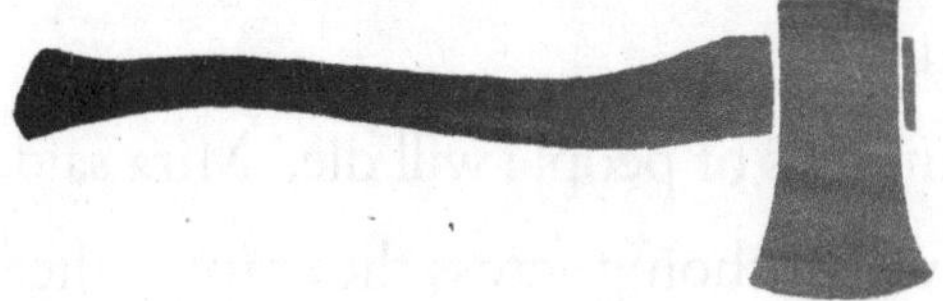

'Petrol?' Luce asked. 'Yeah, sure. How do you think the Sun Warriors got their standing?'

Mira stared at the tanker. 'I'm guessing it wasn't their winning personalities?'

'Not quite.'

The noise from the camp was louder, more raucous. Gunfire crackled in the distance, and two of the trucks burst free of the line, charging toward the convoy.

'Jesus Christ,' Luce said. 'They don't even know what's coming. This is gonna be a bloodbath.'

'You think they could turn back, go down the back streets?'

'Not with those coaches. Back streets are too clogged, full of wrecks.'

'Fuck,' Mira said. 'We need to get to the tanker. If we could take it out, we'd take out half the line.'

'What, blow it up?' Luce scoffed. 'Sure, and you'd likely take out yourself in the process, not to mention your friend in the caravan there. Besides, how the hell do you plan on blowing up a petrol tanker?'

'I dunno. Got to be a way, though.'

'It's not like the movies, kid. Petrol tankers don't just explode willy-nilly. You've got to introduce something to make it go boom. Otherwise you're just spilling petrol everywhere. Our best bet is still to run.'

'We run, hundreds of people will die,' Mira said, sharper than intended, her voice echoing across the empty office.

Instinctively, both of them looked out see if anyone heard her.

'Love, hundreds of people will die, whatever we do.'

Mira stared out at the trucks. 'I can't stand here and do nothing,' she said, finally. 'I need to go get Susan and the others, at least.'

'Hey, no skin off my nose,' Luce replied.

'You're not going to help me?'

Luce fixed her with a scowl, but Mira held her gaze, daring her to abandon her.

'Fine,' Luce said. 'But we need weapons.'

'Let's get some.'

They crept back to the camp, Mira's heart pounding. The attention of the bandits was on the convoy ahead of them, but it would only take one person to spot her, and she'd be back in that caravan.

They stuck to the long shadows, the only light coming from the camp itself. Everyone was either staring forward, or hurrying about, busy being busy.

You out there, Burnett?

Her heart swelled at the thought of being so close to him again. She hadn't seen him in months, but she owed him her life, more than once over. It had been he who had helped her get through the experience of killing Ewen. Of course, she'd been unable to kill anyone since, not for the want of trying.

And you want to try and kill a few hundred more?

They reached the last cover before they'd have to cross the open road.

'Where's your car?' Mira asked, in a low voice.

'No car. Bike.'

A Harley Davidson sat to one side of the tanker. It had saddlebags and a huge water bottle strapped to the back.

'What have you been trading?'

'Water, mainly. Enough to get a day's food, here and there.'

'No weapons in there?'

'Nope. Had some. They got took. Just me and Sally now.'

They crossed the empty street and came to the caravans. They stood unguarded, the Sun Warriors either still inside them or off prepping for battle. Mira hoped it was the latter.

A few men cast glances at the caravan, no doubt weighing up their ability to have their way with the Warriors' property without repercussions. They seemed to think better of it.

'Let's go,' Luce said.

They peered around the side. There were dozens of men, their backs to the caravans, craning to get a view of whatever carnage might unspool in front of them. Luce ducked round and opened the door to the last caravan. Mira followed, and went to the next caravan in the line.

She opened the door, holding her breath. Inside, two women lay on the single bed, huddled together, their clothes torn. At the opening of the door, they both shrank back.

'Come on,' Mira said. 'Let's go.'

The two women looked up, warily. They sat, and tried to recover their clothes, torn and barely wearable. One of the women had a bruise swelling under one eye.

'Head to the back of the caravans, wait for us there,' Mira said.

She turned and opened the door... and walked straight into a Sun Warrior, rebounding off his barrel chest, back into the caravan.

'What's this?' he said. He wore a satisfied grin, which creased the edges of his crude tattoo. 'Looks like our missing girly has...'

One of the other women lunged forward, knife in hand. The steel slashed across his throat, cutting off his smug speech.

Blood spurted from the wound as she took away the knife, spraying over the fallen Mira. The man dropped to the floor.

'Pig,' the woman with the bruise said, and spat on his corpse.

'Thank you,' Mira said, getting up, wiping the blood from her face with her sleeve.

The woman huffed and ran out of the open door. She didn't stop at the rear of the caravans, but plunged into the darkness beyond. The second woman came out and stared at the man's body, her expression blank.

The door to the first caravan opened, and Luce appeared with two other women in similar states of half dress, their expressions a mix of terror and fury.

Luce saw the body at Mira's feet. 'Let's get him moved,' she said to the two women she'd freed. She motioned to Mira. 'Go.'

Clinging to the sides of the caravans, Mira moved down and opened the caravan she'd escaped from an hour or so earlier.

The bed was empty. Mira looked around, worried Susan wasn't there. Then she saw her, curled up on the floor at the far end o the caravan. Blood and bruises covered her face and body.

'Oh god,' Mira said, rushing to her.

Susan stirred. 'Mira?' she said through a busted lip.

'I'm here to rescue you,' Mira said.

'Little short for a storm trooper, aren't you?' Susan said, an laughed a hollow laugh which turned into a coughing fit. 'Hel me up.'

Mira lifted her friend, put her arm around her, and moved t the door. She popped her head out first, to make sure the coa was clear.

'Look what Mister Sunshine had on him,' Luce said, beamin She held up two grenades. Then she saw Susan, and the smile le her face. 'Holy shit.'

They moved back around to the rear of the caravans, Susa supported by Mira and Luce. Once they had their backs to th end caravan they looked at each other, panting. Every woma from around the campfire was there, save for the one who'd ru

Mira sat Susan down. 'You okay?' she asked.

'Mmm,' Susan replied, in the least convincing way possibl 'Can we get out of here?'

Mira brushed the soaking hair from her face, wet with bloo and tears and god knew what else.

'Not yet,' she said. 'We need to help Burnett.'

Susan nodded, wearily.

'You ladies want to help us take these fuckers down?' Luce asked.

There was much nodding from the assembly.

A commotion came from beyond the caravans, and they froze. Luce raised a grenade in preparation for anyone coming round the corner, her finger in the pin. Mira had to concede death seemed a better option than capture at this point.

Mira peered round the corner. Men were jumping into cars, collected their things, and preparing to leave. One of the Sun Warriors looked in her direction, no doubt wondering where his Sun Brother was. He turned back to his friends.

'They're getting ready to make their move,' she said. 'Whatever we're going to do, we need to do it fast.'

'We could chuck the grenades at the tanker,' one of the women said.

'We wouldn't blow it up,' Mira said. 'Might take a few of them out.'

'Shame we haven't got a really long piece of string,' Mira said.

'Why?' Luce asked.

'What?' Mira replied. 'Oh, nothing. I was kidding. You know, like the roadrunner. The coyote used to put the explosives down, and go far away with the fuse, but he was always in the wrong place, and...' She looked around at the faces of the other women. 'What?'

'Everyone,' Luce said. 'Find string, rope, anything. Has to be long. We need to work out how to get the grenades on the rig.'

'What?' Mira asked. 'Wait. No. You saw the roadrunner cartoons, right? These plans didn't work out well for him.'

The women ignored her, ducking back round toward the caravans. Mira was still standing, dumbfounded, when they came back carrying extension cords and a length of rope.

Luce tied them together into one long rope, and Mira got it. This was their fuse, but they wouldn't need to light it.

'I'll take it,' Mira volunteered, once they'd assembled the rope and carefully threaded through the pins on the two grenades.

'Mira, no,' Susan said.

'I'm going, Susan. You've been through enough. Luce, you have to promise me you'll...'

'I promise, okay?' Luce said. She handed the bundle to Mira. 'Hook the grenades in, somewhere, onto the tanker. Pins facing out. Thread the rope, and come back here, okay?'

'Got it.'

She took the bundle, and headed towards the tanker, not daring to look back. Her heart pounded, and she daren't even move her arms lest she arm the bombs.

The bandits were too preoccupied to notice her appearance, and there was nobody between her and the back end of the tanker. Twenty metres.

A man walked right in front of her, too preoccupied with whatever nefarious task he had at hand to notice the sudden appearance of a teenaged Indian girl carrying a bundle of electrical cords and rope.

She reached the tanker and placed the bundle at her feet. She looked for anything she could hook her payload onto, but it was all smooth, domed steel.

'Shit,' she said.

She fell to the ground and found her hook. The rear bumper had a space above it which would serve to push the grenades into. She lifted the bundle, wedging the explosives in place, their pins facing outward. She fed a few feet of rope through her hands, and started back to the caravans, threading the rope through her hands.

When she reached the back of the caravans she even had a few metres of rope left. She let out a sigh of relief.

'Got it?' Luce asked.

'One way to find out,' Mira replied.

'We need to get as much distance as we can,' Luce said. 'If we can hook the end to one of the caravans...'

The sound of a hundred engines coming to life at once cut her off, followed by the deep rumble of the tanker's engine. Luce and Mira fixed each other with a panicked look, as the rope started to curl out of Mira's hands.

In alarm, she dropped it, forgetting for a second that she held the fuse, not the bomb. The rope skidded away before disappearing around a corner. The caravans started to move.

'Shit,' Mira said, and jumped around the side of the caravan, diving for the retreating fuse. She caught it with her finger, gathered it into her palm, and pulled.

The rope gave – pulled from its moorings, or pulling the pins – he had no way of being sure.

How long until it explodes?'

She stood. The women stood, frozen in place, their hiding place removed by the retreating caravans. They stared at Mira with hopeful, expectant faces.

'Run!' she shouted.

CHAPTER TWENTY-TWO

BIRD ON A WIRE

The horizon was on fire.

'I can see the lights,' Burnett said. 'We're getting close.'

'If we can see them, they can see us,' Tyler replied.

They rattled down the road at a fair pace. It was clear — there were wrecks on the pavements, shunted aside, Burnett guessed by people fleeing London in the immediate aftermath.

It was too dark to see anything outside of their own headlights and the glow ahead. They could already be surrounded. The thought occurred to him that the path was clear because the people waiting for them only wanted them to have one option. Into their trap.

If that's what it takes.

'What do we do?' Tyler asked. 'Kill the lights?'

'No point,' Burnett said. 'They know we're coming. There's no way around them. Either we make it through, or turn around and go home.'

'I didn't realise that was still an option,' she replied, chuckling.

'Oh that it were,' he said, with a grin.

Tyler slowed, checking her mirrors to make sure the rest of the convoy hadn't disappeared. They'd deployed the various weapons at their disposal across the fleet, had two Land Rovers either side to protect the flanks, machine guns to the rear, and men with rifles in each of the coaches as a last resort. They'd encircled the two hospital trucks and the supplies on all sides with the coaches.

Burnett's instructions to the passengers had been simple — stay down, stay away from the windows, and once it started, hold on. He hoped when this ended, however it went down, those coaches wouldn't be mass coffins.

The line came into view. Trucks, bikes, lorries, cars, and more spread out across the full width of the M40. A line of bandits, armed with a variety of weapons, stood in front of the vehicles with weapons raised.

'I told you we should have taken the M1,' Tyler said.

'Stop here,' Burnett replied. 'Those guns won't work at this distance.'

Tyler slowed, and the rest of the convoy followed suit. Burnett checked either side to see if there were any surprises, but couldn't see further than a few metres into the murk.

They were close enough to hear the collective roar from the men facing them, but they made no advance. Now it was a question of waiting to see who made the first move.

It sure as shit isn't going to be me.

They sat in silence, scanning for movement.

'Look,' Tyler said, pointing to the far right of the line.

One group had taken it upon themselves to launch the first attack. They moved along the line and disappeared from the end, down a side street and out of the glow of torchlight. Burnett reached into the back seat and pulled out his rifle. He wound down his window and rested the barrel on the door frame, waiting.

Sure enough, after a few minutes, there was movement in the dark beside them. The men reappeared, running at the convoy from the right. There were four of them, until Burnett took his first shot, catching their frontman in the chest. That stopped the other three in their tracks.

A burst of machine gun fire came from the Land Rover to Burnett's right, and the other three men fell.

'Burnett,' Tyler said. 'They're coming.'

Two trucks, each loaded up with men, broke from the line.

'Fuck,' Burnett said.

The trucks sped toward them. Burnett and Tyler readied their weapons. Once the trucks were close enough they both stood, training their guns on the oncoming vehicles. They didn't get the chance to open fire — their attackers were first. Burnett fell back into his seat as bullets ricocheted off the Jeep's frame.

The men in the two Land Rovers returned fire, giving Burnett enough of a window. He swung the rifle round and shot the tyre of the nearest truck.

The truck went toppling, its driver overcompensating with the sudden turn. He collided first with the other truck, then a wreck shunted off to the side. The abruptness of its stop was brutal. The second truck recovered, turned tail, and sped back to the ambush line.

Injured men clambered from the wreck of the first truck, shaking themselves down and running back to safety.

Tyler raised her weapon. Burnett put his hand on the barrel and forced it down.

'No,' he said. 'We might need them to show us mercy before the night is out. Let's be the first to show it.'

They waited.

Burnett scoured the line, waiting for the next attack. Men scurried back and forth, no doubt drawing up plans. The fact they'd repelled two attacks so far might have their enemy questioning their tactics.

Most of the line seemed to be showing little interest in Burnett's convoy. There was a carnival atmosphere. Burnett assumed a fair amount of intoxication was going on.

Good. Let them drink themselves silly and pass out. We'll tiptoe past.

If only they had the time. He watched the sky. There were no storm clouds overhead yet, but he had no idea how long that would last. If there had been, he could at least have pleaded with them, reasoned with them, told them the sky would fall on their heads unless they dropped this bullshit and banded together. Not that it would work, of course. These people were too far gone. Rapists. Murderers. The kind of people he'd spent his whole life before the storm trying to understand.

There wasn't too much to figure out as to what made people bad, Burnett reckoned. Everyone was bad. Everyone was good. In certain situations, given certain options and choices, some people went towards the light, some went to the dark. In the months since the storm these people had made a bad choice, at some time. Maybe some of them had made their choices before the storm. Maybe not. Most of those people would have been shopkeepers, mechanics, librarians, stock brokers. If you'd have told them a year ago they'd end up sitting across from hundreds of innocent people, working out the best way to kill them, they'd have scoffed at you. But here they were, too far gone to re-assimilate.

Broken.

So I have to end them.

The thought hit him like a thunderclap. Everything he'd done was to rebuild and survive. All they wanted to do was destroy.

Is there no other way?

'We need to go on the attack,' Burnett said.

'What?' Tyler replied. 'Don't be stupid. We'd get slaughtered.'

'Would we? What's the alternative? If they keep niggling away at us with these little attacks, we'll be out of bullets before long. Either that or we'll run out of people to shoot the guns in the first place. We need to go out there and kill every single one of them. If we don't, we'll be fighting them all the way to London. And we don't know how much time we have left.'

'What happened to your "all in this together" attitude?'

'These people have no interest in being "in it together". Look at them.'

'So what do you suggest?'

'We put them down.'

'No, I get that part of your strategy. I don't understand how you think we can launch an attack. We haven't got the men, or the bullets. This is a siege, right? Best way to survive a siege is to sit it out.'

'No.'

She looked across at him. 'Are you forgetting those are still people out there? They may have lost their way, but can you blame them? It's not like we're whiter than white.'

'We're not killers.'

'But that's what you want to be? Anyway, you've killed dozens of men. You've made decisions which impact on the lives of hundreds. You sent Greg and Lydia to their almost certain death. You risked the lives of my people to go looking for your friends three months after you knew they'd be gone.' She sighed, and a silence fell between them for a second. 'Don't get me wrong, Burnett. I like you. What you're doing is right, and with the best of intentions. But if you want to try and march us to a certain death and start slaughtering people, you can go fuck yourself.'

She opened her door and got out, leaving him alone with his thoughts. He could see her point, but still, when he looked out at the people between them and London, he wasn't sure there was another way. Negotiation? What the hell did they have that those across the way would bargain for? Sure, they had some supplies, but not enough to satisfy that many bandits.

Across from them, movement started to pick up pace. People darted back and forth, getting into their vehicles, readying their weapons. Burnett checked his rifle. He had less than a dozen bullets left and a single magazine in his pistol. Even if he and the others found their mark with every single remaining bullet, there'd still be bad guys left to spare.

He could always try walking a grenade into the heart of their camp, even up the odds a little, but he'd be too dead to care much about the outcome.

Damn it. How the hell do we get through?

The sound of engines drifted over the gap between them. His pulse spiked as the adrenaline coursed through him.

'Here we go,' he said to the empty Jeep.

He reached over and honked the horn. Tyler came running back from one of the Land Rovers, as a crackle of gunfire burst across the no man's land, one of the bullets rebounding off the Jeep's open door. Tyler jumped in.

'Well,' she said. 'Looks like we're out of time to decide.'

The noise across from them built and built, as they revved their engines. Tyler started the Jeep. Behind them the rest of the convoy did the same.

'Any ideas?' he asked.

'Try not to die?'

'Good plan.'

At the heart of the line, cars and trucks started to part, revealing a petrol tanker, its front lights ablaze, a huge plough jutting from its front. On top of the cab, a man stood behind a mounted machine gun, loading up long trails of bullets.

'Mother of fuck,' Burnett said. 'We need to get rid of that guy.'

'What guy?'

He pointed out the tanker. The colour drained from her face.

The tanker revved its engine, the noise cutting a deeper baritone than its compatriots. It started to move forward, followed by the cars to either side of it.

'They're forming a wedge,' Burnett said.

'Pull back?' Tyler asked.

'Fuck, why not?'

Tyler sounded the horn three times, and put the Jeep into reverse. Burnett stared ahead. It wouldn't matter. There wouldn't be an escape from this.

He was about to voice this thought to Tyler when the tanker exploded.

Chapter Twenty-Three

Them Bones

Everything ached, her teeth most of all. Lydia sat up, or at least tried to. She managed to get about halfway there.

The dog had rejoined her, its head cocked.

'Hey,' she managed, her mouth filling with blood as she spoke

It came forward and licked her hand.

'Thanks,' she said, and ruffled his head.

She tried to stand, but her ankle gave out. She fell onto an already sore knee, putting her hand out to stop from falling on her face, but her wrists weren't working. She fell.

'Fuck.'

The dog came closer and let out a little sympathetic sound.

'Hey,' she said. 'Go fetch me a stick, would you?'

The dog stared at her.

'Fetch? No? I didn't think so.'

The dog looked around and bounded off. He came back a moment later, carrying the remains of a small ball.

She took it from him. 'Good boy,' she said, trying hard not to be disappointed.

She needed to assess the damage before making further attempts at standing. Her face ached, and felt raw to the touch. There was blood in her hair. Her teeth felt like they had tried to chew a tyre. As for the rest of her, both wrists seemed damaged in some way, but weren't registering much pain, which probably wasn't good. Her ankle seemed to have the worst of it, and there were grazes to her arms and her left knee.

Overhead, birds flew in formation, on whatever mission it was birds chose to entertain themselves with. She watched them for a moment, happy to stay there a while nursing the injuries to her body and her pride. But she, too, had a mission, the day wasn't getting shorter, and there was a good chance whoever set those traps would come looking for their catch before long.

She stood, gingerly putting weight onto her other foot. She looked around. Amongst the masonry and debris lay a length of rusted pipe. She hopped over to it and put it under her right side. The rough edge dug into her armpit and it was a few inches shorter than would have been ideal, but it would do.

It didn't help with the pain, though. With every movement of her foot, the pain in her ankle flared up, whether elevated or not. She managed to hobble back to where she'd fallen, picking through the debris until she found her pistol and the radio. She checked them both. That the radio was still turned off and on; she could only hope it still worked.

Not yet though. Not until I've got the bunker in my sights.

How was Burnett getting on? She envisioned him turning up at any moment, chastising her for her tardiness. She limped on, gazing up at the hanging man with contempt, as though he were in some way responsible for her ruined ankle. She hoped it was a sprain, rather than a break. It didn't feel like sprains she'd had before, but she'd always been able to medicate those away, so who could tell?

Painkillers. They were now top of a list which previously covered food, water, one of the Hemsworth brothers, and a functioning Netflix connection. Now the whole realm of her imagination focused on ibuprofen, paracetamol, or something stronger.

After what felt like an age, she turned back to see she'd not even managed a hundred metres. There was a fair old distance left to go –an impossible distance. A raw spot was already wearing through the skin under her left armpit where the end of the rusted pipe rubbed. Lydia was no expert, but rusted metal and open wounds didn't seem like a good combination.

Sinking down onto a wall, or what was once a wall, she looked around. If the rest of London was this bad, what were the odds the bunker had survived? The scenes around her looked like something out of a disaster film, albeit a low rent one with the devastation directed at betting shops, kebab shops, and pubs, rather than national monuments.

The view further down the road wasn't much prettier. A gaze at what had once been the glittering skyline of England's capital showed little more than shards of what once was. Most of the skyscrapers were gone, and those left were skeletons of their former selves — gutted, burned out. Gone.

Birds continued to circle overhead. The thought dawned on Lydia that their dive-bombing antics and formation surges into the sky might be their way of waiting out the inevitable, until their quarry finally succumbed and died.

That would be you.

Her eyes started to feel heavy. The ache running across her body throbbed, bringing on little waves of nausea. She leaned back and rested her sore head on the wall behind her.

I'll stay here for a bit.

Greggles barked, and the world snapped back into focus. Lydia expected a sudden threat, but the street was as empty as before.

The dog considered her once more with the same expression of askance.

'Fine,' she said. 'I'll keep going. But only because you asked so nicely.'

She got back to her feet. The pipe was still a problem. She tore off the right sleeve of her top, wrapped it around the end of the pipe, and slotted it back into her armpit as before. It still hurt like a bastard, but it wasn't rubbing quite so much.

'Come on,' she said, and the two of them set off down the street again.

The clanking of the pipe on buckled tarmac was the only sound. They pressed on, Lydia not daring to take further rests, terrified she wouldn't wake from the next one. Once she found her rhythm it wasn't so bad.

The tight streets started to widen as they wound into the heart of the city. She passed a long park, the dark wilderness of which looked too terrifying to attempt, no matter how much easier it might prove.

The sky started to bruise as day gave way to evening. They were close enough to the river to smell it when the crackle of distant gunfire was carried to them on the breeze, rooting her to the spot.

One burst, and another, echoing around the empty streets, finally scaring off the birds hovering overhead.

The shots came from up ahead, pops and crackles that a year ago she'd have attributed to fireworks.

She hobbled across the street, where a wall offered some shelter. The dog followed, looking around anxiously and cowering at each fresh bang.

'It's okay, boy,' she said, ruffling his head.

You hope.

She shuffled forward, trying to get a better view, but the noise was at least a few streets away. Whatever was going on, it was going on at her bunker. She just knew; not out of a great cosmic intuition, but because that was exactly the way her luck was.

Have to keep going. Have to get there.

She got back into a rhythm, trying to cushion the blow of the metal on the road lest she gave herself away. Halfway down the next intersection she realised she was missing the reassuring padding of gentle footfall.

Greggles hadn't moved. He sat, ears forward, looking around in bewilderment. He winced with every bang.

'Come on,' she called. 'Don't worry, I'll look after you.'

Reluctantly, he followed.

They moved closer to the gunfire. As they did, Lydia could hear both sides of the argument — one side was loud, insistent, firing wildly at the other. The other's muffled, controlled bursts were either some distance away or...

Underground.

The river came into view and with it, the battle. A dozen men in garish clothing fired their guns into what looked to be a pit in the ground. Her heart sank. Not only was her bunker occupied, there were people fighting over it. It didn't matter which side were the good guys and which the bad, she looked doomed to failure.

She ducked out of sight behind a wall. Greggles needed no encouragement to get down. She winced as she sat, ankle jolting against a stray brick. Stretching the leg out, she considered her next move. As uncomfortable as her new perch was, she had little option other than to stay there a while and let things play out. Dealing with one victorious group might be easier than two at each other's throats. On the other hand, if they'd won their turf in a hard-fought battle, they might not be in a sharing mood.

Far from the fighting, a man's head bobbed over a wall. Lydia was half sure she'd imagined it, and craned her neck to get a better look. She stared at the spot for a few moments to see if it would reappear, but it didn't.

She'd have to move round. Getting back onto her good foot, she readied the pole once more and tried to work out how to get a look. She misjudged her footing and went sprawling forward. The pipe flew out of reach and clattered to the ground. A metallic *thunk* rang out.

The gunfire stopped.

She tried to lift herself back up, but her strength abandoned her. She rolled onto her back, in time to see one of the oddly-dressed gunmen bearing down on her, his weapon aimed at her chest.

'Who the fuck are you?' he shouted.

'I-I'm...' she stammered, but couldn't think of an adequate response. Somehow *'I'm Lydia Contos from Leeds. Can I have your nuclear bunker, please?'* didn't feel like it'd have the required gravitas.

'Don't move,' he barked, somewhat unnecessarily.

'I can't,' she said. 'My ankle's knackered.'

Her response didn't seem to compute with him. He looked around, trying to work out what his next move was, or find someone who could make a decision for him.

The gunfire resumed.

'I don't know who you are,' he said, confused. His finger tightened on the trigger.

'Wait!' she cried.

Before she could tell him what he should be waiting for, Greggles appeared from nowhere, and sank his teeth into the man's calf.

The gun barrel swung in the dog's direction, but the man fired early, missing Lydia and her new best friend. The bang was enough to spook Greggles. He let go of the leg, causing the man to yelp in a way unbecoming of his cultivated look of menace. As Greggles dashed off, the man raised his gun again and pointed it at the retreating animal.

'No!' Lydia shouted, again frustrated at her inability to do anything other than shout.

Don't you have a gun?

She went to pull it from her waistband, but it wasn't there. It lay, discarded in her fall, a few feet away. Next to it, shattered under the man's boot, lay the radio.

No.

She lunged for the gun, distracting the man enough to let the dog reach safety, but not quick enough to save herself. The man swung in her direction. She gave up on her own weapon, remembering that it had no bullets anyway, and stared into the barrel, waiting for the pull of the trigger.

Behind the armed man, an even bigger man appeared, the man whose face had popped up from behind the wall. He raised a large piece of concrete above his head and brought it down, connecting with the gunman's skull.

The gunman crumpled to the ground.

'Rude,' the big man said. He giggled, turned, and ran away.

'Wait,' Lydia said.

The man reappeared, joined by an old woman and a younger woman who looked like she'd wandered in from Glastonbury festival.

'Hi,' the hippie said. 'Let's get you out of here, before he wakes up, yeah?' She leaned down and helped Lydia up.

As she put her weight onto her good foot, she looked down at the body of the gunman, his brains dashed across the concrete.

I don't think he'll be waking up.

Chapter Twenty-Four

The Shape Truth Takes

When the first shots rang out, Max's instinct was to run. If the Kurgan had managed to penetrate the bunker complex, there wasn't much hope a bunch of soldiers who'd been sitting on their arses doing nothing for six months were going to be able to stop him. After all, he led a group of men who'd been living on the edge of desperation the entire time, superior firepower or no.

'We should go,' he said quietly to Mouse and Ava, who both nodded their agreement.

'You're not going anywhere,' the Prime Minister said. He turned to one of the soldiers. 'Search them,' he instructed. 'They could be insurgents.'

'What do you mean, insurgents?' Mouse said, indignant, but the Prime Minister had already moved onto other things. 'Insurgents against what?'

An armed guard subjected them to a cursory pat down. He stared at the door with a wary look, as though expecting the bogeyman himself to burst in any second.

'How did they get in?' the Prime Minister barked at a woman sitting at a console.

She stammered a response that sounded like an elaborate, 'I don't know,' before the appearance of an out-of-breath soldier saved her blushes.

'They breached one of the perimeter walls, sir,' he said. 'Bypassed the door, and came through into the corridor.'

'How the hell did they manage that?' the Prime Minister bellowed. 'This place was designed to protect us from a nuclear assault from the entire Russian arsenal. Are you honestly telling me a bunch of bloody savages with guns have managed to get in?'

'The inner door...' the soldier said, and flashed an embarrassed nod to the General Coles, who gave a barely perceptible nod to continue. 'It got jammed with a body, sir. By... removing it, we gave them a moment's advantage. Unfortunately, they seized on it.'

'The bunker was built to withstand a bomb, sir,' Coles said. 'It was not designed to withstand an attack from individuals.'

'Well then what fucking good is it?' the Prime Minister sneered at his officer.

Everyone became interested in their shoes, aside from Coles, who looked to be wrestling to keep his response unspoken. The Prime Minister turned back to the solider. 'You get back out there, soldier, and you bloody well deal with it. Can't be too hard to deal with a bunch of bloody savages.'

'Savages?' Ava said. 'Those are people out there, Prime Minister. Your citizens. If they've turned savage, it's because they've not had any other option.'

The Prime Minister gave her a hard stare. He turned his attention to his cabinet members, staring at the surface of the table in front of them as though trying to magic it into a portal to another dimension by sheer force of collective will.

The gunfire continued. Outside of the control room, people ran about, looking harassed.

'You,' Coles shouted to Max. 'What can you tell me about these men?'

'They're ruthless bastards,' Max said. 'Their leader calls himself 'the Kurgan'. He's either driven away or killed most of the survivors in London. He sees London as his. He's bonkers, but he's made it nigh on impossible to stick around.'

'Why are you still here?' he asked. He almost sounded impressed.

'We were leaving,' Max replied. 'We'd finally run out of food. Kurgan's been stockpiling it. We'd heard outside of London is even worse than the capital, but we figured we had to try it. But we found the bunker. We figured there'd be food, clothes, water. So, we tried to get in.'

'Well,' Coles said. 'I'm sorry to disappoint you...' Gunfire cut him off. He turned to the Prime Minister. 'Prime Minister,' he said. 'We should think about moving you.'

'Where?' the Prime Minister barked in response. 'Where exactly do you plan on moving me to? Back to the surface? No. Deal with these... *men.*'

Ava scoffed.

'What is it you think you've preserved, hiding down here all these months, Prime Minister? What way of life have you guaranteed for your country? You've got politicians and you've got soldiers. I don't see *citizens* down here. I don't see artists down here. I don't see plumbers. I don't see nurses, or doctors, or teachers. There are no children running about down here. Where are the children, Prime Minister? Up there, in the real world, the children are dead. You could have brought children down here with you, but you didn't, did you?'

'The Prime Minister's children are down here,' a woman said, tersely.

The Prime Minister shot her a sharp look of warning.

'Of course they are,' Ava said.

'Prime Minister,' Coles said. 'I must insist. This isn't safe.'

As if to highlight the point, gunfire rang out in the adjacent corridor. Max shot Ava and Mouse a look, and the three of them bolted for the door.

'Stop them!' the Prime Minister shouted, but nobody paid much attention to him. The soldiers grabbed whatever weapon they could and headed for the opposite corridor, toward the fighting. Those who weren't in uniform followed Max and his friends as they headed for the back entrance.

Max tried to recall the way back. He found the inner door, finally, while howls of pain and gunfire echoed off the walls. Max grabbed the handle, but it wouldn't open.

'How do I open this?' he called to the group assembling behind him. There was a crowd gathering, ranging from maintenance men to ministers, anxious to flee the gunfire.

'The keypad,' someone called. 'Three, four, nine, A for alpha, nine, F for foxtrot, six.'

Max keyed the combination, and the door opened with a hiss. It swung out, into the second chamber. Max ran for the door. This time there was no pad, only a heavy steel wheel to turn. It was stiff, and it took him, Ava, and a maintenance man to get it open.

'Can we open it again from the outside?' he asked, remembering it had taken someone on the inside to let them in last time.

'No,' the same man replied.

As the people streamed out into the darkness of the corridor beyond, Max looked around on the floor, and found a piece of flat slate. He wedged it into the doorframe as it closed, leaving a crack of light shining through the frame.

I'm not giving up on this place yet.

They climbed, Ava and Mouse showing the others the way. Muffled gunfire came from behind, distant echoes making their way through the tunnels. The darkness was completely disorientating. People panicked, bumping into one another, knocking others down into the wet ground.

'Look out for each other,' Max shouted. 'It's not far to the surface.'

They climbed out of the corridor into the underground station, and kept going until they saw a dim light. They found the staircase and climbed, the going hard with the stairs cluttered with rubble. There was nothing to get a grip on, and no way of seeing what little there was. Mouse stayed at the rear, helping people up, grabbing those who fell. Max took the lead until they were able to squeeze through the broken entrance and into the street.

The people from the bunker looked around at the desolation, their eyes wide with awe and horror. Max wondered what exactly they'd thought had been going on on the surface all this time. They wandered, dazed, blinking at the sunlight, marvelling at the devastation.

A burst of gunfire, close by, brought them back to their senses. They ducked down.

'Let's find the others,' Mouse said.

'Others?' a woman asked, a look of fear on her face.

'Not them,' Max said, motioning to the entrance to the bunker.

'We have friends here,' Mouse said. 'We left them safe while we looked for a way in.'

Max peered around the wall, towards the clearing where the Kurgan's men had been before. Most of them were gone, no doubt into the bunker itself, but a few remained, their attention directed towards the hole in the ground from which gunfire still sounded.

He looked around, trying to work out where he'd left the others. He clocked the broken wall. He hoped they were still there. 'We won't all make it,' he said to everyone. 'Can you stay here for a while, or find somewhere safe, while me and Ava go back and collect our friends?'

Blank faces looked back at him.

'How can we trust you to come back?' someone asked from the back of the group.

Max turned to Mouse. 'Stay with them. Head in that direction,' he said, motioning to the remains of the Houses of Parliament.

'Try to find shelter. We'll go get the others, come back and meet you. Then we get the fuck out of London, together. Head across the river.'

'Might struggle on that count,' Ava said.

Westminster Bridge was gone, extending a few feet across the Thames before it abruptly ended. To their left, Jubilee Bridge had fared no better.

'Shit,' Max said. 'I don't know. We'll figure it out later. Let's go get the others.'

There were vague rumblings of discontent, but Max didn't care. He and Ava checked the walls, ducked down, and moved across the road to where another wall gave them cover. They picked their way round, pausing every time there was a crackle of gunfire.

They came to a clearing, in which lay the body of one of Kurgan's men, his brains dashed in by a large piece of concrete. Alongside the body lay a pistol and the smashed remains of what looked like a walkie-talkie. Max picked up the gun and gave Ava a look.

Not a good sign.

They moved on, until the broken wall was across from a clearing. Max stopped, his back to some rubble.

'Hey,' he called, in a hushed tone. 'Jess?'

Darren's head popped up, his face breaking into a wide smile. Relief washed over Max. He motioned for Darren to get down. Ava's hand slipped into his for a second, and gave it a squeeze. He squeezed back and turned to her. She gave him a relieved smile.

'Let's go,' he said.

They moved, low and slow, and managed to cross the distance without taking fire. They ducked round the wall, running along it to their friends.

Nana sat with her eyes closed. Darren sat, cross-legged, a big smile on his face, a collection of weeds in his lap. Jess tended to a fourth person, a woman with dark hair and olive skin, covered in more scrapes and bruises than Max thought possible on one person. Her leg was in a rudimentary splint. A scruffy looking Labrador sat by her side.

'Max!' Darren said, louder than Max would have liked. He stood, spilling the weeds over the ground.

'Hey, fella,' Max said, and went in for a hug. 'Is Nana...'

'Sleeping,' Jess said with a smile.

Max looked down at the new woman. She as crying, tears streaming down her face as she looked away from him.

'Hi,' he said. 'I'm Max, and this is Ava.'

'Lydia,' she replied, giving a weak smile as she looked up at him.

'What's the matter?' Ava asked.

'Not sure where to start,' Lydia said, wiping away her tears. 'There's another storm coming. Unless we get into the bunker, we're going to die. I have friends coming, hundreds of people, and they're counting on me getting in there. But I can't contact them anymore. I lost my friend to this mission, and I've failed. Oh, and I've broken most of my body.'

'Another storm,' Ava said.

'On the plus side I have a dog.'

The dog barked appreciatively.

'I don't know about anything else, but I can get you into the bunker,' Max said. 'All of us. I just don't know how we get to stay there.'

Chapter Twenty-Five
Sun Grows Dim

Their big mistake was deciding the North Circular would be quicker than the M25. They'd debated it until the last possible moment, Tana of the opinion that three lanes of the motorway would be less congested than the two of the circular, which would offset the extra distance. Tom thought the shorter distance gave the circular the edge, especially given the motorway's fame as the country's longest running traffic jam. Chen at least admitted he didn't have a clue one way or the other, and just wanted them to choose so they didn't have to argue anymore. In the end, as the deciding vote, he sided with Tom because coming at the problem from the side might give them a better chance than coming up behind Burnett's convoy.

There was slim chance of that, however, with the pace they now crawled along the circular road, which was almost completely impassable at times. More than once, Tana and Chen had to get out and push a car or two out of the way, while Tom squeezed the vehicle through gaps almost too small for their car.

Tana had refrained for the most part from gloating, mainly because it was too frustrating a situation to gloat over. Now the sky was dark, and the way much harder to find as a result.

'Fuck's sake,' Tom said as he weaved between two SUV's, both of which had crashed into the cars in front of them, leaving Tom little way to navigate through.

'There goes the right light,' Tana said. 'Add that to both wing mirrors and the indicators.'

'Glad you're keeping score,' Tom said. 'When we get through this, how about one of you take over? My leg is fucking killing me.'

'Sure,' Chen said from the back seat.

'What's that?' Tana said, leaning forward to look through the smeared windshield.

Tom peered through the murk. Up ahead, the horizon looked to be aflame, a thin red glow rising up like steam. He stopped the car, having made it through the squeeze, and the three of them got out. Tana climbed up onto the bonnet to get a better look.

'What can you see?' Tom asked.

'We're not far. I can see lights. Some fires, too.'

'We should kill the lights,' Chen said.

'I've got a better idea,' Tana said.

They got back in, Chen at the wheel, Tom beside him, Tana in the back seat. They set off, picking their way forward under the light of the stars, while Tana prepped their weapons. They had taken quite a collection from the last village, with shotguns, knives, pistols, and more bullets than they could possibly use. Tana handed Tom a pistol and a shotgun. Tom checked both and watched as the oncoming ambush grew closer.

'So what's the plan?' Chen asked.

'Well,' Tana said. 'These guys are grade A, top-notch arseholes, right?'

'It's a fair assumption,' Tom said.

'Well, we can pull off arsehole, I reckon.'

'Tom can,' Chen said under his breath.

'Nice,' Tom said. 'So, what, we join the ambush, and when it kicks off we turn on them?'

'It's our best bet for finding the girls, and it'll be the biggest help to Burnett.'

'Tom looks the part,' Chen said.

'Hey,' Tom said, as the other two burst into fits of giggles. 'I have feelings, you know.'

Tana's hand patted Tom's shoulder. 'You do look pretty fearsome.'

'Fine,' Tom said. 'If nothing else, we give the others a fighting chance.'

They drew closer until a lorry blocked their path, parked up across the lanes. Standing in front of it were three men. Each sported a thick beard, a shaved head, and a sawn-off shotgun. Their clothes didn't round off the look of menace — one wore filthy jogging bottoms, another, what looked like slippers.

'Here we go,' Tana said.

Tom rolled down his window as they pulled up. 'We miss it?' he asked the approaching men, who eyed their car warily.

'Miss what?' one of the men asked in a thick West Country accent.

'The fight. We heard the message, but we've been stuck in Norfolk. Took us fucking forever to get here.'

'Who are you then?'

'Us?'

'Yeah. What faction you belong to?'

Tom paused for a second. He hadn't considered they might need some kind of gang name to gain entry. 'We're the Lebowski's.'

'The who?'

'Not heard of us?'

'No, mate.'

'Hmm.'

The man speaking scratched his beard, sending a cloud of dandruff flying. 'What you got to trade?'

'Ammo? Got plenty of that.'

Tana held up the box of ammo in the back seat. The man leaned in to the car to appraise it. His beard smelled of shit.

'Okay,' he said. 'On you go.' He signalled to the truck behind him, which moved back across the road enough to let them through.

Tom tried to convey his thanks with raised eyebrows, not wanting to open his mouth while the shitty beard was in such close proximity to it.

'You're just in time,' the man said, smiling through rancid whiskers.

Tom wound the window back up, and they drove through. Beyond the truck lay a carnival of different gangs, stretched out in a line as far as Tom could see. People ran about the line, clambering into cars, rushing about with ammunition. Somewhere off in the distance, engines revved.

It wasn't the ambushers, however, who drew the eye. A hundred metres or so down the road, packed together, was Burnett's convoy. It looked tiny in comparison to the line of enemies allied against it.

'Fuck me,' Tana said from the back seat, craning between them to get a better view.

'He's got no fucking chance,' Chen said.

A man walked in front of the car and held his hand out to stop them. Given the shotgun in his hand and ring of grenades over his shoulder, it made sense to comply.

'We're going at them in a wedge,' he said. 'Sun Warriors are leading the charge, mad bastards. Don't get ahead of whoever's to your left. Chances are you won't see much action from here, so you don't get much of the spoils either. Serves you right for turning up late.'

'Right,' Tom said.

Chen pulled them up alongside the next vehicle, an old people carrier retrofitted to look like something out of *Mad Max*-. They'd replaced the roof with an improvised machine gun nest, although that seemed too grand a term for something held together with gaffer tape. The open side door revealed a bunch of chavvy-looking oiks hiding within a billowing cloud of weed smoke. Tom felt a pang of jealousy — he hadn't had a joint since Leon had died.

'So what do we do?' Chen asked.

Tom shifted in his seat. 'Play along, I guess. Look for an opportunity.'

'If we move too soon we'll be dead before we can help anyone,' Tana said.

'You think we can make a difference, the three of us, against this?' Chen asked. 'Feels to me like we turned up just in time to see our friends die.'

'We can try,' Tom said.

A roar went up, far along the line, spreading outwards. A great revving of engines followed. A wave of excitement rushed along the line. People high-fived each other, beat their chests, and generally readied themselves to go to war. That they were going to war against a group of innocent people trying to flee to safety didn't seem to dampen their enthusiasm.

From the heart of the line, a huge petrol tanker rumbled forward, flanked at either side by two trucks laden with armed men.

'Here we go,' Tom said.

Chen put the car in gear and revved the engine.

A strange *pop-pop* sound came from somewhere, followed by a deep, bellowing boom, and the sky filled with fire.

The tanker had exploded.

The force of the blast sent their car skidding sideways. The windows cracked, distorting the fireball rising into the sky into a thousand shattered flames.

The tanker shot forward and into the air, head over heels, its rear end pulling into the sky and toppling over the front end.

'Woah,' Chen said.

'Fuck,' Tom added.

Something burning hit the bonnet of their car. It took Tom a moment to realise it was a leg, still aflame. It was followed by a rushing sound.

Chen screamed and hit the wipers, trying to rid the windshield of the appendage. The car filled with the smell of burning flesh.

Screams came from everywhere, a shrill note of total collective panic, and Tom realised what the rushing sound was. Spreading out from what remained of the tanker was a lake of liquid fire.

'Drive!' Tom shouted, as billowing smoke shrouded the car, smothering everything else. To their left, several smaller explosions boomed.

Chen put the car into gear and spun the wheels, trying to get away from the oncoming fire lake. They lurched forward, but too late. The flames caught both left tyres, which burst, slamming the chassis of the car to the ground.

'Get out,' Tom said, as the right side tyres popped.

'Where too?' Tana shouted.

He was right. Flames rose around them, and the temperature started to rise. If they left the car they'd be jumping into burning gasoline, but with the petrol tank below them heating up, staying in the car wasn't an option, either.

Chen popped the driver's side door open, pulling back from the heat immediately. 'Fucking hell!' he screamed, holding his hand.

'What the fuck are we going to do?' Tom shouted.

Hot wind blew in from the left, filling the car with smoke, choking the three of them. The water in the radiator started to steam, whistling out the front of the car. Tom opened his own door, careful to wrap his sleeve over his hand first. He looked down and saw the ground beneath him was no longer aflame.

'It's burning itself out,' he shouted.

He jumped out, remembering to take his weapons with him. The moment his shoes hit the tarmac the soles started to sizzle, so he started to half run, half tiptoe away from the car. The fires were out, burned through as quick as they had started, but the tarmac had melted, giving off noxious, acrid fumes which caught in the back of Tom's throat.

'Over here,' Tana shouted.

Tom ran to the big man, who had found a patch of tarmac unaffected by the fire. They'd been at the edge of the lake's reach. Chen joined them, and they watched as flames started to lick around the seats in their car, the heat enough to get the upholstery burning.

The bearded guards had come round from their post, staring into the clouds of black smoke. A gust of wind cleared the cloud for a moment, revealing the devastation before them.

'Well,' Tana said. 'Looks like our job got a lot easier.'

Everything in front of them was chaos. The fires still burned around the tanker, now little more than a wire frame with a couple of melted wheels jutting off it, adrift on a sea of flames. The trucks that rode out with it lay on their sides, knocked over by the force of the blast. Smouldering bodies lay around the wrecks. Everywhere else, people tried to flee the fires – those not trapped inside burning cars, that is. One of the cars must have held a stock of ammunition — it exploded in a hail of deadly fireworks that made everyone duck for cover until it had stopped.

Tana stared across to where the convoy had stood before the explosion, but everything that far away was still shrouded in smoke. 'You think Burnett survived?' he asked.

'Only one way we can find out,' Tom replied.

'What about the girls?' Chen asked.

There's no way they survived that. If they were even in there.

'Burnett could be readying himself for a charge, seize the moment,' Tom said. 'He wouldn't even know they're there.'

'Okay,' Tana said. 'Let's go tell him.'

Tom handed Tana his shotgun and pulled the pistol from his waistband. Chen checked his rifle, and tested the melted tarmac with his toe.

'Let's go,' he said, and the three of them ran into the smoke.

Chapter Twenty-six
When Forever Comes Crashing

It started with two pops, a flash, and a boom. The windshield shattered, spraying Burnett and Tyler with tiny shards of safety glass.

'Drive!' Burnett shouted, somewhat unnecessarily given Tyler was already in the process of getting them the fuck out of there. He hoped everyone else in the convoy was as alert as her, as she put the Jeep into reverse and slammed her foot down.

The sudden acceleration joined with the force of the blast, smacking Burnett's head against the seat as their Jeep smashed into the coach behind them. Tyler didn't take her foot off the pedal for a second. The wheels span uselessly underneath them until the coach, too, started to reverse.

Opposite them, the tanker rose on a pillow of fire, its rear accelerating into the sky until it started to tip, the arse end going over the front, forcing the cab into the road.

'Move!' Burnett screamed.

The rear end was headed in their direction, fast. The convoy started to retreat, moving backwards as one. Burnett could only imagine the panic running through the coaches as hundreds of people watched, powerless.

The tanker completed its full flip and smashed into the road. The convoy put distance between it and the wreckage, but not fast enough.

As the tanker, aflame, hit the tarmac, it burst. Petrol washed out of both sides in a wave, catching alight as it went, a tsunami of burning liquid hell pouring out along the road. A splash flew through the air and landed on their bonnet, causing Tyler to lose control of the Jeep. It swayed from side to side in its retreat.

The lake of fire spread out in both directions, swallowing the ambush line as it went. Car after truck after jeep after minibus caught aflame almost instantly, fuel tanks rupturing beneath them in the sudden heat. It was like a firework display, especially when the vehicles carrying ammunition or grenades caught, sending secondary explosions into the sky.

A volley of gunfire came across the void between them, whether by judgement or accident Burnett couldn't be sure. None of the bullets found their mark.

The lake spread out, finding the outer limits of its devastating surge and falling back. In the end, they escaped its wrath by some distance, the force dissipating sideways rather than forward. The fires started to peter out almost immediately, but the damage they left in their wake was breathtaking.

Despite the slowing fires, Tyler pressed the accelerator, and they again smashed into the coach behind them, knocking Burnett's head against the dashboard. Dots of light rushed through his field of vision. They didn't seem out of place with what was going on in front of him.

The Jeep came to a halt. In the absence of squealing tyres and a protesting engine, the screams of people burning, dying, falling, reached them through the smoke.

'What the fuck happened?' Tyler asked, nursing her own head.

'I don't know,' Burnett said. He couldn't quite process it himself. 'Should we help them?'

'Why?' Tyler asked.

'Tyler, look at them,' he replied. 'There are people dying out there, in the most unimaginable way possible.'

'Well,' she said, unbuckling her seatbelt. 'You make your bed...'

Burnett got out of the Jeep and stood in front of it. Behind him, the doors to the coaches opened. People poured out, straining for a better view of the carnage.

A car burst through the smoke, going faster than it should have been capable of on melted and deflated wheels.

'Back on the coaches!' Burnett shouted, raising his pistol.

Tyler got out, raising her rifle toward the oncoming car.

A man leaned out of the passenger window, or at least, it looked to be a man – with the burns covering their face it was hard to tell. Burnett thought for a second this could be someone fleeing the carnage, willing to give them the benefit of his considerable doubt – until they raised a weapon, which immediately began to unload in the direction of the convoy.

Burnett and Tyler opened fire, followed by two of their armed guards. Bullets pinged off the vehicles around them. One caught a man trying to climb back onto his coach, hitting him in the back. He fell forward onto the steps and slid onto the street.

The approaching car fared worse, riddled with bullets within seconds. The windshield misted with blood and the man hanging out the side sagged, his body spilling from the car. The car swerved, careening out of control.

'No!' Burnett shouted.

It headed straight for them.

He jumped back into the Jeep, thankful Tyler had left the engine running, and accelerated hard. He only had a split second, the oncoming car speeding up as it barrelled toward them.

I'm going to be too late.

Wheels spinning, the Jeep just managed to clip the rear of the car as it sped past him. Without a seatbelt, he smashed into the steering wheel, but sat back up, ignoring the sudden protestations of pain. He accelerated hard. Something scraped, latching on. Their bumpers had entwined. He pressed on, dragging the car away from the convoy by a matter of inches. He kept going, until they smashed into a wrecked minibus. His face connected with the steering wheel again, and something cracked.

A cheer went up somewhere behind him, but Burnett wasn't able to appreciate it. Without the distraction of impending death, the pain in his face blossomed. His hands went to his nose, gingerly feeling it to assess the damage. Given the pain he felt, he half expected his fingers to find nothing more than a gaping hole where his face used to be, but everything was still there, although not in the same shape it normally was. The pain was so bad it almost blinded him.

'Boss?' Tyler said, reaching into the car.

'Fuck me, that stings,' he replied.

'Let's get you out of there,' Tyler said, and forced open the door.

His knees buckled at first, but he managed to get hold of himself enough to steady them. They walked back to the convoy.

'Well done,' someone said.

'Let's get out of here,' he said. 'We've still got work to do.'

He leaned against one of the coaches, trying to catch his breath. Tyler went to try to find the doctor. Burnett stared across the road. Most of the fires were out and, with the smoke, he couldn't tell what was going on over there. Hopefully, the remaining survivors would have weighed up their options and decided to call it a day.

All was silent for a few moments, until a single, angry cry went up, followed by another, and another. Burnett peered through the smoke. One, two, dozens of men came charging across the smoking tarmac, their faces filled with anger, their hands filled with weapons.

'Well,' Burnett said. 'Shit.'

Chapter Twenty-Seven

The Hurt That Finds You First

They found an old street sign, its paint burned off, its edges harsh, and used it to improvise a stretcher. Loading Lydia on as delicately as they could, Darren took one end while Max and Ava carried the other. The sign cut into their hands, but none of them complained, given the obvious pain their load was in. Still, there was more than one occasion when Max felt the sign slipping away from him. Given the state of Lydia's injuries, dropping her didn't seem wise. It didn't help that Lydia's dog insisted on weaving between their legs, trying to make sure his owner wasn't manhandled.

The silent walk at least gave him half a chance to collect his thoughts. Over the course of the last six months he hadn't thought much about the first storm. It was something which had *happened*, and knowing how or why wouldn't have changed anything. Sure. They'd spoken about it for the first few weeks, but when no answer presented itself, they'd simply... *adjusted*.

Now, knowing how, knowing why, and knowing there could be more on the way — his head buzzed with fresh knowledge and unanswered questions. As for how to take the bunker, he had no idea. He could get them back inside, but whoever had the upper hand, they were unlikely to take Max's reappearance well, let alone the hundreds of others Lydia said were on their way.

They crossed back over without detection. The Kurgan's men looked to have gone into the bunker. They carried on until they reached Mouse, guarding the Underground entrance from a small pile of rubble. The others from the bunker milled around, some working to clear the gap from the entrance in case their colleagues tried to follow their escape.

That's good, because otherwise how the hell are we going to get Nana down there?

Mouse jumped up the moment they came into view and rushed over, stopping in his tracks when he saw Lydia.

'Who's she?' he asked.

'Play nice, Mouse,' Ava said, shooting him a look.

'This is Lydia. She's come to tell us we have to take back the bunker,' Max said.

'Why?'

'Long story.'

'The storms,' Lydia said. 'They're coming back.'

'Apparently not that long,' Max said.

They lowered Lydia to the ground and two women rushed over to attend to her, no doubt medical staff from the bunker.

'There's no way Nana's going to be able to make it down the slope,' Ava said, in a low voice. 'Lydia, either.'

'We could try the way the Kurgan went in,' Mouse said.

Everyone stared at him. Max wanted to admonish him for such a patently terrible idea, but he couldn't think of a better option.

'Fine,' Max said. 'We need to scope it out first. Ava, come with me. Mouse, stay here with the others. Spread the word about what's happening. If we get in, we'll signal for everyone to follow.

'Why do I have to stay here?' Mouse asked, pouting.

'We need you to look after everyone,' Ava said.

'If it helps, it means you're in charge,' Max said.

Jess put an arm around Mouse and led him away, the boy looking displeased but not pushing it further. As she walked away, Jess turned to Max and mouthed that she was still in charge, right? Max nodded.

'Some of us don't need looking after,' a man said, striding up to Max. Max recognised him from the control room, where he'd been sat around the huge central desk. From his strident air of authority Max guessed he must be a person of some importance. 'And what gives you the right to think you can order us about?'

'Nothing,' Max replied. 'By all means, feel free to fuck off and die in a horrific manner when the storms come back.' He turned away, allowing himself the briefest of looks at the man's face, and headed back to the edge of the wall, followed by Ava, who smirked at him.

'You know,' she said. 'You can be a sexy motherfucker, sometimes.'

'Thanks,' Max said.

He peered round. There was still no sign of the Kurgan, or his men. The fighting seemed to have stopped.

'Right,' he said. 'Let's do this.'

They ran to the opening. Up close, they saw how the Kurgan had made his way in. The collapse of the building had damaged the walkways and corridors leading to the bunker, and a section of the floor had collapsed, exposing a steep staircase below.

Here was me thinking the Kurgan must have employed some dastardly cunning to get in, turns out it was his idiot men stomping around for hours over a cracked floor.

The way the floor had collapsed allowed them access through a steep but manageable ramp. Max poked his head through first, knowing the Kurgan's love of booby traps. It looked clear, so the pair of them walked down.

Bodies littered the staircase – the Kurgan's men – allowing them both to arm themselves. Ava picked up a pistol, Max a rifle. He placed his own pistol into his waistband.

'This feels better,' Ava said, checking the chamber.

Halfway down the corridor was another of the huge steel doors, propped open by bodies. At a certain point the bodies of the Kurgan's men stopped, replaced by dead soldiers.

They stepped over the bodies and entered the main bunker. All was silent inside. Max checked every corpse along the way in the hope one might be the Kurgan, but knew full well none would be be. If the government had won this fight, the door would have been closed.

The bodies became sparser as they moved deeper into the complex. The only sound came from the hum of the electrical lighting and the air vents, which recycled endless stale air.

‘Stop right there,’ a voice called. ‘Turn around.’

They did as instructed. Behind them in the corridor was one of the Kurgan’s men, with a long scar down his weasel face; what remained of his hair in a matted pink Mohawk; and big, black panda eyes. He looked ridiculous, like an eighties pop promo gone homeless. The shotgun in his hands, pointing straight at Ava and Max, was less ridiculous.

‘Guns on the ground,’ he said.

They laid their weapons down.

‘Well, it was nice to hold one for a few seconds,’ Ava muttered.

The scarred man ushered them to turn round and head back down the corridor. They trudged, the man breathing heavily behind them, the wheeze in his chest pronounced enough to make Max wonder how the how the hell he’d snuck up on them.

At the end of the corridor they turned right, and approached the main control room, this time from the opposite side. The bodies of government guards thickened here again, thirty or so, some stacked on top of each other.

Stepping inside, the situation was as dire as Max had suspected it would be. Despite their inferior numbers, the Kurgan and his men most definitely held the upper hand. The Prime Minister and everyone else still alive were in rows, on their knees. Each had their hands interlocked behind their heads, save for the woman Max recognised vaguely as the Prime Minister’s wife, who sat, her two young children sobbing in her arms. Some of the people wept, while others stared forward with jaws set in grim determination. The Prime Minister was in the latter camp, his eyes fixed on the Kurgan.

'Well,' the Kurgan said, as the man ushered Max and Ava into the room. 'If it isn't my least favourite little pissant, and his lady friend. Where's that little rodent of yours, I've got some payback to give him.' He smiled, sitting in the Prime Minister's chair. Max said nothing, trying to assess the situation and look for anything which might give him hope of turning the tables.

The Prime Minister's gaze flitted between the Kurgan and his wife and children. Max wondered if the Kurgan had actually sussed the scale of the prize that had fallen into his lap. He didn't strike Max as the sort of person who'd be particularly au fait with who the leader of the country was. Then again, neither was Max, and he'd recognised him as soon as he'd set eyes on him.

'What brings you to *my* lovely bunker?' the Kurgan asked, spreading his arms out to convey the *his*-ness of the space around them.

'There are more storms coming,' Max said, which got the Prime Minister's attention, as well as many others in the room.

'Bollocks,' the Kurgan scoffed.

'We need to get everyone down here. Every survivor we can.'

'Not on my watch,' the Kurgan replied. 'This is my gaff. I reckon there's enough stuff down here to keep me and my boys living fat and satisfied for a good few years.'

'How noble of you,' Ava said. 'You're a real humanitarian.'

'Listen, darling,' the Kurgan replied. 'I don't give a fuck about anyone 'cept me and my boys. That's not to say we couldn't find room down here for a beautiful black mama such as yourself.' He blew Ava a kiss.

'I'd sooner die,' Ava said.

'I can arrange that.'

'What do you mean another storm is coming?' the Prime Minister asked, addressing Max.

'I don't remember saying you could open that fat face of yours, Your Highness.'

'I don't need your permission,' the Prime Minister replied.

This is going to go south.

Max scoped out the opportunities available. Even if he managed to turn the tables on one of the guards, it was pretty clear things would become bloody. He wouldn't put it past the Kurgan to open fire indiscriminately, just to prove he could.

One of the kneeling men caught his eye, motioning to Max's left. At the end of one of the workstations encircling the room sat a pistol, alone and unguarded. Max looked back to the kneeling man, who tired to convey some elaborate plan with his eyes. Max had no idea what that may be. There was no way Max could make it across to the weapon.

'So what's the plan here, Kurgan?' Max asked, playing for time. 'You've got a load of hostages, but nothing to trade them for. Are you expecting the police to come and negotiate for their release? You can forget about that.'

'Plan is this,' the Kurgan replied. 'Either every wanker in this building agrees to bend their knee to me, or I kill every fucking one of them. Then, we lock the door and wait for the world to be rebuilt. *Then* I ransom their precious Prime Minister back to them.'

Max couldn't help letting out a hollow laugh. 'He stopped being the Prime Minister the moment the first storm hit,' he said. 'There's nobody the least bit interested in him, apart from the people here too caught up in the way things used to be to notice.

As for rebuilding, you heard me mention the new storm? So who is going to do that? Everyone not in this bunker when it hits is going to die.'

'I'm not saying it's a perfect plan,' the Kurgan replied, smiling. 'But it's a plan.'

Max started to move over to the right-hand side of the room, drawing the attention of the Kurgan and his men away from the gun. The Kurgan made no move to stop him.

'It's not going to work,' Max continued. 'The best thing to do, the *smart* thing, is to let everyone down here. Sit out the storm, and go back to the surface. The Prime Minister can get back to work, and we — *all of us* — can start to rebuild. If you want to be a part of that, show how important you can be, you should think about that.'

The Kurgan appeared to mull it over, as Max continued to move towards him.

Max turned to the Prime Minister. 'I'm sure when this is over we can give the Kurgan here a place of importance in keeping with his stature, yes?'

'Well, I...' stammered the Prime Minister.

Max tried to signal him to play along, but was apparently as good at conveying his intentions with a raised eyebrow as the man across the room was. Max looked across to the man, and gave him a curt nod.

The man stood and lunged for the pistol. Max charged at the Kurgan, hoping to take him unawares, forgetting the Kurgan was neither stupid nor gullible. He met Max's dash with a swift thump to the chest, driving the air from his lungs. He fell to his knees, gasping for breath.

The other man reached the pistol and aimed at the Kurgan's head. The Kurgan saw it coming, and ducked. The bullet ricocheted off the wall, and took out one of the Kurgan's men, who fell to the floor clutching his throat.

Screams erupted, as the two young children and their mother took in what was happening. She made to cover her children with her own thin frame, but in two strides the Kurgan was over to them. He picked up the youngest by his top and held him up.

'Right!' he bellowed.

Silence cut through the room, followed by a low, desperate moan from the Prime Minister's wife. The Kurgan held the child, a boy of no more than four years, brandishing him as a shield. The pistol in his other hand came up, and pressed into the boy's temple.

The child, already weeping, darkened his trousers. His eyes locked, pleading, onto his father's.

'Please,' the Prime Minister begged, his arms outstretched. 'Whatever it is you want, I can make it happen for you.'

'Of course you can,' the Kurgan said. 'But how's about first we calm the fuck down, yeah?'

Behind the Kurgan, Ava moved, silent. She stepped up to one of the Kurgan's men and took the pistol from his belt. The man didn't even notice. She raised the gun, and pressed it into the base of the Kurgan's skull.

'Put him down,' she said, in a low voice.

'Darling,' he said, moving the barrel from the boy's temple.

She pulled the trigger. The Kurgan's brains splattered across the crowd kneeling before him. The boy dropped to the ground, screaming, as the Kurgan's body fell onto him.

Then the battle really began.

Chapter Twenty-eight

Dead Leaves And The Dirty Ground

Mira hit the tarmac with such force that she skidded along for a few metres before coming to a halt, her knees and arms scraped red raw by the tarmac. Then the heat came, and for a second she assumed she must be on fire. It seemed a reasonable assumption, since everything else was.

'Mira, get up!' Luce screamed.

The women stood together in their torn clothes, motioning urgently to her. None of this made sense – she was sure there'd been a line of caravans between them a second earlier. Now those caravans were a hundred metres down the road, what remained of them.

She blinked. The interminable ringing in her ears didn't help much. As least it drowned out most of the noisy chaos behind her. Most of it. She could still hear Luce, her nasal voice the only thing to break through.

'Huh?' she said.

Susan stood up, directly in Mira's eye line. She stared at Mira, took in a huge lungful of air and shouted at the top of her voice.

'RUN!'

This finally shook Mira from the dazed confusion. She got to her feet, and ran. She couldn't quite manage full pelt, but a few seconds later she'd caught up to the other women, who as one, gathered her into their group and turned, running as fast as they could. Behind them, the tanker completed its arc through the air, and slammed into the ground, spilling liquid fire. She heard a *'whoosh'*, a sound so alien it chilled her to the core. She had no idea what that sound heralded, but it couldn't be anything good.

Her legs ached with every movement, but before she could think about stopping, things started to explode behind her. She pushed the pain as far to the back of her mind as she could, and kept running. When she finally did chance a look behind, nothing of what she saw made sense. A mélange of fire and heat and death too jumbled, too incoherent in its scope. Had she done that?

Me?

Little old me?

What the hell have I done?

The other women started to ease off, so she did the same. They had outrun the fire. They stopped, deep in the darkness beyond the flames, and turned to watch.

The whole of the ambush line was on fire, the trucks and cars and everything else which had been there moments before reduced to different shapes of burning orange. Men staggered about, burning, trying to find any way out of their situation. Smoke billowed up, swept into the wind and carried across the way.

The convoy.

'Can anyone see the convoy?' she asked, breathlessly.

'I think they're okay,' someone responded, but Mira couldn't see how they could possibly know that.

She felt sick, nausea swelling through her.

You just killed hundreds of people.

Killed them in the worst way imaginable. Her mind went back to the fire in the farmhouse, when she'd lost Sam. She hated knowing he burned up in there. She'd never gotten to say goodbye to him. Now she had consigned who knew how many people to that same fate. Worse even.

She leaned over and retched. There was nothing in her stomach to spill. She felt weak, dizzy with the weight of it.

Susan clung on to her, helping her up. 'You did it,' she said, voice full of pride.

How could she be proud? How could anyone be proud of what Mira had done? Mira shrugged her arm away.

The fires started to die down. People – survivors – spilled from cars and trucks, desperately trying to get away. A car sped off toward the convoy, disappearing into the smoke. A man, staggering and wounded, started toward them.

'Oh shit,' Luce said.

'Can he see us?' a woman asked.

The man raised his gun in their general direction. 'Fucking bitches!' he screamed, and opened fire.

He might not be able to see them, but one of his wild bullets hit a wall above them. The women ducked to the ground, scrabbling for cover. Abruptly, the man stopped, and fell forward. Whether he was dead or unconscious, Mira couldn't tell, but he didn't look to be getting up.

They waited, watching the carnage, expecting the survivors to turn in their direction and exact their revenge. There might not be hundreds of bandits down there anymore, but judging by the numbers still scurrying around, there were enough left to mount an assault on seven unarmed women hiding behind broken walls.

Unlike the others, every person she saw still walking made Mira's spirits soar, even if they crawled from a wreck, or stumbled around. She couldn't process the sheer volume of death she'd doled out, and every person still alive was another life she could subtract from her guilt.

'We should get out of here,' Luce said.

'We need to help Burnett,' Susan said, her words followed by a racking cough.

'I'd say we've helped enough already,' Luce replied. 'You want to stay here and die, be my guest. But if you've got any sense, you'll get the hell out of here.'

'And go where?' Mira asked. 'Burnett is the only hope we have. There are more storms on the way, and if we don't get him and his people through this we all die. You want to go hide and wait for it, knock yourself out.'

'Hey!' Luce said, squaring up to Mira. She pushed Mira to the ground. 'I saved your fucking life, and the lives of every one of these bitches, okay? So don't fucking lecture me.'

Mira picked herself up and dusted down her jacket. 'Do what the hell you want,' she said, and turned her back. The women around her stared Luce down.

'Hey,' Luce said. 'Look, I'm sorry, alright. You saved my life too. I'm not a complete idiot. You think there's gonna be more storms coming?'

'Burnett says so,' Mira said. 'I know him. I trust him. If he says that's what's happening, that's what's happening. Besides, he's not going to try to drag hundreds of people down here and risk death unless he's got a damn good reason.'

Survivors started to come together, forming little packs, looking around them in bewilderment at the chaos engulfing them. All around, bodies still smouldered. The groups called to each other. Before long they'd be deciding whether to turn tail and get the fuck out of there, or stay and lash out.

Sucking air through her teeth, Mira turned to the others. 'We have to try.'

The other women looked at their feet, except Susan.

Luce turned back to them. 'Fine,' she said. 'I'm with you. So what do we do?'

Susan stood, a little unsteadily, but Mira could tell some of her friend's strength was returning. 'We get to Burnett.'

'We could go down the back streets to the side,' one of the women offered.

'There's a good chance your friends will think we're bandits if we come at them in a sneak attack,' another said.

Mira tried to get a sense through the smoke as to whether Burnett and the convoy were even still there. She thought she could make out their headlights through the smoke, but with the carcass of the tanker still billowing out heavy black clouds between them, it was hard to be sure.

The survivors had formed a single group, and one man tried to take charge, rallying them together, raising his fist in the air. Mira couldn't make out the words at this distance, but it didn't seem to be a treatise on how they should lick their wounds somewhere else. Around him, dozens of other hands went up, and a low roar of anger washed over the distance between them.

'Whatever we're going to do,' Mira said, 'we need to decide, and fast.'

'Oh shit,' Luce said.

Men passed guns around the group. By contrast, the women had zero weapons between them. Mira tried to think of some way they could alert Burnett and the others about what was coming their way.

'We can't just stand here,' Mira said, more out of a desire to motivate herself than chastise the others.

Another roar went up from the crowd before them. Arms went up to the sky, some holding guns, some holding blades. They turned to the smoke between them and the convoy, and ran toward it.

'Fuck!' Mira shouted.

She ran after them.

'Mira!' Susan called after her.

Mira ignored her. When she reached the man who had taken potshots at them, she grabbed his gun, and carried on. She sensed Luce running behind her, but had no idea how many others had followed.

The tarmac had cooled enough to no longer be sticky underfoot, but it was rough, like frozen mashed potato, and she nearly went over on her ankle as soon as she crossed the line. It was a mistake to have rushed down here. She hadn't prepared herself for the carnage enveloping her, nor the crushing realisation the bodies, the men *she'd killed,* would be still smoking, still burning, and in some cases still moaning in pain. They were dying all around her.

She stopped. Her head swam. She bent over and heaved again, before sinking to her knees, the hot tarmac warming her broken skin. Tears streamed down her face, and she let out a moan of despair.

An arm went round her shoulder, picking her up. She looked up into Susan's face.

'I did this,' Mira said. 'I killed all these people.'

'Come here,' Susan said, and pulled her into a tight embrace. 'You did what you had to do, and you saved lives. You're the bravest person I know.' She pulled away, and looked deep into Mira's eyes. 'Jen would be proud of you.'

Mira wept again.

'Come on,' Luce said, breaking the spell. She picked up a pistol discarded by bandits. 'Let's go get those fuckers.'

Chapter Twenty-nine
When We Were Younger & Better

Tom moved forward slowly into the darkness. Away from the glow of the fires behind them, and not yet in sight of Burnett's convoy, they could barely see a few inches. The lack of visibility wasn't helped by thick wafts of smoke engulfing them every few seconds.

The noise around them was no help. There were distant screams of dying men, occasional pops of gunfire, and explosions. To Tom's ears, the battle continued to rage.

'Chen,' he whispered, and got no response. 'Chen,' he repeated, more urgently.

'What?'

'Can you see anything?' Tom asked. In truth, he wanted to know his friend was still there with him.

'Nothing,' Chen replied.

'Tana?' Tom asked. Chen was to his left, out of sight but close by, but he had no idea where the big Samoan was.

'Oh shit,' Tana said. 'Get down!'

Tom ducked. A car burst from the smoke and went tearing past them, the three of them briefly illuminated by its headlights. The car ignored them and swept past, up the road to where the lights of Burnett's convoy were barely perceptible.

Tom broke into a run, trying to catch up with the careening vehicle. A gun battle broke out between the two sides. Tom's legs ached almost immediately, and his lungs felt like they might burst. Tana and Chen ran past him. He kept running.

As soon as it had started, it was over. He was close enough to see it unfurl, see a Jeep peel off from the convoy and slam into the oncoming vehicle, and the whole thing come to a chaotic conclusion. A cheer went up from the convoy. Tom slowed.

Looks like he's getting on fine without you.

Tana and Chen slowed up too, and caught their breath. They were closer to the convoy. Behind them, the ambush line was little more than a glow through the smoke.

'We should go see if Burnett's okay,' Tana said.

'If he's not,' Chen said, 'they're not going to know who the hell we are. What if they assume we're hostile, and start shooting before we get round to explaining it to them?'

'Let me catch my breath a second,' Tom said, struggling not to faint from the exertion.

I'm really not in good enough shape for the apocalypse.

'You okay?' Tana asked.

'Did someone set fire to my lungs and muscles and I didn't notice?'

'Not that I can see.'

'Then I'm probably fine. Let's go.'

They started to walk. The smoke swirling around them blocked off the convoy once more.

The roar which came from behind stopped them in their tracks. Tom turned back. There was no sign of where the noise came from save for the dim glow of the remaining fires, but the sounds coming over the gap were clear enough. They were war cries, the desperate howls of desperate men.

'We should find cover,' Chen said.

The first of the rampaging men came into sight, face red with blood and burns, clothes ragged and burnt. He held what looked like a butcher's knife in one hand and an automatic rifle in the other, waving both in a primal rage.

'Holy shit,' Tana said.

There were a few wrecks scattered nearby, so the three of them ducked behind them, sheltering from view.

Dozens of others joined the man. The marauders were not far from the convoy, where people scurried about, taking cover or trying to get back on the coaches.

'They'll massacre them,' Tana said.

'Not if we can help it,' Tom replied. 'Everyone loaded?'

They checked their guns. None of them had much in the way of ammo, but they could make a dent if their shots were well aimed. They readied themselves, unseen by the approaching wall of angry men whose battle cries died out as they approached the point of no return.

A man dressed head to foot in camouflage gear, half of it burned away, was the first to shoot. He lowered the barrel of his heavy-duty machine gun at the convoy and opened fire. A second later, Tom, Tana and Chen did the same.

One of their bullets hit the man square in the chest, while two others took out the leg of one attacker, and the neck of another. More profound than the deaths themselves was the effect their shots had on the approaching horde. They had expected to meet gunfire straight on, not to their flank, and several of them stopped, trying to work out where the shots had come from.

Tom hesitated for a split second, not wanting to give their position away too easily, and opened fire again, his second shot missing its target completely.

The crowd shot back, peppering the cars around them with gunfire. Tana and Chen tried to return fire, but couldn't get out from their cover. Bullets struck around them, shaking the car, shattering the windows. It occurred to Tom this wasn't the smartest place to provide covering fire from.

Gunfire crackled from the convoy as they shot back at the distracted men. The attackers split into two groups, and started to fan out, one wedge moving toward Tom and the others, the other heading toward the convoy.

A tyre popped at his feet with a loud hiss.

'Motherfucker!' Chen exclaimed to Tom's left. 'I'm hit.'

Tana ducked down and crossed to Chen, who clutched his arm, wincing at the pain.

'How bad is it?' Tom asked. He tried to get up to take a shot; a volley of gunfire pinned him back down.

'Clipped him,' Tana said. 'He'll be fine.'

'Thanks for the fucking concern,' Chen spat. 'It fucking hurts, okay?'

'Diddums,' Tana replied, smiling. He took back his position.

'I'm sick of getting fucking shot,' Chen said.

The gunfire continued in their direction. Tom shot over the top of the car, but if he hit anything it didn't diminish the gunfire coming their way.

He peered round the car's bumper. The battle over by the convoy seemed to be going better. Burnett's people weren't pinned down and hiding behind their cars, for starters. As for their attackers, they held a V shape, each arm taking aim at their respective sides. Satisfied Tom and the others weren't going anywhere, some of the attackers turned their attention back towards Burnett's convoy.

More people swelled the ranks of their attackers, moving into the space between the two flanks.

Reinforcements. We're doomed.

'Hey!' one of the new arrivals shouted, her voice carrying through a gap in gunfire.

The gunfire stopped. Some of the attacking force turned around to see who had called to them.

'Fuck you!' the woman snarled.

Mira.

The new arrivals opened fire. Tom, Tana, and Chen did the same, as did Burnett's group, catching the attacking mob in a three-way assault. They were dead before they could work out where to point their guns. Tom took out one man with a shot to the head. He moved round from behind the car, moving and firing towards the line. Tana and Chen followed.

Another man fell to Tom's gunfire, taking one in the back as he raised his gun towards the women in front of him. Tom didn't feel even the faintest twinge of guilt at shooting the man in the back, and readied himself to do the same again.

There was nobody left to fire at.

The women stood facing them, defiant, their guns raised, their clothes torn and filthy, their faces covered in cuts and bruises. They clustered together so none had their backs exposed. They appraised the men coming toward them with hard, unforgiving eyes.

Tom raised his hands.

'Stop right there,' a woman called out, her voice thick with an Australian accent.

Tom stopped.

'I'm putting my gun down,' he said. 'Mira?'

The young girl spun round from where she'd been scanning Burnett's convoy. She took in the sight of the three of them, her face not quite registering them.

'Tom?'

Another face turned to them, badly bruised.

'Tana?' Susan said.

Mira broke free of her group and ran toward them. Tears streamed down her face, and Tom felt his own tears starting to fall. She crossed the distance and practically knocked the three of them over.

'I thought you were dead,' she sobbed.

'Nah,' he replied. 'You should know better than to write me off.'

She pulled away, gave him a smile which filled his heart with joy, and went to give Tana a hug. Susan hobbled over to them, met by Chen.

'Hey,' Tom said, giving her a gentler hug. 'You know, it's considered rude to mock a crippled man by hobbling over to him.'

She laughed. Tears welled in her eyes. They hugged again.

'You okay?' he asked.

She nodded. 'We both thought the three of you must be dead,' she said.

'We survived. Had a hell of a job tracking you down.'

'We rode on a tractor,' Chen said. 'That bit was alright.'

'You found us, though,' Susan said. She flashed the three of them a warm smile.

'Might not be all we found,' Tana said, looking back to the convoy, where people watched this strange reunion, their guns not raised but still in hand. No doubt waiting to see how it played out. Tom scanned the line of people, but couldn't see Burnett.

'You think he's over there?' Susan asked.

'Let's find out,' Tom said, and started towards the convoy.

Chapter Thirty

Replenish The Empty

Gunshots rang out in the distance, far underground. Lydia sat bolt upright.

'Shit,' Mouse said, moving over to the hole and peering in. 'Whatever's going on, it's pretty far down.'

Lydia had been getting to know her new friends, both Max's group and the ones from the bunker. The latter seemed incapable of taking in their surroundings, blinking at the sky even hours after leaving. Presumably they thought they'd never see the outside again. Most were support staff, secretaries and the like, although there were a few uniforms among them. They didn't seem in a desperate hurry to get back into the bunker and help their fellow soldiers out, however, so Lydia had to assume they weren't fighters. Engineers, perhaps, or communications officers.

Communications.

'Hey,' she called out. 'Anyone work in communications?'

'Um, me,' a uniformed man said, raising his hand.

'Come here,' she said, motioning him over. She edged herself up, glad to find her body didn't scream at her for doing so. 'Did you hear those broadcasts, from CERN?'

He shook his head. 'No. We've not been monitoring channels other than military since...' he tailed off, and shot a look to another uniformed woman. 'No,' he added, finally.

She frowned. 'What channels have you been monitoring?'

'Military ones.'

'Not civilian channels? CB?'

He shook his head again. 'No, ma'am. Only military. We were under instructions to ignore civilian channels.'

'Wait,' Mouse said. 'You've been down there for six months, your sole job to monitor communications channels, and it never occurred to you to scan civilian frequencies?'

'That's not what I said,' the man said, his cheeks flushing red. 'That's what the Prime Minister *ordered* me to scan.'

'Never mind,' Lydia said. 'If we can get you back down there, can you get onto the civilian frequencies? Could you broadcast on CB channels?'

'I-I...' he stammered.

'I could,' Mouse said.

'You could?' Lydia asked.

Mouse nodded. 'Not a problem.'

'Wait,' the soldier interjected. 'It's not that simple. All broadcasts need authorisation, and only on military channels. The Prime Minister...'

'Not sure if it's escaped your attention, mate,' Mouse interrupted. 'But your Prime Minister isn't in a position to dictate fuck all.'

'Wait a minute,' the soldier said.

'Officer,' Lydia said, flashing Mouse a look to get him to back down. 'Look around you. What power do you think he still has?'

'He's still the Prime Minister!'

'I reckon if we threw a snap election, he'd lose it,' Mouse scoffed.

'While we're on the subject,' Nana said, from the stone she'd been sitting on. 'What kind of a leader is he anyway? Lets his people, his country, go through hell for six months? Not exactly Churchill, is he?'

'He...' the soldier started to stammer again, but there was more gunfire, and they went back to staring at the hole in the ground, waiting to see what came back out.

I need to get to those radios.

'What do you want to do?' Mouse asked.

She tried to move. Everything still felt damaged, but she might be able to stand.

'I need to get down there, get word to Burnett.'

'Here,' Nana said, holding out her cane. 'I'm not in a rush to get down there. You take it.'

Lydia took the offered support and stood, careful not to put too much pressure on her left side. Something inside groaned, and for a second she thought she might pass out. She took a deep breath and started to walk. It was clear that at least one of her ribs was broken, but her leg didn't seem too bad. When all this was over she'd need to thank whoever strapped it up for her. She was glad of the walking stick, however.

Mouse walked alongside her, but nobody else volunteered to come forward.

'You okay?' he asked.

'I'll manage,' she said. 'You're not going to be in trouble, are you? Max asked you to stay here.'

'Nah,' he said. 'Max isn't our leader. We're like a family, and he's everyone's big brother. Well, except Nana. And Ava, for different reasons. But if this is what we need to do to save everyone, that's what we've got to do, right?'

It was difficult to manoeuvre Lydia down the ramp, but between them they managed it. They set off down the dark staircase. Neither of them had thought to ask the soldiers for one of their guns. Lydia had hoped the fallen soldiers on either side of the battle might have dropped their weapons, but she didn't see any.

The sporadic bursts of gunfire grew closer. A stray bullet knocked off some plaster on a wall not far down from them.

'Wait,' Mouse said.

She stopped. Everything hurt more. She wished she could sit down, but unless she perched herself on a corpse she was out of options.

Mouse moved forward, and peered round a corridor. He pulled back. 'They're right through there,' he whispered.

'Who are?' Lydia replied.

'Kurgan's men. They're facing away from us.'

'What about Max?'

He moved forward and peered round once more.

There was a crack, and Mouse fell back, hit full in the face with a rifle butt, blood spurting from his nose. Two men appeared, both wearing the ludicrous attire marking them as the Kurgan's men. Both carried machine guns. One pointed at Lydia's face, while the man carrying the other aloft scooped Mouse up in one oversized arm.

'Stay fucking quiet,' the first man said, his voice deep with an Essex twang.

Lydia put her hands up in compliance, but the pain in her ribs made her lower them immediately.

'What the fuck do we do?' the other hissed, still carrying Mouse like he was a bleeding rag doll.

Mouse's eyes lolled about in their sockets; the hit to his nose had knocked him clean out.

'Don't fucking ask me,' the first man said, still aiming at Lydia, sizing her up. 'Who the fucking hell are you?'

'Lydia,' she said.

'Fucking bitch shot the Kurgan,' the second man said, pacing.

'Only the two of us left,' the first man said. 'Good job we got ourselves some hostages.' He stared at Lydia with dead eyes. She did her best to stare right back.

'Really?' she asked. 'Hostages? The way out is that way, and there's nobody stopping you from leaving. Or do you mean to barter an entire nuclear bunker for the safe return of two people? Two people those down there couldn't give a fuck about, for that matter.'

Mouse regained consciousness, and found himself dangling above the floor. He started to flail about in a panic, convinced he was falling. The two men ignored him, and he stopped. He looked up at the man carrying him and the colour drained from his face.

'What do you suggest, love?' the first man asked her.

'Go,' she said. 'There's no way the two of you alone can take the bunker. So, either you die trying, or you find somewhere else.'

'Somewhere else?' he replied, his face reddening. 'Have you fucking seen it out there? There is no fucking *other place.*'

'You've not been outside London?' she asked, adding a note of incredulity to her voice to try to mask her fear.

'Outside London is a war zone,' the other one said.

'In places,' she replied. 'Other places are doing better. What's more, there's plenty of room out there, for everyone.'

'Bullshit,' the first man said, but the certainty had fled his voice. He looked at his friend, who shrugged.

'Fuck it,' the other man said. 'They've got the fucking Prime Minister back there. Army and shit. Ain't no Kurgan holding us here no more. Let's fuck off.'

The first man considered it, then shrugged and lowered his weapon. The other man dropped Mouse, who fell to the ground with a thud. Without a word, both men headed up the corridor.

'You okay?' she asked Mouse, as he stood and dusted himself off.

'Fine,' he said, wiping his nose on his sleeve and trailing a long streak of red along it. 'That wasn't so hard.'

Two shots rang out back the way they'd came.

'Not for them,' she said.

'Let's go,' Mouse said. He walked to the end of the corridor and strolled round the corner.

'Mouse, no!'

The bullet caught him right between the eyes. Mouse's body fell backwards, dead.

Lydia screamed.

'Oh fuck,' someone called out. 'Sorry!' he added.

'Hold your fucking fire!' Lydia shouted, and rushed to the boy's body. His face, shorn of its usual smile, looked even younger.

'What the fuck did you do?' a woman shouted from somewhere.

Ava and Max charged down the corridor towards them. Ava knelt down beside her and cradled Mouse's head in her hands, weeping. Max stood dumbstruck, and Lydia saw his hand tighten around the grip of his own weapon. He looked back down the corridor, to where a soldier stood staring at the body on the floor.

'No,' Lydia said. 'Max.'

Her voice seemed to break the spell.

Max looked back at her, his eyes filling with tears. He turned back to the soldier. 'You fuck!' he shouted, spitting a mix of his own tears and saliva to the floor. 'What the fuck were you thinking?'

'I'm sorry,' the man offered in response, the guilt plastered over his face.

'What was he even doing down here?' Max said, turning to Lydia.

'He said he could help with the radios,' she said. 'He wanted to help.' She looked down at the lifeless body, torn between guilt and anger that her last chance to contact Burnett was dead on the concrete floor before her.

Ava stood and wiped her eyes clean with her sleeve, her face falling into an emotionless mask. 'Come on,' she said, taking Max's arm. 'Let's get back in there. Still work to do.'

Max nodded and turned back down the corridor. But he'd barely stepped forward a pace when the heavy steel door at the end swang shut.

'No!' Max shouted, dashing down the hall. He slammed his hand into the thick round glass. Behind it, implacable, the Prime Minister stared back, before turning on them and heading back the other way.

'Motherfucker!' Max shouted, throwing himself against the door.

Lydia leaned against a wall, and stared at the door.

It's over.

Chapter Thirty-one

Waging War on the Forevers

Max stared back through the window, breath fogging up the thick pane. He raised his pistol to the unforgiving glass and contemplated opening fire, but knew it'd be useless. Once the door shut, it was over.

This door...

'Quick,' he said, turning to the others. 'The other door.'

After taking a moment's pleasure in the upturn in Lydia's face, he hustled back up the corridor with the others, and up to street level. He could see his breath as he climbed the ramp.

The escapees from the bunker and the rest of the Shitty Six —

Five

— huddled together, trying to keep warm. Two of Kurgan's men lay dead between them.

'What's going on?' Nana asked, as he and Ava appeared, with Lydia hobbling not far behind.

'We've got to go back in through the other door,' Ava replied. 'The Prime Minister has decided he doesn't want to share his toys.'

'Where's Mouse?' Darren asked, peering behind them.

'He's gone,' Max said.

'Gone where?' the big man asked.

Max put his hand on Darren's shoulder. 'He's gone, Darren.'

Nana let out a whimper. Ava hugged Darren. He pulled away from her in disgust and turned to Jess, wrapping his arms around her instead. Ava looked affronted by his spurning, but Max understood. It was Ava's job, and his, to protect their little brother. They had failed.

'Come on,' Max said. He turned to the others, who watched this family reunion uneasily. 'Has anyone got the ear of the Prime Minister?' he asked.

Nobody answered.

'Fine,' Max continued. 'I need as many of you as can manage to get back down there, but I need a couple of people to stay here with Nana, and anyone else who doesn't think they'll make it down the ramp.'

'I'll stay,' Jess said.

'Me too,' Darren said, half sobbing.

Lydia's dog barked.

'Okay,' Max said. 'With luck, we'll be coming back out through this door soon and go in together.'

'We'll be waiting,' Jess said.

Max turned to the others. 'Lydia, are you going to be able to make it down? This way isn't as easy.'

'I don't have a choice,' Lydia said.

'We need to move,' Ava said. 'He might realise there's an open door.'

The entrance to the Underground station might be wider, but the way down was just as dark, just as terrifying. The cold started to permeate everything, the walls like ice to the touch.

'About the storm,' he said to Lydia. 'You think you can reach your friends if we get in there?'

Struggling down, her every step made her wince. 'I hope so,' she replied.

As they got to the bottom, Max found the gap in the floor and jumped down to the corridor below. Ava jumped down beside him, and together they helped Lydia down.

Max dashed to the outer door. The wedge was still there. He stopped by the door, and turned. The corridor was full.

'You've spent more time with the Prime Minister than I have,' he said to the group. 'Correct me if I'm wrong, but I don't think he'll welcome us with open arms.'

'You know him well enough,' a woman said, staring at her feet.

'Right,' Max continued. 'Well, it's not like we have a lot of choice. Another storm is coming, and either we make it into the bunker, or we die. All or nothing. Anyone got a problem with that?'

The woman who had answered gave him a curt nod.

Max pulled open the door and led them into the corridor beyond. The florescent lights above them stung his eyes. He moved toward the second door, pistol in hand.

'What's the combination?'

'Three, four, nine, A for alpha, F for foxtrot, six,' a man said, in a quiet voice.

Max keyed it in.

'Let's hope they've not changed the locks on us,' he said.

The little light above the keypad stayed red for a moment. It changed to green. A hiss of air escaped the bunker.

'Right,' Max said, pulling open the door. 'Here we go.'

A blast of stale air hit him in the face. Stepping through, he found himself back in the same corridor, faced again by two flanks of armed guards, their weapons raised and pointed in his direction.

There are a lot fewer of them this time.

The faces on the men and women facing them were stony, but he sensed a skittishness which wasn't there last time. As the space around him filled with their former friends and colleagues, this unease seemed to grow.

'You going to kill your friends?' Max asked.

They stood, unmoved. Lydia stepped forward.

'There's another storm coming,' she called out. 'A bigger one. The people up there, on the surface, they've got no hope unless we can get them in here. Into this bunker.'

'How many of you knew there were survivors up there?' Max asked. 'I bet they kept that from you, didn't they? If you'd have known, you'd have wanted to leave, go looking for your families. Help people. For whatever reason, your Prime Minister didn't want that. But you can still help.'

'Nice speech,' a voice called out, ensconced behind the wall of armed guards. Max peered over the line of guards, and saw the sneering ruddy face of the Prime Minister. 'You should have gone into politics.'

'I don't have the requisite taste for bullshit,' Max replied.

'Pity. You know we can't let you in, don't you?'

'Why not?' Ava asked. 'It may have been a long time since my civics lessons in school but I remember learning that you serve the people, not the other way round. Well, here we are. Your people. Without your help, the country ends right here.'

'No,' the Prime Minister replied. 'We will prevail, but not with a rabble of psychotic looters and hooligans.'

'That's how you see us?' Max said. He snorted a derisory laugh. 'How does everyone here feel about that? I'd like to see how our esteemed leader would have dealt with life up there, above ground, these last few months. You try facing six months of the apocalypse, and see how well you keep your stiff upper lip.'

'We managed well enough.'

'With a stocked larder, comfortable beds, and a shitload of armed guards,' Lydia said. 'People have been dying, Prime Minister. Every day. We've had to deal with death, hunger, bandits, fake governments. Every. Day. Your people, Prime Minister; every single one of whom will die, unless you let them down here.'

'Then they'll die.'

The guns surrounding them, already wavering, started to falter, their barrels pointing to the floor. Glances started to flit between the soldiers. Max thought, he *hoped,* that the Prime Minister had misread his audience.

'How long have you known, Prime Minister,' Lydia asked, 'that the storm wasn't what you thought it was? That people were alive up there? Why didn't you want the others to know?'

The Prime Minister had no reply. Max let the question sit with the crowd a moment.

'Kill us,' Max said. 'You want our blood on your hands? Don't send us back out there. Shoot us. Have at it. Make murderers of these men and women.'

Silence fell between them, until the Prime Minister gave a weary sigh.

'Very well,' he said. 'Guards. Fire at will.'

A gasp rose from behind Max. Across from him a few guns rose, but no shots came.

'You don't want to do this,' Max said to the soldiers. 'You don't have to do this.'

'These are traitors, bandits,' the Prime Minister said, his voice booming in the corridor, his face reddening further. 'If we let every vagabond in the country down here we'll all die, you mark my words. Take the shot.'

'Prime Minister,' one of the soldiers said. It was General Coles. Max hadn't noticed him beside the Prime Minister. He dropped his rifle on the floor, and turned to his leader. 'Sir, this is madness.'

'Fine,' The Prime Minister said, and picked up the rifle awkwardly, looking down at it as though he'd found some alien artefact. He soon got the hang of it, however, and strode forward. He pointed the gun at Max.

'No!' Ava shouted.

The silver haired soldier grabbed the barrel, and forced it up. The Prime Minister pulled the trigger, and rubble rained down on Max from above.

Coles wrenched the gun from the politician's grip, following up with a swift, efficient punch to his leader's nose. The Prime Minister fell back, blood smeared across his stiff upper lip.

'You bastard, Coles, I'll have you fucking court-martialled for this, you arrogant pissant.'

'Oh yeah?' Coles replied, in a roar that rebounded off the walls, cowing the Prime Minister. 'With what authority? Because it looks to me like your impressive mandate went up in smoke six months ago.'

'I am your fucking Head of State!' the Prime Minister shouted back, his voice more of a cowed whine than the soldier's bark.

'Actually,' Ava said. 'I think you'll find the Head of State died six months back. Unless... she's not down here, is she?'

The Prime Minister leapt forward at the soldier. Coles was too quick for him, raising the rifle's butt and catching him in the chest. The Prime Minister fell back, slamming against the wall.

Coles swung the gun round to face the Prime Minister. The Prime Minister sneered, and readied himself to leap at Coles once more.

Coles fired. The bullet caught the Prime Minister straight in the heart. He stopped, his mouth opening into a silent 'o'.

He fell to the ground, dead.

The only sound in the corridor was the echo of the shot, bouncing off the walls. Everyone stared at Coles, whose face wore a grim expression.

'Anyone have a problem with what I did, feel free to take me to the brig,' he said.

Nobody stepped forward.

'You did the right thing,' Lydia said, stepping forward, limping as she leant on Nana's cane.

'No,' Coles said, shaking his head. 'No. I've committed treason. If you don't mind, Ma'am, can we get to doing whatever it is you need to be doing to bring your people here?'

'Of course,' Lydia said.

'I need to get back out the front,' Max said. 'I still have people out there.'

Coles nodded again.

'Take this,' Lydia said, offering the cane back to Ava. 'Nana is going to need it.'

Ava took it, and she and Max turned away from Lydia and started to run down the warren of tunnels, until they got to the main control room, where several people who had no idea their leader was dead looked up, startled. Max ignored them and ran though the room, back into the corridors on the far side. He opened the heavy door and kept running until he came to Mouse's body. They both stopped a moment. It seemed cruel to leave him here.

'It's cold out there,' Ava said. 'I hope Nana's okay.'

'Me too.'

He ran back and propped the door open. He was a lot happier knowing Lydia was in there to let him back in, and that the scumbag he'd once been stupid enough to vote for wasn't. Still, he wasn't taking any chances.

Back in the rubble-strewn outer corridor, lights danced, and Max's heart sank. He ran, climbing the broken ramp to the surface and back into the street.

Jess, Nana, and Darren were still there, along with a handful of others. They stared upwards, where the first veins of light played across heavy clouds.

CHAPTER THIRTY-TWO

PEDESTAL

The wind caught the burning embers of the fires behind them, scuttling them along the expanse between Tom and the convoy. Smoke obscured their vision for a moment, but when it cleared, the guns were still aimed in their direction. They were within calling distance, but Tom didn't want to do anything to spook the people behind those weapons.

He raised his own gun in the air, to signify he wasn't a threat. He didn't drop it, in case they decided he was. Behind him the others did the same. They'd fallen into a wedge shape, with Mira, Tana, Chen, and the woman named Luce directly behind him, the other women behind them. Two of these carried Susan, who was not in a good way. Hopefully, Burnett's people had a doctor. Chen clutched his arm, his top a deep red despite Tana once more declaring the wound to be 'a nick'.

Across from them, a short, austere-looking woman with dark hair raised a shotgun into the air, and fired. The shot rang clear across the distance between them, bringing Tom and his group to a stop.

Tom kept his hands aloft, his finger remaining firmly on the trigger.

'That's close enough,' the woman called out to them, aiming her shotgun back in their direction.

'We're looking for Burnett,' Tom shouted back.

The woman paused.

'Don't know any Burnett.'

'Funny,' Mira shouted back. 'He was the one leading your convoy. Remember, he made a broadcast?'

The woman considered this for a moment.

'You think something's happened to him?' Tana asked, quietly.

'I hope not,' Tom replied.

'Who are you?' the woman shouted back.

'Friends of the Detective,' Tana called back.

'Friends?'

'I was his partner,' Tana called back.

She laughed, the sound carrying across the distance. 'His partner? Well, I wondered about that.'

'I've got a bad feeling,' Mira said.

'His police partner,' Tana shouted back.

'Can you tell us where he is?' Tom called. 'Is he still with you?'

'Where did you last see him?' the woman asked.

'Scarborough,' Mira shouted.

She paused a moment. 'He's here.'

'Can we see him?' Tana asked, struggling to keep the frustration out of his voice.

'How do I know we can trust you?' she called back.

'How about we fought on the same fucking side?' Tana called.

'Can you tell him we're here?' Tom interjected. 'Tell him Tom, Tana, Mira, Susan, and Chen are here.'

She stared back at them, weighing up her options. Either side of her, armed men and women looked on, weapons at the ready. 'Alright, come forward,' she said. 'Slowly.'

Tom moved forward, never breaking eye contact with the woman. Her gun remained trained on them until they reached her.

She looked them over, a motley crew of mostly women, led by armed men.

'These your hostages?' she asked Tom, motioning to the women.

'Friends,' Tom replied.

'Good.'

'You want to tell us where Burnett is?'

'Sure. He got shot. He's with the doc.' She said this without much concern.

'He going to be alright?'

She shrugged. 'Let's go find out. I'll need your guns first.'

Tom handed his over, and the others did the same, though reluctantly.

'I'm Tom,' he said, holding his hand out to the woman, who looked down at it as though he'd offered her an unsolicited dick pic.

'Tyler,' she replied, giving him the most cursory of handshakes.

He couldn't blame her. He hadn't seen a mirror in a while, and hadn't been too impressed by what he'd seen in it the last time he had, despite Tana's hairdressing skills. It was a shame, though; she was a hell of a good-looking woman.

She turned, and they followed.

The convoy had taken a bit of a battering, with the coaches sporting bullet holes, a few with shattered windshields to boot. Inside the coaches, hundreds of faces peered out of the windows, watching events outside with a mixture of fear and intrigue, voyeurs to the chaos.

She led them along the convoy and into the heart of it, to a battered van. Tyler pulled open the rear door, which creaked open on rusted hinges, releasing a pungent cloud which billowed outward. Inside, three mattresses lay squashed into each other, each occupied by a patient. Their doctor scurried about over them. Burnett occupied the central mattress, his shirt thick with blood.

'Tyler,' the detective growled. 'It fucking reeks in here; get me the fuck out of here. What's fucking going on out there? Is it done? I need to get the fuck out of here. Doc!'

'Jesus Christ,' Tyler replied, wafting the smell away. 'It's done. And you've got visitors.'

Burnett sat up, with some effort. He rubbed his eyes.

'Tom?' he said, recognising them. 'Tana?'

'Detective,' Tana replied.

'Get me the fuck out of here,' Burnett growled back.

'No,' the doctor said, seemingly noticing her restless patient for the first time. 'You stay.'

'Fuck's sake, Doc, I'm fine. It's just a nick.'

'See?' Tana said, turning to Chen.

'Oh, fuck off,' Chen said. 'Good to see you, detective.'

'Chen!' Burnett said, getting up. 'Fucking hell, you're all here? Susan, good to see you.'

'You too,' Susan said, a wide smile spreading across her bruised face.

'Mira! Hello, sweetheart. Where's Jen?'

He'd been expecting it, but Tom's cheeks still flushed red with guilt and embarrassment, and his mouth dried up. He felt a sudden and unquenchable thirst come over him, one he knew the water bottles stacked against the van wouldn't satisfy.

'She didn't make it,' Mira said.

Burnett jumped down from the back of the van, wincing. 'Oh, honey,' he said, taking Mira into a hug. 'I'm so sorry.'

She gave him a smile. 'It's okay. Well, you know, not really. But I'm fine.'

'Have you been together this whole time?'

'Mostly,' Tom said. 'But not recently. Your broadcast brought us back together.'

Burnett took turns handing out hugs. He looked like he'd aged a decade since Tom had last seen him.

Haven't we all?

'Listen,' Burnett said. 'I'd love to catch up, but we need to get moving.'

'We heard,' Mira said. 'There's more storms on the way?'

'I don't know, but some intelligent-sounding scientists seemed to think so, so I figured it best to play it safe.'

'Let's hope this isn't the biggest Catfish in history,' Mira said. When everyone stared at her dumbly, she added: 'Sorry. Young person reference.'

'What am I,' Tom laughed, 'Old Man River?'

Tyler reappeared, out of breath. 'Hate to break up this touching family reunion, but we've got company.'

Burnett sighed. 'Never a dull moment.'

He limped off, wincing and holding his side. Tyler went with him, leaving the rest of them standing together by the hospital van.

Tom looked at the others.

'What do we do?' Chen asked.

'We should let the doc look at Susan,' Mira said.

'Hey,' Tana said. 'You can ask the doc here about your arm, maybe it needs amputating.'

Chen leaned into the van, and pulled away again at the smell. 'No thanks,' he said.

'I'll pass, too,' Susan said.

A shotgun blast rang out somewhere behind them. They turned in its direction. The action, wherever it was, remained hidden by the rest of the convoy. Several armed guards ran past them, carrying the guns they'd taken off Tom and the others a few minutes earlier.

'Maybe we should…' Mira said.

'Yeah,' Tom agreed.

Tom felt naked walking towards a fight without a weapon, but had to see what was going on.

Beyond the back of the convoy, stretching along the winding main road, headlights shone back at them.

'Ah, fuck,' Tom said.

'Is it a second wave?' Mira asked, going onto her tiptoes for a better look.

The convoy's guards arranged themselves into a line, looking about wildly, trying to take in the breadth of the problem. Tyler and Burnett stood, Tyler holding the shotgun aloft in warning.

The sun crept above the skyline, and Tom could make out the cars a lot clearer. These weren't the souped-up cars and trucks of bandits; these were a mish-mash of whatever was available, crammed with desperate-looking people.

They pulled up, their engines idling. Doors opened. People got out, their hands raised, their eyes surveying the line of gun barrels aimed at them.

'Is this the convoy?' a man shouted. 'Are you going to the bunker?'

'Who are you?' Burnett called back.

'We've come from Manchester,' the woman replied. 'We heard your message. We picked up others along the way. We want to join you.'

Silence fell between them.

'How do we know we can trust you?' Burnett called.

'I guess you don't, but you put out the call, remember? We're just looking to survive here.'

Burnett looked at Tyler, who shrugged, then back at Tom and the others. 'I guess we'd better get you seen to,' he said, turning back to them.

The faces relaxed, and other doors started to open. A woman climbed on the bonnet of her car, took out a hankie, and waved it at the convoy. People streamed out of their cars. At the rear of their convoy, another woman stood on her bonnet and did the same. Three more coaches rolled into view.

'Shit,' Tana said. 'I hope it's a fucking big bunker.'

Chapter Thirty-three
Wasteland

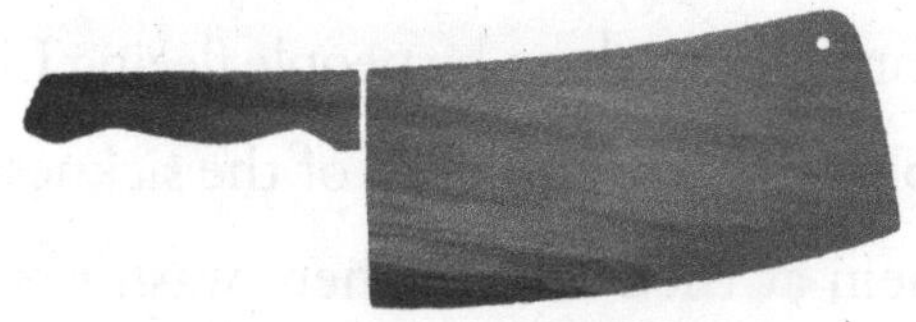

The wound in his side hurt like a bastard, but the headache pounding in his skull was of greater concern to Burnett. He needed to change his shirt; the blood on this one clung to the dressing the doc had put over the bullet wound.

Where in the hell am I going to get a fresh shirt?

He should probably work out the logistics of getting close to a thousand people into the centre of London first. Then he'd have to work out how to get them into the bunker, and hope to hell it was roomy.

He'd not yet heard from Lydia or Greg. He'd have at least expected them to check in. The only logical conclusion was that they'd not made it. Either they'd run into trouble before they got to London, or they'd found the bunker but died trying to get in. Or their radio had broken. Perhaps they'd shacked up somewhere. Any way he cut it, he doubted the bunker would be open and waiting for them when they got into the city.

He rubbed at his temples. That wasn't even the most immediate concern. The Mancunian convoy were in a bad way. They'd run out of food on the way out of the city, and their leaders, a stern black man called Charles and a sterner white woman called Sally, had begged him to share what Burnett's convoy had with them.

This, Sally had explained, was pretty much their last throw of the die, storms or no storms. Manchester had not fared well in the first storm, and a sickness had run through the survivors a few months back, brought to them by people fleeing Liverpool. They said their people were free and clear of the sickness, but Burnett had to take them at their word. There wasn't enough time to check it out.

People were everywhere. The road no longer represented a war zone; it had turned into a refugee camp. The coaches had emptied and dazed people milled about. Tyler had taken Tana, Chen, and Luce to scout out what remained of the bandit's ambush line, trying to salvage guns, ammunition or other supplies that might have survived the fires.

The thought of Mira being responsible for that devastating salvation roused a chuckle from Burnett, and people around him looked at him, horrified. He supposed it wasn't funny. He was bloody glad to have his friends back, though. It sounded like they'd gone through every bit as much of hell as he had in the last few months, but that was probably true of every single person here.

'Hey,' Tom said, appearing through the crowd like a shaven-headed spectre of death. Mira and Susan were with him, making Tom look even worse by comparison. 'So, what's the plan?'

'Fuck knows,' Burnett said. 'Any thoughts?'

'Oooh, no,' Tom chuckled. 'My days of making big decisions are long behind me. Besides, I could barely run a camp with a handful of people, let alone however many you've got here.'

'I don't want to think about it.'

'People seem pretty frightened,' Mira said, looking about.

She was right. People seemed especially scared of him, he noticed.

Perks of leadership.

'If those scientists are right, they ought to be,' Burnett said.

'Did they give any idea when it might hit?'

'No. Soon though. I think we're running out of runway.'

They instinctively looked to the skies to check, but there was barely even a cloud up there.

'We'll let you get on,' Susan said.

'Cheers.'

His people unloaded food supplies to feed the assembled Mancunian ranks, as well as their own people. He would let them eat, but they needed to get back on the road.

Tyler and Tana returned, carrying two large rucksacks laden down with supplies.

'Good hunting?' Burnett asked.

'Lots of presents,' Tana said.

'We need to get moving,' Tyler said.

Burnett nodded. 'Get things prepped. Find Charles and Sally.'

She frowned and headed off.

'She's a character,' Tana said, staring after her.

'You're in love, I assume?'

Tana laughed. 'A smidge. What about you, you found love in the time of apocalypse?'

Burnett snorted. 'Not exactly top of my priorities, and besides, if it was hard trying to size up if a guy's gay before the storms, it's nigh on impossible now.'

'Fair point. So what's the plan?'

'I wish people would stop asking me that.'

'You should get used to it.'

'Head to London, take it from there.'

'You think this bunker's even there?'

'If it isn't, I don't know what we'll do. Head into the underground tunnels, I suppose, and cross our fingers.'

'We could conjure up some of the famous Blitz spirit.'

Charles and Sally appeared.

'So what's the plan?' Charles asked.

Tana gave Burnett a smile and left him to it.

Word got round that it was time to go. Everyone got back on the buses, and Burnett commandeered one of the Land Rovers for himself and Tyler. Tom and Tana wanted to ride with him, much to the chagrin of the men they stole it from in the first place. Burnett relegated them to the coaches.

Mira's annihilation of the tanker meant there was a hole for them to squeeze through, so Tyler guided them, and they were on their way.

As soon as they passed into London the scenery changed. Fires had devastated most of what was around them. Heavy clouds rolled in above them, and the temperature dropped as everything drained to dull grey.

'Doesn't bode well,' Tana said, pointing to the skies.

They drove through streets filled with trash, bodies, and destroyed buildings. The roads were thick with parked cars and broken buses, each of the latter turned into charred metal mausoleums. Dead littered the pavements — wherever there had once been a pub or restaurant the corpses were denser.

This scene was familiar enough, but didn't last long. As they reached the heart of the city, the scenes became more and more desolate. The fires which devastated the city had burned so fiercely they'd left little standing.

They passed two whole streets taken out by downed aeroplanes, and the road itself changed to a rippled and warped mess. Around them the buildings weren't just burned out, they looked like they'd been smote by some invisible hand. Masonry and debris lay everywhere, and the convoy had to stop every few minutes to allow people to clear the way.

London's famous skyline was another casualty. Where once glittering skyscrapers had ridden high in the sky there stood jagged spikes of metal, twisted and ugly.

'Do you think a nuclear bomb went off, somehow?' Tom asked from the back seat.

'No,' Burnett said. 'But something terrible happened here.'

'I can't imagine how anyone could have survived this,' Tana said.

They hadn't seen a soul so far. Whether down to a genuine absence of people or because they hid whenever a giant convoy came into view was unclear. Nothing they saw was even halfway habitable. It could be nobody had survived.

'Burnett,' Tyler said. Unlike the rest of them, her focus was on the road ahead and nothing else.

In front of them, blocking the road completely, was the toppled remains of a building. The way was completely blocked.

'Shit,' Burnett said, as Tyler pulled up in front of it.

He got out and stepped into the street, looking at the damage. A crashed plane had clipped what had once been a tall apartment building. The plane had ended up a few streets over, or at least the warped tail of the plane had, but the building looked like a giant Jenga failure knocked into the street.

'What do we do?' Tana asked.

'There's too much to clear,' Burnett said. 'But I can't see we can back up, either.'

'Hey, boss,' Tyler said. 'You know you've got hundreds of people in coaches behind you who haven't been able to feel useful in days, right? Let's put 'em to work.'

By the time they could see a path through the rubble, several hundred people milled about, either helping clear the path or getting in the way of those who were. Tyler sat, stony-faced, behind the wheel of the Land Rover, waiting to be able to move forward again. Burnett shared her eagerness; the clouds gathering above them had an increasingly portentous look about them.

'Keep it going,' Tana shouted to the men and women in the thick of the rubble, handing back pieces of brickwork and steel, the remains of chairs and cabinets, televisions and bones.

'We should be clear soon,' Tom said, limping back to the Land Rover.

'Good,' Burnett replied. 'How's your leg these days?'

'Hurts like a motherfucker,' Tom said. 'I'm getting used to it. I've had tougher things to get past in the last few months.'

'That fuck, Ewen, has a lot to answer for, doesn't he?'

'He sure does.'

Tom hobbled off, and Burnett thought again about the first storm. He'd been inside a police cell when it had hit. He had wondered off and on what it must have looked like. Now he found he didn't want to find out.

When the first flickers of blue light danced in the clouds all he could do was stare. Panic started to ripple through the crowd.

'Let's keep it going,' Tana shouted. 'You want to avoid the storm, we'd better get this cleared.'

Everyone not involved in clearing the debris started to run back to their buses, cars and coaches, running with their eyes on the sky.

We're too late.

'Burnett,' a voice said, small and distant.

'What?' he asked Tyler.

'I didn't say anything.'

He pulled out the radio and stared at it.

'Burnett?'

He pressed the button. 'Lydia?'

'Detective,' Lydia replied, her voice crackling, distant. 'Thank God.'

'Lydia!' Burnett shouted into the speaker. 'You're alive!'

'Just about. Where are you?'

'Making our way to the bunker. We think.'

Crackle buzzed.

'...bunk...read...'

Silence.

'...dead...'

The line spluttered, and the radio died.

'No!' Burnett shouted.

He hit the button, smacked the radio against the door rest, and gave it a shake, to no avail.

'What does it mean?' Tyler asked.

'It means let's get a fucking move on.'

Tyler fired the engine. One of the Mancunians moved the last piece of masonry out of the way. People ran back to their vehicles. Tom and Tana climbed back in, and they pulled away, each of them watching lightning play through the clouds rather than the road ahead.

Chapter Thirty-four

Teardrop

'How's this supposed to work?' Coles asked, taking Lydia's hand to support her.

'I get to a radio, let my people know I've made it inside,' Lydia replied.

She tried to ignore the body of the dead Prime Minister as she stepped over it, blood still oozing from the bullet hole, dead eyes staring forward.

'No,' Coles said. 'I mean, how are we going to fit everyone down here? You said there's a few hundred people?'

'How many can you fit down here?'

'We've room for a hundred and fifty bodies, rations for less, but I dare say we could fit a couple of hundred down here for a day or so. It'd be tight. How many hundred is a few?'

'Hard to say. Burnett put out a call to try to save as many people as he could, so who knows?'

'So there could be many more?' Coles said, with a sigh. He stopped. 'What if we can't fit them in? Do we turn people away?

What if some of the people who hear the message have less noble intentions than your friend?'

'What's the alternative?'

Coles considered this. 'Fair point,' he said, stroking his moustache.

'It's not going to be easy. Who knows, maybe we're too late. But we have to try. We could well be talking about the survival of the species.'

They walked on down the corridor. Around them people made preparations — lifting boxes out the way, stacking things high. In the bunk rooms, people packed their personal belongings and stashed them out of harm's way.

'General Coles,' a voice called out.

They turned around. The Prime Minister's wife stood, two children trying to hide behind her white skirt.

Lydia gasped. She hadn't seen children in so long, and yet here were mirror images of her own. Not twenty metres away, down a turn in the corridor, their father's body lay. In an instant, everything he'd done made sense. He didn't care about the rest of humanity, or the other people in this bunker, even. It wasn't about his power, or his position. Everything the Prime Minister had done had been about one thing — keeping his family safe.

Humanity be damned.

'Ma'am,' Coles said. 'A word in private, if I may?'

He motioned to Lydia, a barely perceptible nod.

'Kids,' she said, crouching to their level as best she could, ribs protesting vehemently. 'Hi. I'm Lydia. Do you want to come with me while the General and your mum have a chat?'

The Prime Minister's wife gave them a look of dawning horror. 'It's okay, children. I'll be with you in a second.'

Lydia flashed what she hoped was a smile conveying both embarrassment and condolence. The children detached themselves from their mother and Lydia led them into a room down the corridor. She closed the door and motioned for them to sit. She gave them both a smile.

'The soldier needs to speak to your mummy,' she said.

'General Coles,' the little girl said, precociously. 'Where is Daddy?'

'So,' Lydia said, ignoring the question. 'How do you two like it down here?'

'It's stupid, and boring,' the little boy said.

Lydia welled up. They were so much like Cassie and Nico her chest hurt.

'Well,' she said. 'Hopefully, soon, we'll be able to go back to the surface and you can both play again.'

The little boy's face lit up at this, but the girl was unmoved.

'I asked you a question.'

'What's your name?' Lydia asked.

'I'm Sylvia, and this is Harry. Where is my father?'

A scream filled the air, a howl of anguish from the corridor outside.

'Mummy?' Harry asked, scared.

'Listen,' Lydia said. 'No matter what, you remember this. Your dad did everything to keep the two of you safe, you hear me?'

Both children burst into tears, and the door flew open.

'Come, children,' the Prime Minister's wife barked, and the two children ran to her. She flashed Lydia a look that could melt steel beams, and left the room.

Lydia wiped her own tears away and tried to compose herself.

'You okay?' Coles asked, appearing at the doorway.

'Oh, terrific, thanks,' she said, wiping her eyes.

'You got kids?' he asked.

'Had.'

'Me too,' Coles said. 'It's been driving me mad seeing the pair of them running around here for the last six months, not being able to check.'

'Why didn't you leave?'

'Not that simple.'

'You knew, though? That it was habitable above ground? Or did the Prime Minister keep that one to himself so you'd stay down here?'

'I knew.' He sighed. 'It's a complex thing, duty.'

She nodded. She couldn't begin to fathom it, but she wasn't going to argue. 'They smokers, your family?'

'No,' he replied.

'Then I'm sorry,' she said. 'Come on, let's go.'

'What do you mean?' he asked, as they moved along the corridor.

'You lot don't know anything down here, do you? Look, I'm sorry. I will clue you into everything the minute we get through this, but I need to phone a friend.'

'Fair enough.'

The control room was a wide circular space surrounded by banks of computers, each of which seemed to show variations of nothing. People stared at them, passed each other papers, and generally tried to make themselves look busy. As a former office drone, Lydia knew full well the practice, having had years to perfect the technique herself.

Coles seemed oblivious to this as he strode to the desk in the centre of the room. 'Perkins!' he barked, making a young man with immaculate hair jump in his chair.

'Yes, sir?'

'You can pull up civilian CB channels, correct?'

'Uhh, I believe so.'

'You believe so, or you know so?'

'The latter.'

'Good. This young lady needs your assistance.'

He ushered Lydia forward as she tried to ignore the small flash of excitement at such an authoritative older man calling her 'young lady'.

'What channel do you need?' the man at the desk asked.

Her mind went blank. She remembered Greg telling her, but couldn't for the life of her remember what he'd said. When she tried to focus on the memory it got jumbled with images of his sweaty body against her own and his lifeless one lying in a road.

'I...uh...seventeen!' she cried out.

'Seventeen what?'

'I don't know,' Lydia said. 'Channel seventeen.'

The soldier frowned, and turned back to his console, turning knobs.

'Civilian channel *seventeen* for you, sir,' he said, turning back to Coles.

'After you,' Coles said, motioning her to step forward.

She took the handset from the officer, and pressed the button. 'Burnett?'

Static.

'Detective Burnett?'

The room fell silent. Everyone turned to stare at her, and she felt her neck flush red. She was about to try one final time, when the speaker crackled to life.

'Lydia?'

'Detective,' she said. 'Thank God.'

'Lydia!' Burnett screamed. 'You're alive!'

'Just about,' she replied, a surge of relief washing over her. 'Where are you?'

'We're ma... way to the b... Think.'

The line cut in and out.

'Burnett?' She looked at Coles. 'I'm in the bunker. You are okay to proceed. Do you read me?' She shook the handset, and pressed the button again. 'The line is going dead. Burnett?'

There was a fizz, a crackle, and the static stopped.

'We've lost signal, General,' the soldier said.

'Figured that out on your own, did you, Sergeant?' Coles muttered. He turned to Lydia. 'You think you got through to him?'

'I don't know,' she said, staring at the piece of plastic in her hand.

All that effort. Everything I did to get here. For what?

Coles put his hand on her shoulder. 'He's alive. And he knows you are. I'm sure he'll make it.'

She nodded.

'Right!' Coles shouted, turning to the rest of the room. 'We are going to be having guests soon. There are going to be more of them than we can fit in here. We're going to find somewhere for them to go, am I understood?'

Faces stared at him.

'So we're clear,' he growled. 'I am in charge of this operation.'

'Sir,' a woman called, running into the control room. 'The Prime Minister's family. They're gone.'

Across the room, Max ran into the other entrance, eyes wide, Ava in tow. His breath was ragged. Behind him, Jess trailed, followed by Darren, who cradled Nana in his arms, the old woman looking white as a sheet. Lastly, Greggles padded after them, panting.

'The storm,' Max said. 'The storm is back.'

The lights went out, and the room plunged into panic.

CHAPTER THIRTY-FIVE
DOWN BY THE WATER

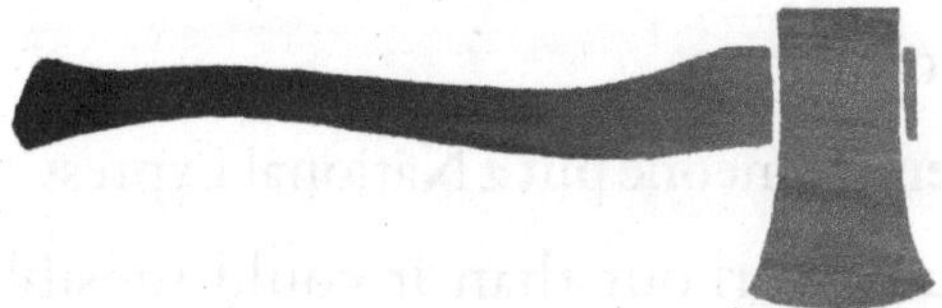

'Anyone got a cig?' Chen asked from back of the bus.

'I haven't had a fag in about a month,' Luce said, somewhat wistfully, from the driver's seat.

'I'm serious,' Chen said. 'We survived because we were smokers, right? Given the sky looks like it's about to go full-on *Exorcist* again, I'd like to be juiced up on nicotine, in case.'

Mira turned round from the front passenger seat, and frowned at him.

'What?' he said, smiling. 'Oh, alright, I want a fag. It's stressful, this.'

'You think this is stressful?' Luce said. 'Yeah, mate. You sit there in your comfortable back seat while I try and squeeze a minibus through gaps smaller than a gnat's arsehole. It must be dead stressful for you.'

'Yeah,' Mira said. 'Poor baby.'

'You're not too old for a smacked bum, missy,' he said, smirking.

'Just you try it,' Mira said. 'You might be on the wrong bus though.'

Chen was the only man on the minibus Luce was busy testing the suspension of with every sharp turn or uneven street. Outside their windows London was completely devastated, but they were in too much of a rush to take notice. Too focused on the intensifying storm above.

Ahead of them, someone put a National Express coach through a more rigorous workout than it could sensibly withstand. Burnett's Land Rover led the charge, with Tyler at the helm, their convoy cutting a dangerous swathe through the abandoned city.

In the minibus with them were the rest of the women who had escaped the bandits. They apparently looked like enough of a collective bunch of badasses that the Mancunians had given them the van. Mira felt pretty good about that. She'd always wanted to be a badass.

She kept that thought front and foremost in her head. The minute she started to think about men burning and lakes of fire, she started to shut down. She couldn't afford to do that. That was one of the reasons she was glad Chen had asked to join them. She'd hoped to stay with Tom and Tana, too, but could understand Tana wanting to be with Burnett again. As for Tom, either he had the taste for power again or he wanted to be somewhere nobody stared at his scars.

Behind Mira, Susan slouched in her seat, staring out the window. Mira turned, smacking her head on the roof as Luce went over some masonry without slowing down.

'Ow!' Mira shouted, before she turned to Susan. 'You okay?'

Susan stared at her for a second with a lost look. 'Fine,' she said and went back to staring out of the window.

'We're almost there,' Luce shouted.

They went past a battered sign. The City of Westminster was up ahead. Mira craned and could see the river glinting in the reflection of the storm. A thick vein of red light worked through the clouds, changing to a deep blue as it capillaried across the sky.

She thought back to the night of the first storm, but pushed the image back down. Another memory that would serve no purpose.

Up ahead, Tyler pulled up next to a ruin; huge slabs of building scattered like an amphitheatre flicked to death by an angry deity. To their right stood what little remained of the Houses of Parliament. Mira pressed her nose to the window, breath fogging her view.

'Holy shit,' she muttered.

'Guess we know what happened to the government,' Chen said, moving forward, as Luce pulled up behind the coach.

'We're here,' she announced.

Chen pulled open the door and jumped out, followed by the other women. Mira opened the door and stepped out. A coach pulled up beside her, almost knocking her over. She waited for it to come to a halt and moved round the minibus to the other side. Susan was still inside the minibus, head leaning against the glass. Mira knocked on it, but Susan didn't even flinch.

'Hey!' Mira said, tapping again.

Susan stirred, her eyes meeting Mira's.

'Come on,' Mira called.

Susan gave a faint smile and shook her head.

Mira skirted back round, moving against the current of people spilling from every vehicle. She climbed back into the bus.

'Hey,' Mira said. 'Come on. We've got to go.'

'I'm staying here.'

'Don't be daft,' Mira said. 'Come on. We've got to go.'

'No,' Susan said, turning her face back to the window.

'Hey, I'm not fucking around here. You're coming with me.'

'I'm tired,' Susan said. 'I'm tired of running, and I'm tired of things not getting better. Six months, Mira, and we keep stumbling forward, from one shit pit to another. That caravan.... You know what my first thought was, when I heard the storms might be back? Thank *God*. I don't want you to think I regret getting you out of there. I don't. But... I can't do this anymore.'

Mira squeezed her hand. 'I know.' She opened her mouth to say something more, but couldn't.

'Every time I see bodies in the street, from the first storm,' Susan said, staring out the window again, 'all I can think is... they were the lucky ones, not us.' She turned to Mira and smiled. 'You go. I'll be fine.'

Mira hesitated for a second, and started to leave, but remembered Sam, and Jen, and everyone else she'd lost along the way. She clasped onto Susan's wrist and pulled. 'No. I'm not losing you. Not today. You can't do that to me. You're coming with me.'

Susan pulled her hands away and shot Mira a dark look. She was about to protest in more vehement terms, when a scream rang out somewhere outside. A high, howling noise joined it.

'What the fuck?' Susan asked, turning round in her seat.

'I don't know,' Mira said. 'Let's not stick around to find out, eh?'

Susan nodded, and they climbed out of the minibus, into the street, where the clouds seemed even lower, like the storm weighed down on them, squeezing the air. People ran about, sprinting in every direction, without purpose.

'Where's Burnett?' Mira asked, looking around.

Someone else screamed. Behind Mira, a low growl sounded, freezing her to the spot. She turned. In front of her, its body so thin you could count the ribs, teeth bared, eyes cold, stood the meanest-looking dog she'd ever seen.

'Stay still,' Susan said, in a low voice.

'Uh huh.'

Another growl. To her left, two more dogs approached, their hackles raised and teeth bared.

'You know the romantic notion you had of letting the storm take care of you?' she asked.

'Yeah?'

'How does it compare to wild dogs ripping you to pieces?'

'It was definitely a better plan.'

A sharp pain burst in Mira's head, and she winced. Beside her, Susan did the same, along with everyone else running about. It must have had a similar effect on the dogs because as one, they howled. These were not the howls of ferocious hunters, these were howls of pain. Blinking, Mira forced her eyes open. The dog in front of them tried to bury its head in its paws, scrabbling frantically to get at whatever pain had appeared in its head.

She grabbed Susan's hand. 'Run,' she whispered.

They ran, every step sending spikes of pain to the front of her brain. Spots of light flashed at the edge of Mira's vision. She couldn't be sure if they were the storm, or some trick of her overwhelmed mind.

She stumbled, falling hard onto her hands, scuffing them on the hard concrete. She held them up to examine the bright pinpricks of red blossoming on her palms. Someone else's hand wove into hers, and pulled her up. She looked up and saw Tom, his scarred face smiling down at her.

'We should get out of here,' he said.

'Susan,' Mira said, weakly.

'Right here,' her friend said, hand lacing into Mira's free one, helping Tom to pull her to her feet.

'We stick together, yeah?' Tom asked.

Mira nodded, the action sending a wave of nausea breaking over her.

Around them dogs — dozens of them — chased their tails, howling, clawing at their heads. One or two tried to growl menacingly, but their hearts were no longer in it.

'Poor things,' Mira said, barely able to form the words.

'Poor things?' Tom replied, showing none of the effects of the storm. 'A minute ago, they were going to eat you.'

'Can't blame a hungry animal for trying to eat,' she said.

A woman ran past them, sobbing, blood streaming from her mouth and nose. Instinctively Mira's hand went to her own face. It came away flecked with red.

'Tom?' she said.

'Nope,' Tom replied. 'I'm getting you out of here, Missy, no matter what you or the storm have to say about it.'

'Okay,' Mira said, before the world went dark, and she was falling.

Chapter Thirty-six
Crown of Storms

'Are we going to die?' Nana asked, breaking Max's gaze away from the sky.

'I...' he started to say, but he didn't have an answer, so he went back to staring at the clouds.

It was mesmerising, as it had been on that first night. The sky turned into a canvas, on which endless colourful flourishes danced in and out of each other before fading, leaving little imprints on Max's retinas.

'We need to go,' Ava said beside him.

Lydia's dog barked at the cloud, tail tucked between his legs. He pressed into Darren. Darren reached down and ruffled his head, his eyes never leaving the sky. The big man, usually so happy, wore a concerned frown. It occurred to Max that Darren was the only one of them who hadn't shared his story of the night of the first storm. He'd simply said 'storm' and that was that.

Ava's hand slipped into Max's. He looked at her, her beautiful hazel eyes staring back at him, and tried to think how long it had been since he'd woken next to her. Only a few days, but it felt like a lifetime ago. Theirs was always a relationship of convenience, but under the light of the storm, he realised how much she meant to him.

Aren't you an idiot?

'Come on,' he said. 'Jess, you look after the dog. Darren, can you carry Nana?'

'Nana,' Darren repeated, nodding, his broad smile returning.

Gingerly, they made their way down the slope together, descending to the bunker. Max kept Nana and Darren in front of him, with Ava in front of them in case the big man should stumble. Nana kept looking back, terrified, as though the storm could reach out and smite them. The dog started to bark more, emboldened by their move away from the storm.

'How the hell are they going to get hundreds of people down here?' Jess asked. 'I mean, that's how many Lydia said were coming, right?'

'If they don't get here soon,' Ava said, 'I don't think it'll be an issue.'

The electric lights of the bunker urged them forward, until they came to Mouse's body.

Jess screamed.

In his haste, Max had forgotten they'd be walking right past the body of their friend.

'Mouse?' Darren asked, and started to stoop, Nana still in his arms, to try and rouse his friend.

'He's gone, Darren,' Ava said, placing her hand on his shoulder. 'Remember?'

Darren looked up at her with eyes brimming with tears. 'Mouse gone?'

'Sorry, buddy,' Max said. 'But we've got to go.'

Darren nodded solemnly.

They ran the rest of the distance, down the long winding corridor, lit by overhead lights flickering more than they had before, and through the steel door, still propped open. They ran into the control room, where Lydia and Coles stood, staring at another soldier.

'The storm,' he called out, needing to get their attention. It worked. Every face turned to him. 'The storm is back.'

Mouths dropped open. Coles looked like he was about to launch into questioning when the lights went out.

An audible fizz overloaded every light at once. A hum echoed as the equipment shut down. A scream rang out. The darkness was total.

The dog's barking intensified.

'Max?' Darren said softly.

'I'm right here, buddy.'

'Put Nana down?'

'Sure, but do me a favour and hold her hand?'

'I'll look after you, Darren,' Nana said.

'Everyone stick together,' Max said.

Ava's hand slipped into his own again, and Jess grasped the other.

People started to panic. There were sobs and cries, and the sound of shuffling feet. A pane of glass shattered somewhere, causing a few people to shriek. Probably whatever idiot had panicked so much they'd run into plate glass in the first place.

They edged their way along the back wall. Unlike everyone else here, Max and his friends were used to darkness. When the candles had burned down to nothing in the house they'd felt their way rather than open the blinds and be seen by their enemies. Now they moved slowly, methodically, their backs against the smooth concrete.

'Everyone stay still, for fuck's sake,' Coles' voice boomed across the room, trying to regain a control he was evidently not used to losing.

'In here,' Ava said, leading the way. 'There's a room.'

They moved through the door and into the room beyond.

'Where are my backup generators?' Coles barked, further away.

Once they were in, Max closed the door as quietly as he could.

'Everyone here?' he asked.

'I think so,' Ava said. 'Darren?'

'Darren here.'

'Jess?'

'Just about.'

'Nana?'

'Yes, dear.'

'Good,' Max said. 'Whatever else happens, we made it.'

'Not all of us,' Jess said, solemnly.

'Shouldn't we be out there, helping?' Jess asked.

'Helping who?' Max replied. 'The people who sat down here in luxury for six months while we starved? Or the strangers who may well have died on their way here?'

'I mean...' Jess said.

'No,' Max said, cutting her off. 'I set out to keep my family safe, and here we are. What's left of us. As close to safety as we're likely to get. If you think I'm about to jeopardise that for strangers...'

'Don't cut her off,' Ava said. 'Like you said, we're here, we're safe.'

'Who knows what happens if we go out there,' Max said. 'What if Lydia's people aren't the shining beacons of humanity she's made them out to be? What if the government want to force us out again?'

A whir sounded somewhere, and the lights flickered on. Max's family stared at him with a look of horror or disappointment. Except Darren, who sat on the floor ignoring them, playing with the dog.

'Oh, I'm the bad guy?' Max said

'You don't sound much like a good guy,' Ava said. 'You want to tell me how your attitude is different to that of our ex-Prime Minister?'

'Besides,' Nana said. 'What are we going to do, barricade ourselves in this room forever?'

'Darren need toilet,' Darren said.

'Okay,' Max said. 'Fine. We'll go be good people. You happy? But I can't lose anyone else.'

Ava squeezed his hand. Jess came over and kissed him on the cheek, and he felt it flush.

A wide window fronted their room, so they could see outside into the control room, where hell seemed to have broken loose. Everyone ran, panicking, or trying to stop everyone else from losing their shit. Max had no desire to get out there, but the others were right.

'Oaky,' he said. 'Nana, you stay here with Darren. Big man, you think you can clear as much space as you can in here?'

Darren looked at him, puzzled.

'We're going to need to fit a hell of a lot of people in here.'

Darren nodded, and immediately set about moving things.

'Jess, Ava, let's go help.'

They opened the door and the volume trebled, an indecipherable babble of panic and anger.

'Lydia,' Max called out across the room. 'What the hell's going on?'

'The children, they're gone!' Lydia cried out in return, picking her way across the mass of people.

'Shit,' Ava said.

'Wait,' Jess said. 'There are kids here?'

'The Prime Minister's,' Ava said.

'Wait, the Prime Minister's here?'

'Not any more,' Max said.

'Their mother took them. We need to find them,' Lydia said, struggling for breath and holding her ribs.'

'You need to lie down,' Max said.

'Fuck that,' Lydia said. 'Ava, will you help me?'

'Sure. Jess?'

'Count me in, but could someone please tell me what the hell is going on?'

Lydia turned to Max and grasped him by the shoulders. 'Help my people.'

Max nodded.

'You promise?'

'I'll do whatever I can, I promise.'

The three women turned and headed off toward the back entrance.

Great, now what do I do?

He walked into the centre of the control room. People either ran about like lunatics or stood uselessly, staring at the chaos. It took him a moment to notice a third group, the ones trying to melt into the walls, hiding under desks. The end of the world was here, and they wanted nothing to do with it.

He thought back to the first night, and his position, watching it from several storeys up. Was this what it was like on the ground? Or was this storm too loaded with the knowledge of what was to come? Perhaps back then everyone had been like him, staring at the marvel in the sky until it was too late.

Closing his eyes, the sight of a jumbo jet heading straight for him flooded his vision. He snapped his eyes open.

You can do this.

'Listen up!' he shouted, and everyone froze, falling silent. They turned to him. He climbed up on a desk.

'None of you were above ground for the last storm, right?' he asked. A few heads bobbed in agreement. 'Good for you,' he continued. 'It wasn't much fun. You survived, because you were down here. Now there's another storm and guess what? You're still down here. So pull yourselves together, for fuck's sake, because any minute there's going to be hundreds of people wanting to get in here and share in the safety you enjoyed before. These people didn't get the easy ride last time, so how about you stop running about like headless fucking chickens, and make sure we do as much as we can to be ready for them, yeah?'

They stared at him for a second, and started to go about their business. The not-at-all-well-hidden men and women climbed out from their hiding places, looking sheepish, dusting themselves off.

General Coles walked over to him, as Max jumped down from the table.

'Well said,' the General said, and offered his hand.

Max took it. 'Thanks. I have a question for you, General.'

'I'll answer it if I can.'

'Why didn't you ever look out? Six months down here, it never occurred to you to check the surface?'

Coles sighed. 'Of course it did. I had a family up there too. In the aftermath of the storm, with the fires, it broke most of our sensors. The fires were too hot. The radioactivity monitors failed. Everything pointed to a nuclear detonation. After that, the Prime Minister wouldn't risk opening the seals. His family, I suppose. We heard from military channels across the world, but when the Prime Minister heard a broadcast from this country... well. He convinced me to keep it quiet. Ordered comms to only scan military channels. I...' He sighed. 'When you appeared at the door, it was a shock to many people down here.'

'You were the one who let us in?'

Coles nodded.

'Thank you,' Max said. 'But... we could have done with some leadership up there.'

'I know. If we can help these people, save who we can, who knows, maybe I can work that debt off.'

A soldier ran into the control room.

'General,' he said. 'They're here.'

'Good,' Coles replied. 'Let's get moving.'

'No, General,' the soldier said, his eyes wide. 'You don't understand. There must be thousands of them.'

Max looked at Coles, who shrugged. 'Well,' he said, smoothing his moustache. 'We'd better clear some room.'

Chapter Thirty-seven

With Every Light

Despite the pain in her leg, Lydia moved through the corridor almost as fast as Ava.

'Where are we going?' Jess asked, trailing behind.

'They went out the back entrance,' Lydia said.

The three women turned down the last corridor, past the place where the Prime Minister had died. His body was gone. An ugly red smear remained on the wall.

'Jesus,' Ava said.

'Why would she run?' Jess asked.

'Because Max and I got her husband killed,' Lydia said. 'I hope the body was gone before she took her kids down here.'

'She's probably not thinking straight,' Ava said.

'I don't give two shits about her,' Lydia said. 'I just want to get those kids back to safety.'

They reached the doors, which stood wide open, a draft of dank air coming from the tunnels outside.

If those doors close...

'Jess, can you stay here and make sure nobody closes these doors?' Lydia said.

'I wanted to help,' Jess said, pouting.

'If that door closes and we can't get in, we all die,' Ava said. 'Including those two children.'

Jess nodded. 'Fine.' She crossed her arms.

Lydia and Ava carried on, into the dark corridor.

'What's her story?' Lydia asked.

'You know how they say you can choose your friends but you can't choose your family?'

'Yeah?'

'Why do you think we refer to each other as a family?'

Lydia snorted.

'She's not that bad,' Ava said. 'She's lovely. But she's never had to work a day in her life, and she...' She trailed off, as they found the crack leading to the underground tunnel. 'I'm just being a bitch.'

They stared through the gap into the darkness beyond.

'I know the type,' Lydia said.

Ava nodded and pulled herself up through the gap. 'You going to be okay getting up here?'

'Let's find out.'

Ava grabbed her hands and helped Lydia up. Her ribs protested, and she let out a cry of pain that reverberated off the damp walls.

'Hello?' a voice called out. A child's voice. Even if it was exactly what they wanted to hear, in the pitch black it couldn't help but creep Lydia out.

'Hello?' Ava called back.

Footsteps echoed through the tunnel.

'We're not here to hurt you,' Ava called out, in the general direction of the noise.

'Mummy,' a tiny voice said, far away. 'I'm scared.'

'I know,' a woman answered. 'Keep going.'

'Wait!' Lydia called out.

She and Ava started to pick their way through the darkness, toward the voices.

'Leave us alone!' the Prime Minister's wife called back, her voice high and terrified.

'Ma'am,' Ava called. 'You can't go out there. The storm is coming back.'

'Says you. Why should I believe anything you say? Bitch. Murderer!'

'Think of your children, please!' Lydia shouted.

They were getting closer. The patter of small feet on the ground rebounded off the walls, trying to keep step with those of their mother's impractical heels.

'Mummy, my head hurts,' a tiny voice whined.

'You have to stop!' Lydia shouted. 'Your children are going to die if you don't fucking stop!'

Ahead of them a shadow turned, and they could finally make out the fleeing woman, her white skirt reflecting the fraction of light available.

'How dare you speak to me like that?' the woman screamed. 'Don't you know who I am?'

'I've had enough of this,' Ava said in a low voice.

Lydia felt Ava move past, towards the indignant mother.

'Hey!' Ava called out. There was the crack of a thrown punch, a guttural cry, and the noise of someone hitting the ground.

'Mummy!' two small voices called out in unison. The boy's voice rose into a wail, and the girl screamed.

'Hey, kids,' Lydia said, moving toward them. 'Remember me? Remember my voice?'

'Uh-huh,' the boy replied, his wail cut off by the simple recognition of a voice.

'You've got a headache?'

'Mmm-hmm.'

'Well,' Lydia said, finally reaching them, kneeling to their level. 'If you and your sister come back with me back into the bunker, we can sort it out for you, okay?'

'What about Mummy?' the little girl asked.

'We'll bring her too.'

'Great,' Ava sighed.

'You want to make them orphans?' Lydia shot back.

'Easy for you to say,' Ava replied, bending down to lift the unconscious woman. 'You're not the one who's going to have to carry her back.'

The way back to the bunker was better lit, but the going seemed harder, especially with the headache Lydia had brewing. It moved from a dull ache to a needling throb. The storm. They weren't deep enough yet.

They reached the gap to the tunnel below. In the growing light, the children could see what a mess Ava had made of their mother's face. Her eye was swollen, her nose broken. When Ava turned, Lydia could make out a long red stain down the back of her top where the woman's nose had bled in transit.

I hope that's from the punch, and not the storm.

Ava laid the woman down on the ground.

Both of the children looked in a bad way. Faces drained of colour, their gaits woozy, almost drunken. Sweat poured off their faces. Their hair lay matted against their skin and the boy looked on the verge of pitching forward into the dirt.

Ava lowered herself into the tunnel first, and Lydia lowered the two children down. The little boy immediately sat down, cross legged, on the floor. The little girl stood, waiting for Lydia to lower her mother down.

Lydia bent and hooked the unconscious woman's arm over her shoulder. She lifted her, but something cracked.

'Motherfucker!' she screamed, releasing the woman's arm. She fell down to the ground beside her. Both children burst into tears.

Lydia's whole chest filled with pain. 'Oh shit oh shit oh shit oh shit,' she muttered to herself, as she tried to cling onto consciousness.

'Wait here, kids, please?' Ava said, and climbed back up. 'What happened?' she asked Lydia.

'I think I broke a rib,' Lydia replied, her breath getting shorter. 'Oh fuck. What do we do?'

'Hang on,' Ava said. She reached out and touched Lydia's side, but her touch sent a fresh surge of pain.

Ava lifted Lydia's top, exposing her side. She sucked in air through her teeth. 'It's badly bruised, at least' she said.

'Go,' Lydia said. 'Take the kids into the bunker and send some people out for us.'

'I'm not leaving Mummy,' the little girl said, half indignant, half terrified.

'Jess!' Ava screamed down the corridor.

There was no response.

'Go,' Lydia said. 'There's no time.'

The pain in her head started to intensify. Ava rubbed at her own temples as she tried to think.

'Wait here,' she said, and climbed back down. 'Kids,' she said, trying to sound calm. 'We have to go back to the bunker, okay? I promise I'll come back for your mum, but I can't take you all at once.'

Lydia couldn't see down into the tunnel, but could hear footsteps receding. She stared at the ceiling. Stars danced in the darkness and her head swam. The calm certainty of impending death washed over her. She felt at peace. She'd saved the children. She'd made it to the bunker. It would have to do.

'No!' Ava howled down the corridor.

Lydia instinctively tried to sit up, but the pain overwhelmed her and she fell back down. She tried to focus on the ceiling as footsteps ran back down the corridor.

Ava's head popped up next to her. 'Fucking bitch!' she spat. 'She's shut the fucking door.'

'The kids?' Lydia asked, weakly.

'I've put them into the first chamber. I need to get both of you down there.'

Tears welled in Lydia's eyes. 'No,' she said. 'Stay with the children. Close the outer doors. Maybe it'll be enough.

'Nope,' Ava said, and climbed up.

She straddled the children's mother and slapped her, hard.

The Prime Minister's wife moaned and sat bolt upright, almost knocking Ava over as she did.

'What?' she asked, groggily. She started to look around for her children.

'They're safe,' Ava said. 'But you need to come with me.'

'You...' the woman said, as she remembered what Ava had done.

'You can hate me as much as you want, but we saved the lives of your children.'

'My head,' she said.

'It's the storm,' Lydia said, her voice little more than breath.

'Oh, God,' she replied. 'I was going to take them up there.'

'Good job we were there to stop you, eh?' Ava said, standing up. 'Now, help me get my friend back down there, and we can all try to survive this.'

'I'm sorry,' she said, as Ava pulled her to her feet. 'I...'

'It's okay,' Lydia said. I understand.'

Together they lifted Lydia to her feet. She tried to bite down the pain, but only succeeded in drawing blood from her lip. Ava climbed down and the other woman lowered Lydia into the hole. Her head smacked off the side, but she was already in so much pain she barely noticed. She struggled to keep conscious, fighting with every fibre of her being to stay with it.

In the corridor, they lowered Lydia onto her feet, and each took one of her arms, draping her between them. As they headed toward the light of the bunker, the walls of the corridor started to shake. A crack appeared in the ceiling above them, dusting them with plaster.

They reached the first door and pulled it shut behind them. At the far end of the corridor, both the children cowered against the locked door. They looked up and saw their mother.

'I'm coming, darlings,' their mother said, puffing at the exertion of keeping Lydia upright.

They reached the end of the corridor. They sat Lydia down against the wall, next to the children. She tried to flash them both a reassuring smile, but it must have come out as a grimace, because they shrank back.

Ava turned to the door. 'Shit,' she said, staring at the keypad. 'I can't remember the fucking code.' She turned to the woman fussing over her children. 'Do you know it?'

'No, sorry.'

Ava hammered on the door and screamed at it.

Lydia's headache eased, but didn't disappear. She looked at the children, who didn't look much better than before.

Ava stopped hammering on the door and stepped back, either weighing up her options or trying to burn through it with mind bullets.

There was a hiss. The door opened, swinging outwards. The sudden movement made them jump.

Jess stood in the doorway. 'I'm so sorry,' she said. An ugly welt swelled under one eye. Behind her, a man lay prostrate on the floor, clutching between his legs. 'I had a few issues.'

Ava embraced her. The children ran into the bunker, followed by their mother. Jess and Ava lifted Lydia up, and carried her inside, where they were immediately engulfed by a surging mass of people. Fighting for air, Lydia wondered if she'd have been better off staying in the corridor.

Chapter Thirty-Eight

At The Age Of Decay

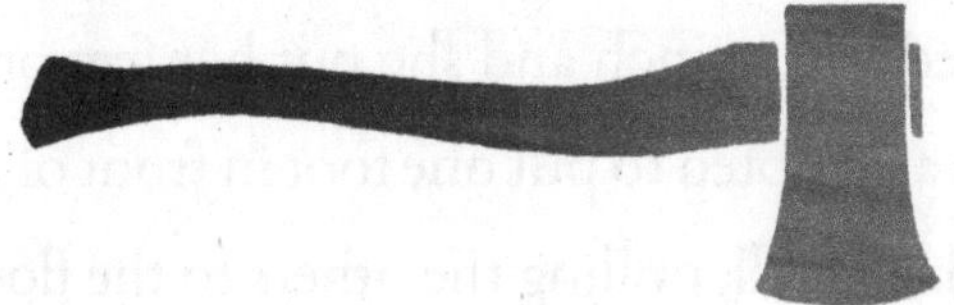

Mira found herself dragged forward, her toes the only part of her touching the floor. She blinked, trying to focus. Tom and Susan carried her along a dark corridor, draped between them.

She opened her mouth to speak. 'Mnnnhhh,' was all that came out.

'It's okay,' Susan said, struggling. 'We're going to get you inside.'

She tried to focus, to get her feet under control. She was being carried by a man half crippled and a woman who'd been badly beaten. She needed to get her shit together. The darkness didn't help. She could hear and feel the throng of people they moved alongside, but couldn't make sense of the random shadows and shapes on the walls and ceiling of the corridor.

Her top lip was wet. She went to touch it, to see if it was blood, but remembered her arms were being used by her friends to keep her upright.

'Where are we?' she managed to say. Her mouth felt alien, completely dry and not under her control.

'We're heading into the bunker,' Tom said, through gritted teeth. He struggled to carry her, and as Mira became more aware, she realised how badly he was limping with each step.

'Let me walk,' she said.

They lowered her an inch and she put her feet on the ground. As soon as she attempted to put one foot in front of the other, her knees buckled. She fell, pulling the others to the floor. Her knees smacked against the concrete floor, and Tom's head bounced off the ground.

She didn't even have a moment to collect herself before the people behind, blinded by the darkness, tripped over their fallen bodies and landed on top of her. A large woman's shoulder drove into the small of Mira's back, knocking the air from her lungs. Something snapped. She hoped it wasn't anything of hers.

You're going to die now.

As unbidden as the voice was, it sparked something inside, something primal. Once more she was standing by the tanker, grenades in hand. Once more she was striding into a room and putting a gun to Ewen's temple. The fear drained away, replaced by something else.

Belief.

Strength.

Pushing up from the ground, she rolled the woman from her back.

'Tom,' she called out, and heard a groan to her right.

She put out an arm and found him. Dragging herself up, she pulled him with her. She reached down and dragged the unconscious Susan to her feet, draping her arm around her friend. People jostled them, bumping into them, off them. Mira stood tall. She wiped the blood from her nose with her sleeve, and took Tom's hand.

'Come on,' she said, and started forward.

The people who'd tripped over them got to their feet, too, and together they surged forward.

The walls around them started to shake. Whatever was going on outside was reaching its peak.

'You okay?' she asked Tom, through gritted teeth. Her calves burned with the weight of Susan.

'I'll be better when we're safe,' he replied. 'Let me take the other side.'

'I'm fine,' Mira said.

A light appeared over the heads of the people in front of them. They were close, the electric glow of strip lighting only a doorway away. Dust fell from the ceilings. Somewhere ahead a cry of panic rang out, and Mira ran into the woman in front of her. As the person behind did the same, Mira realised what was happening. They crushed forward, several hundred people trying to fit through the same small doorway.

'Stop fucking pressing!' someone shouted. It was Burnett. Mira could just make out his unshaven face and shaggy hair in the light of the door.

'Move back!' Mira shouted, and the pressure behind her started to ease.

They stood, waiting for the crowd to clear, staring up at the ceiling, which threatened to buckle completely. They started to move forward again. The light grew stronger, and Susan started to stir.

A tearing sound rang out, and rubble fell onto them. A huge crack wound its way along the roof of the tunnel, prompting a fresh sense of panic in the crowd, who pushed forward again.

They went through the door, into the bunker. The crack stopped at the doorway; the bunker itself enjoying a greater reinforcement than the corridor outside.

I hope it's enough.

Inside the bunker was bedlam. Every inch of the place was full, with people hardly able to move, and more pouring in. People climbed onto tables, desks, anywhere they could find unclaimed space.

'Move through, people!' Burnett shouted from somewhere. 'There's still space in some of the rooms. Move down the corridor, or we can't get everyone in.'

People looked around, terrified. The lights flickered, and a gasp rippled through the crowd.

'Tom!' Burnett called out. 'Mira!'

'Burnett?' Mira called back. She couldn't see him at first, but finally made out the tall frame of Tana, his head popping out above the rest of the crowd.

They moved through the people, swimming against the tide, until they were in a large circular room. Broken glass crunched under Mira's feet, and she saw the walls must have been windows at one time. Now they were just empty spaces.

'Fucking hell,' Mira said, finally reaching the two policemen, who stared at the chaos. With them was an older man in military uniform, sporting a pepper-grey moustache, his brow furrowed as he took at the scene before him.

'Tell me about it,' Burnett said.

'Were there many still behind you?' Tana asked, taking Susan from Mira.

'No idea,' Tom said, rubbing his leg and wincing.

Mira took in the scene from her new, central position. She could see into one of the rooms leading off the chamber where people were crammed in so tightly they looked like they were on a commuter train, albeit one where they couldn't read some terrible free newspaper or stare at their phones. Instead they stood in studious silence, using every ounce of their ingrained Britishness not to make eye contact with each other.

Across the other side of the bunker, two young children had climbed atop some large cabinets, their legs dangling inches above the people crammed below. People cried, or muttered, or looked generally pissed off. She could sympathise. If this did end up being the end of the world, it was hardly the most dignified way to go.

Chen appeared through the crowd. 'You made it,' he said to Mira, and gave her a hug. He looked at Susan, who Tana was still holding up. 'Here,' he said. He took Susan from Tana and led her to a table, where he shooed away some people to clear space to lay her down.

Although the bunker was much better insulated, they could still hear every rumble from above them. Mira wondered what was going on up there. Was it like that first night? In six months, she'd never told a soul about what had happened. Not even Jen, who'd no doubt assumed they'd get around to it eventually. Not

Sam. Not Tom. Nobody. It was too painful a memory. Not that there was anything remarkable about it. She'd gone into the garden with her mum and dad and little brothers to watch the storm. They had looked up at the sky with amazement, while her dad had tried to explain the wonder of electromagnetism to children who'd rather look at the pretty colours. She'd not gone through what the others had. There were no fires, no plane crashes. But still, she couldn't bring herself to tell anyone about waking up next to her family, imploring her Ammaa to please wake up.

Would that be her fate now? To always be the last one to wake up, surrounded by the bodies of the people she cared about? She was a different person to that little girl – they all were – but she didn't think she could take that kind of heartache again.

Her gaze went back to the two kids perched on top of the cupboard. She hoped they'd still have someone the next day.

The walls shook, and the lights dimmed again.

'Damn those generators,' the army man said.

'Shit,' Burnett said. 'We need to get the door closed.'

Together they picked their way back over to the entrance, where the last few people staggered through. Men and women jostled them as they tried to pass, but Mira tucked in behind Tana, who made an effective shield.

They helped the last few people through, the straggler's noses bleeding. Their eyes widened as they saw what they needed to cram into, but they moved past without a word, until Mira, Tom, Tana, Burnett, and the soldier were the only ones by the entrance. They stared down the corridor. They could only make out ten metres or so; beyond was a darkness so deep it sent shivers down Mira's spine. People lay all along the corridor.

'We need to help them,' Mira said.

Another deep boom. In the corridor outside, more paintwork and debris fell from the ceiling, exposing further cracks.

'It's acting as an echo chamber,' Burnett said, stroking his stubble. He turned to the soldier. 'You think there's a risk it'll come down on us?'

He shrugged. 'There's a chance.'

'We'd better get a move on,' Burnett said. 'Mira, you stay here, okay? If the corridor collapses while we're gone, you close the door, okay?'

'No! I'm not going to leave you out there.'

Burnett took her by the shoulders. 'If you don't, every single person in here could die. You understand?'

He turned to the soldier. 'General, no offence, but you should stay here too. After the storm, these people are going to need you.'

The soldier nodded and offered his hand to Burnett, who took it in a firm handshake.

'I expect you to return, Detective.'

'Hey,' Mira said, as Tom, Tana, and Burnett went through the doorway. 'Don't be heroes, okay?'

Chapter Thirty-nine
A Final Storm

Tom nodded. He was too tired to play the hero. In fact, he had no desire to head back into the corridor. For the first time today, the desire to rummage through the contents of the bunker until he found the secret whisky stash the top brass hid from the rest of their men overwhelmed him. He pushed that particular need down and promised himself once this was over, he'd allow himself a wee dram.

People littered the corridor. Most were still conscious, blood streaming from their noses. Some tried to inch themselves forward to the door, while some were as close to death as made no odds.

Tana was first into the corridor. He hauled a woman to her feet and lowered himself to pick up a skinny looking man, who he lifted over his shoulder.

'You don't expect all of us to be able to do that, right?' Tom asked.

'Come on,' Burnett said. 'Let's get this done.'

They ferried people back and forth, Tom's strength waning with every step. As they moved deeper into the corridor, they had to resort to calling out for survivors and feeling the pulses of the bodies they tripped over. As the tunnel grew darker, fewer of the bodies had pulses.

'Should we go back?' Tana asked, out of breath.

'I second that,' Tom said. The headache had that started as a low buzz at the back of his head had moved front and central.

'No,' Burnett said. 'We can't leave anyone out here to die.'

Tom had enough light to see Tana nod and trudge off. Tom picked up a middle-aged man, who started to come to before passing out again. Tom threw the man's arm over his shoulder and started to drag him back to the door. When he got there, Mira took him.

'You okay?' she asked.

'Peachy,' Tom replied. He smiled, and headed back into the corridor.

He shook his head, trying to shake off the dizziness. Along the corridor, Burnett and Tana staggered back. Tana's footsteps were that of a town drunk.

That's my role.

'It that it?' Tom asked.

'Huh,' Burnett said, swaying. Blood trickled from one of his nostrils. 'Oh. Yeah. Think so.'

A groan came from somewhere farther down the corridor.

'Guess not,' Tom said. 'Come on, let's get this one and fuck off, yeah?'

They headed back into the darkness.

'Hey,' Tana called out. 'Where are you, mate?'

Another groan. They worked their way down to it, Tom keeping his fingers running along the cracked paintwork to stay orientated. Finally his foot connected with a body, which gave an 'oof' in response.

'Sorry, chap.'

Tom leaned down and tried to lift the man, but his knee went out from under him. Tana lifted Tom with his free arm. Tom's knee cracked on the way up.

Definitely done playing Good Samaritan.

Once Tom was on his feet again, Tana helped Burnett, who struggled with the unconscious man. The light picked up as they headed back, Tom bringing up the rear in case the two staggering policemen dropped their cargo, who the light revealed to be heavyset and balding.

A loud boom reverberated across the corridor, shaking the walls. Above them, the crack widened, and the roof started to buckle.

A tear wrought open the ceiling, splitting it in two.

With all his might, Tom lunged at his friends, shoving them in the smalls of their backs. Even with Tana's size, and their passenger's bulk, the three of them went sprawling forward, as a huge chunk of the roof collapsed onto the ground in front of Tom.

'Run!' he shouted.

A scream issued from the end of the corridor, as it dawned on Mira what was happening.

Tom looked up. The rest of the roof buckled. Earth fell through the new gap.

A cluster of brickwork landed to his left.

Time to go.

He turned and ran from the falling debris, away from the bunker. He couldn't muster much of a sprint, but hauled himself forward with as much energy as he could, as the ceiling above him stared to collapse. With his knees protesting, his side burning, he ran. Dust covered him and filled the air; he took great gulps of it into his lungs, but kept pushing forward, even as he gasped for breath. He ran toward a shard of light, until he came to a staircase and realised the noise behind him had ended.

He tried to stop, but his momentum carried him forward. He sprawled onto the steps, knocking his arm hard on the rough concrete, his head smacking off the hard floor.

Struggling into a sitting position, he looked back down the corridor, except the corridor was gone. In its place was an arch filled with soil, brickwork, and the end of Tom's hope. He stared at it a second, trying to see if there was a way back to the bunker. There wasn't.

It was over.

His head pounded and his vision started to swim. He looked up the steps, to the raging storm outside.

Fuck it. May as well go out in style.

He climbed the staircase and up the ramp, the chaos of the outside world revealing itself to him.

Everything was on fire.

When he had stood on his terrace six months ago, he and Leon had stared up at clouds dancing with electricity, but this lightning wasn't confining itself to the sky. Sustained pulses of red, blue, and green light struck the ground, burning red hot, and going out.

It might be night, for all Tom could tell, as he stepped up into the street. The only light came from the storm, but there was enough of it to illuminate the city. Still, there was no rain, no moisture in the air.

To his right, fire burned. There were pockets of it everywhere, where the lighting had struck the ground, setting even the rubble ablaze. A bolt of green light slammed into the river in front of him and a great plume of steam rose up from the Thames, before falling away once the strike ended. The steam rolled across to him, then cleared.

An odd thought struck him, and he reached into his pocket. He pulled out his wallet. He'd not opened it in months, but had dutifully transferred it from trouser to trouser since the storm, not able to say goodbye to that most ordinary facet of normality.

He opened it now, and popped the button to the coin holder. Inside, pressed as flat as paper, was the remnant of a joint. Leon had passed it to him, the night before they took down Baxter. He'd squirrelled it away, to smoke another day, and completely forgotten it was there.

Now's as good a time as any.

Walking over to the fire, he tried to coax the flattened dry tobacco to life and held it to the flame, until the end burned red.

He took a drag, and hobbled over to a small pile of rocks. It tasted like shit. The hit of smoke made him cough, and the weed, dead and dry as it might be, flooded his system, immediately easing the aches in his body and head.

The stars in his vision intensified. He didn't have long left.

'Well, buddy,' he said to the wind. 'I guess this is as far as we go.'

'Guess so,' Leon said.

'We gave it a good go though, right?'

'Not bad for a couple of fuck-ups.'

'Too right.'

'Tom?'

'Yeah?'

'You've got red on you.'

Tom looked down at the hand holding the roach. Blood speckled his skin. He wiped his nose on his sleeve. It was tacky, wet. He didn't need to look at it to see the blood that would be smeared across it.

The stars intensified, and stopped, bringing only darkness. His body slumped forward, as the fires around him burned.

Chapter Forty
Surrender

'Motherfucker!' Burnett shouted, scrambling to his feet.

'Boss,' Tana said, as a piece of the ceiling landed behind them. 'We've got to go.'

They scrambled to their feet, and ran for the door. Mira stood there, dumbfounded. The man they'd been trying to carry back didn't make it, his body consumed by the falling roof. As, presumably, had Tom's.

'Tom!' Burnett screamed at the top of his lungs, but his voice bounced off the dirt and bricks filling the corridor. The deluge of falling earth and debris came to a halt, leaving them staring at a flat mound which ran to the ceiling.

There was no way Tom could have survived. Even if he had, there was no way back through the landslide.

He kicked out at the debris, his toe catching a metal pole. He didn't care.

'Tom!' Mira shouted, behind him.

'He's gone,' Burnett said.

'No!' Mira screamed, and leapt forward, removing bricks and tossing them behind her.

'Mira,' Tana said, placing a hand on her shoulder.

She pulled away and returned to the debris, scooping out handfuls of dust and dirt, tears streaming down her cheeks.

Burnett rubbed his temples. His headache had eased, but a dull ache remained. Stars no longer danced at the periphery of his vision. He leaned against the doorframe of the bunker and took a deep breath.

The General returned. 'Detective,' he said, sizing up the scene. 'We need to get this door closed. Nothing is secure until we do.'

'No,' Mira said, turning round and squaring up with the older and much larger soldier with a ferocity that made him step back. 'Our friend is still out there.'

Coles looked to Burnett, who nodded.

'I'm sorry, ma'am,' Coles said. 'But as harsh as this might sound, your friend is gone. If you don't want your other friends to die we need to close this door.'

Mira fell to the ground, and wept. Tana went to her and scooped her up in his large arms. She hugged him, burying her head in his shoulder.

They went through to the bunker, and Burnett shut the door. Coles spun the large lock, until it locked into place. The headache eased immediately.

'We still have a problem,' Coles said, under his breath.

'What's that?'

'This bunker can hold a few hundred people for a sustained period of time, not this many for a short period. The air purifiers are not designed to work that hard. And the power went out when the storm hit. We're on backup generators, but your guess is as good as mine as to whether they last the night. Even if they do, the system won't be able to keep up with the demands of nearly a thousand people.'

'So we could suffocate?'

'Exactly.'

'Great.'

Coles gave him a shrug, and moved away. Burnett went back to the window. He could barely see the rubble through the thick plastic. He stared through the glass, willing the pile to move, for a hand to spring free of it begging for rescue.

It never came.

Hours passed. Everywhere he turned he could see a mass of people trying to coexist in the same space as the people next to them. Before long the air filled with a putrid mix of sweat, fear, and lingering farts. Eventually people tried to negotiate a sitting or lying position, resolving it with glares or the occasional, immediately snuffed-out scuffle.

Burnett thought back to the time he'd spent in the back of an old horse cart, squashed in with a dozen others, unsure whether he'd ever get out again. This wasn't so bad in comparison.

Tana moved through the crowd, helping people where he could. Chen and Susan, back on her feet, distributed water. Mira sat on top of a filing cabinet with two small children, making them laugh. Coles stood in the middle of his command centre, glowering at the world around him, at the disruption to his ordered world. He couldn't see Lydia and Greg, still. He hoped they were in here, somewhere. When they'd arrived he'd asked around after the pair of them, but it was too much of a maelstrom to try to start finding people. If they survived, he'd find them and give them both the hug of a lifetime.

Burnett's gaze went back to the window. What was next? Even if they survived the night, what kind of world waited for them out there? How long would it be until the next storm?

One thing was for damned sure — he was done playing leader. Leave it to better men and women than he. He was going to find a house in the countryside and stock up on beans and books.

He sat down and rested his head against the steel door, and closed his eyes.

He awoke to a low buzz. Whether it existed in his head or outside, he couldn't tell. His head pounded, and as he opened his eyes, the harsh glare of strip lighting forced them closed again.

He raised a hand and tried again.

People began to stir, sitting up as the realisation hit them that they were still alive. Judging by the lack of whooping and hollering, they seemed to be largely ambivalent about this. Perhaps it was the paucity of air. Burnett's lungs ached, and his fingers and toes felt numb. It would explain the headache too, although that could be the storm raging on.

He stood. Mira and the others had come close to the doorway in the night, so he checked on each one, rousing them. Susan and Chen had their arms around each other. Mira stood and stretched her willowy frame.

'We made it, then?' she asked, yawning.

'Looks that way,' Burnett said. He realised how dry his throat was the moment he tried to use it.

General Coles walked over, his uniform looking somewhat less pressed than it had the day before.

'Good morning, Detective,' he said.

'General.'

'I think it's time we cracked the doors to this place, let some air in. What do you say?'

'You're asking me?' Burnett said. 'This is your gaff, General.'

'Yes, but you're in charge, are you not?'

Burnett shook his head. 'I don't think so.'

'Knock it off,' Tana said. 'You're the big man. The head cheese. You've saved the lives of every sodding person in this tin can. You think they'll look to anyone else?'

'I don't want it,' Burnett said.

'Don't see you've got much choice in the matter, son,' Coles said.

'What about you, General?' Burnett said. 'You're much higher ranked than me.'

'Oh no,' Coles said. 'I'm a man to serve, not a man to lead. I can be whatever you need me to be, except that. Besides, these people don't know me.'

Burnett sighed. 'Let's get out of here and worry about it later.'

'How exactly are we going to do that?' Mira asked. 'Last I checked there were several tonnes of dirt and brickwork between us and some fresh air.

'There's another entrance,' a woman said.

Burnett turned and saw Lydia, flanked by a young black couple. Behind them trailed a man who made Tana look small, a blonde woman, and a little old lady. A dirty Labrador padded alongside them.

'Lydia!' Burnett said.

They embraced, Lydia wincing as he squeezed her.

'Where's Greg?' he asked.

Lydia shook her head. Tears welled in her eyes.

'I'm sorry,' he said. 'You did it, though. I never lost faith.'

'Another entrance?' Tana asked.

The young black man nodded. 'Presuming it didn't collapse like the other one, it's back here.'

He led them down a corridor, people parting to let them through. Lydia opened a door, which led into what looked to Burnett like an air lock. When Lydia opened the second door at the far end, a rush of fresh air came through, dank and smelling of dust, but nectar to them nonetheless. They let it wash over them for a second, before stepping out into the darkness.

Guided by Max and Ava, who Burnett learned had been instrumental to their survival, they worked their way to the surface. The Underground station above the tunnels seemed to have protected them from further collapses, and they picked their way up, a long line snaking behind them out of the bunker.

They found themselves at the bottom of a long staircase, burned out and charred.

'Some of this has changed,' Max said, running his hand along the wall. 'Storm must have done more damage.'

They reached the surface. The entrance to the station had partially collapsed, so they had to clear it before they could taste their freedom once more.

Stepping out into the morning air, they saw what an understatement Max had made. Even in the ruins of London, the damage caused by the storm was almost impossible to take in. Every building had been completely levelled. The Thames ran clogged with burnt timber. Around them, small fires still burned.

Burnett looked at his friends, who surveyed the damage with open mouths.

'Right then,' he said. 'Let's get to work.'

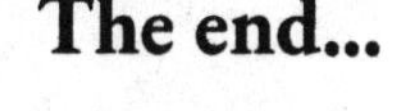
The end...

Leave a Review

I really hope you've enjoyed reading *A Final Storm*.

If you did, the nicest thing you could do for me right now is to leave a review, on this or any of the books you've enjoyed. Reviews are absolutely crucial for discoverability, and social proof. If you could take a second to rate and review this at the store of your choice, I'd hugely appreciate it.

Thanks,

Paul

START THE CHRONICLES

Plague. Murder. Unrest. Humanity's future looks far from bright.

The year is 2115, and Earth is dying. For Wyn, Lois, and Judd, that's the least of their problems.

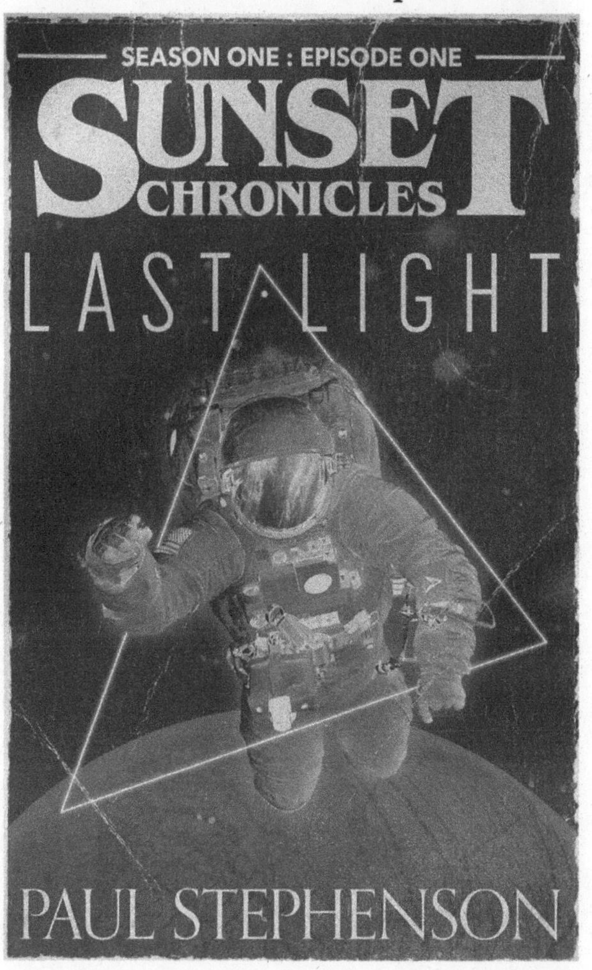

Get the first episode in the monthly sci-fi horror serial that's guaranteed to knock your socks off...

AUTHOR'S NOTE

It's with a heavy heart that I write this, knowing that it means that the Blood on the Motorway saga is finished. I've spent as much time with Tom, Leon, Jen, Mia, Sam, Burnett, Tana, Chen, Lydia, Greg, Samira, Max, Mouse, Ava, and the rest of these characters as I'm going to spend.

Well, for now.

The Blood on the Motorway story has been part of my life for the best part of a decade now, and there's a lot of people that I need to thank for it reaching the end.

Firstly, Ellen, always, for being a wonderful support to me, picking me up every time I felt like I couldn't make it, never letting me give, up, believing in me, and letting this endeavour dominate far more of our lives than it has any right to do.

Mum and Dad, for always believing in me, for letting me know from such an early age what a joy there is in reading, and always encouraging me when I started trying to scribble stories of my own.

My brother, Vince, whose unbridled enthusiasm for this story has pushed me harder to give it the ending it deserves.

My online writers group, Writers United, for being my fellow soldiers in the trenches. We've been there, man, we know. Onwards and upwards!

The indie author community at large. It's impossible to overstate how it's felt to discover this whole world of writers, each willing to go beyond sensible limits to help each other. If the traditional world is one of cut-throat competition, enforced scarcity and envy, then the indie community is truly the opposite, full of people willing to give up ridiculous amounts of their time to help out people lower than them on the ladder. The SPF guys, Joanna Penn, Mark Dawson, and all the other leading lights, yes, but it's the long tail of indies out there helping each other out, they're the true heroes of this movement. I see you all on FB forums and Kboards and elsewhere, and it makes me strive each day to be better, so thanks.

Ro, my wonderful editor. If you've enjoyed this story, a huge chunk of credit has to go in her direction.

Libby and Lydia, always the first set of eyes on anything I write. I don't know where this story would have ended up without your input, but I doubt it would have been half as good.

Lastly, you, dear reader. Every writer dreams of fame and fortune and awards and everything else, but there is nothing like getting an email from a reader telling you what your book meant to them. I've been privileged over the course of this story to have received messages of support and encouragement, reviews that have made my heart soar, and more beside. Every one of you who have taken the time to read this story, I love you, sincerely.

One day I might return to Burnett, Mira, and the others, to see how they're getting on, but for now, this is the end. My next series will be different, a sci-fi series, but I hope you'll join me on that story, too.

Until then...

JOIN MY READER'S GROUP

Join my reader's group and
I'll send you an exclusive collection
of short stories you won't find anywhere else

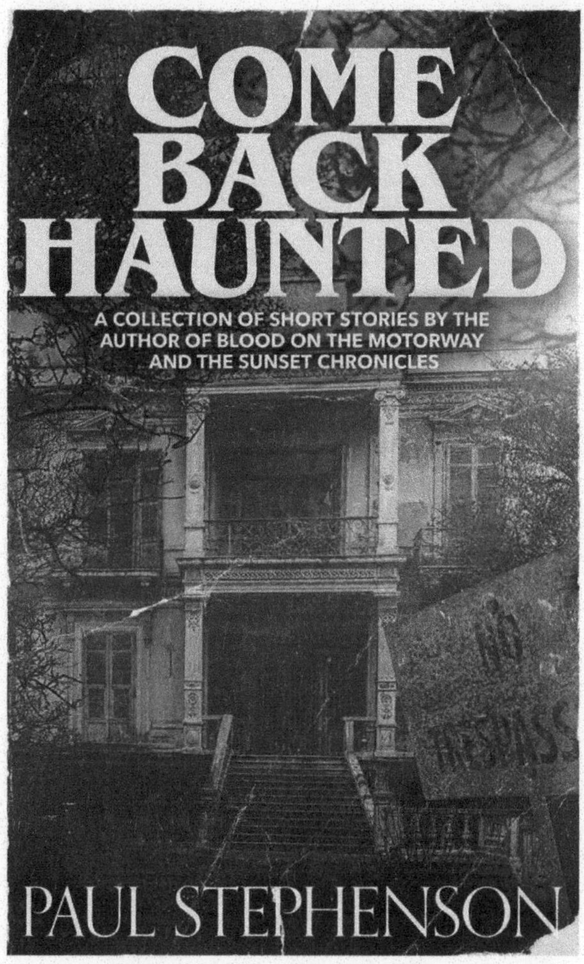

You'll also get a 10% discount on all ebooks bought directly from my website (that will last you forever), be the first on the planet to hear abou new releases, and get exclusive content you won't find anywhere else.

About the Author

Paul Stephenson writes pulp fiction for the digital age. He is the creator and narrator of Bleakwood, a horror podcast, and his first novel series – the apocalyptic Blood on the Motorway trilogy – has been an Amazon bestseller on both sides of the Atlantic.

His work has been featured on the chart-topping horror podcast, The Other Stories, and his new eBook serial, The Sunset Chronicles, is a dystopian sci-fi thriller that will delight and terrify fans of science fiction and horror alike. He lives in England with his wife, two children, and one hellhound.

To keep up to date with his books, please visit his website PaulStephensonBooks.com

ALSO BY PAUL STEPHENSON

The Sunset Chronicles

Plague. Murder. Unrest. Humanity's future looks far from bright.

The year is 2107, and Earth is dying. For Wyn, Lois, and Judd, that's the least of their problems. Each holds a key to Earth's cure and humanity's survival in The Sunset Chronicles, the new sci-fi horror thrill-ride from Paul Stephenson, author of the bestselling British horror saga, Blood on the Motorway.

Non Fiction

Welcome to Discovery Park

Chronicling one man's increasingly frustrated attempt to listen to every album on Rolling Stone's Top 500 Albums of all time list, this comic and acerbic book looks at why we feel the need to quantify and rank our art, revels in the complex musical world we live in, and wonders why anyone would voluntarily listen to Bono.

Lightning Source UK Ltd.
Milton Keynes UK
UKHW041843160522
402956UK00003BA/14/J